Painting Time

Also by Maylis de Kerangal

The Heart

The Cook

Painting Time

Maylis de Kerangal

Translated from the French by Jessica Moore

Farrar, Straus and Giroux
New York

Farrar, Straus and Giroux
120 Broadway, New York 10271

Printed in the United States of America
Originally published in French in 2018 by Éditions Gallimard, France,
    as *Un monde à portée de main*
English translation originally published in 2021 by Talonbooks, Canada
Published in the United States by Farrar, Straus and Giroux
First American edition, 2021

Library of Congress Cataloging-in-Publication Data
Names: Kerangal, Maylis de, author. | Moore, Jessica, 1978– translator.
Title: Painting time : a novel / Maylis de Kerangal ; translated from the
    French by Jessica Moore.
Other titles: Monde à portée de main. English
Description: First American edition. | New York : Farrar, Straus and Giroux,
    2021. | Originally published in French in 2018 by Éditions Gallimard,
    France, as Un monde à portée de main. | Summary: "An aesthetic and
    existential coming-of-age novel exploring the apprenticeship of a young
    female painter" —Provided by publisher.
Identifiers: LCCN 2020052403 | ISBN 9780374211929 (hardcover)
Classification: LCC PQ2671.E64 M6613 2021 | DDC 843/.92—dc23
LC record available at https://lccn.loc.gov/2020052403a

Our books may be purchased in bulk for promotional, educational, or business
use. Please contact your local bookseller or the Macmillan Corporate and
Premium Sales Department at 1-800-221-7945, extension 5442, or by email
at MacmillanSpecialMarkets@macmillan.com.

www.fsgbooks.com
www.twitter.com/fsgbooks • www.facebook.com/fsgbooks

10 9 8 7 6 5 4 3 2 1

*Does the wind make a sound
in the trees when there's no
one there to hear?*

Painting Time

PAULA KARST APPEARS IN THE STAIRWELL, she's going out tonight, you can tell right away, a perceptible change in speed from the moment she closed the apartment door, her breath quicker, heartbeat stronger, long dark coat open over a white shirt, boots with three-inch heels, and no purse, everything in her pockets—phone, cigarettes, cash, all of it, the set of keys that keeps the beat as she walks (quiver of a snare)—and her hair bouncing on her shoulders, the staircase that spirals around her as she hurries down the flights, swirls all the way to the lobby, where, intercepted at the last second by the huge mirror, she pulls up short, leans in to fathom her walleyed irises, smudges the too-thick eyeshadow with a forefinger, pinches her pale cheeks, and presses her lips together to flood them with red (indifferent to the hidden flirtatiousness in her face, the divergent strabismus, subtle, but always more pronounced when evening falls). Before stepping out into the street she undoes another shirt button—no scarf even though it's January outside, winter, *la bise noire*, but she wants to show her skin, wants the breath of night wind against the base of her throat.

AMONG THE TWENTY-ODD STUDENTS WHO trained at the Institut de Peinture (30 *bis*, rue du Métal in Brussels) between October 2007 and March 2008, three of them stayed close, shared contacts and warned each other about sketchy deals, passed along contracts, helped each other finish rush jobs, and these three—including Paula with her long black coat and smoky eyes—have a date tonight in Paris.

It was an occasion not to be missed, an exquisite planetary conjunction, as rare as the passage of Halley's Comet!—they got all worked up online, grandiloquent, appending their messages with images pulled from astrophotography sites. And yet, by the end of the afternoon, each one was imagining the reunion with reluctance: Kate had just spent the day perched on a stepladder in a lobby on avenue Foch and would have happily stayed sprawled at home in front of an episode of *Game of Thrones*, eating taramosalata with her fingers; Jonas would have preferred to keep working, to get ahead on a tropical jungle fresco he had to deliver in three days; and Paula, who had just flown in that morning from Moscow, was jet-lagged and not so sure the meeting was a good idea after all. But something stronger than them propelled them outside at nightfall—something visceral, a physical desire, the desire to recognize each other, faces and gestures, timbre of voices, ways of moving, drinking, smoking, all the things that would be reconnecting them any minute to the rue du Métal.

Bar thick with people. Clamor of a fairground and dim light of a church. They show up on time, all three, a perfect convergence. Their first movements throw them against each other, hugs, sluice gates open, and then they wend their way through the crowd single file, welded together, a unit: Kate, platinum hair with dark roots, 6'1", thighs bulging in ski pants, motorcycle helmet in the crook of her elbow and big teeth that make her top lip look too thin; Jonas, owl eyes and grayish skin, arms like lassos, Yankees baseball cap; and Paula, who is already looking brighter. They reach a table in a corner of the room, order two beers and a Spritz—Kate: I love the color—and then immediately begin that continuous pendulum movement between the bar and the street that sets the night's cadence for smokers, cigarettes between their lips, flames in the hollows of their hands. The day's weariness disappears in a snap, excitement is back, the night busts open, there's so much to talk about.

Paula Karst, fresh off the plane, you first! Tell us of your conquests, describe your exploits! Jonas strikes a match and his face flutters for a fraction of a second in the light of the flame, skin taking on a coppery glow, and in a flash Paula is back in Moscow, voice husky, back in the huge studios of Mosfilm where she spent the fall, three months, but instead of panoramic impressions and sweeping narration, instead of a chronological account, she begins by describing the details of Anna Karenina's sitting room, which she had to finish painting by candlelight after a power failure plunged the sets into darkness the night before the very first day of filming; she begins slowly, as though her words escort the image in a simultaneous translation, as though language is what allows us to see, and makes the rooms appear, the cornices and doors, the woodwork, the shape of the wainscotting and outline of the baseboards, the delicacy of the stucco, and from there, the very particular treatment of the shadows that had to stretch out across the walls; she lists with precision the range of colors—celadon, pale blue, gold, China White—and bit by bit she gathers speed, forehead high and cheeks flaming, launching into the story of that long night of painting, that mad crunch. She describes the hyped-up producers, their black parkas and Yeezy sneakers, how they cracked the whip over the painters in a Russian full of nails and caresses, reminding them that no amount of delay would be tolerated, none, but letting them glimpse possible bonuses, and Paula suddenly understood that she would have to work all night. She was in a panic thinking about painting in the dark, convinced that the tints couldn't possibly turn out right and that the seams between panels would be visible once they were under the lights, it was insane—she taps her temple with her index finger while Jonas and Kate listen, rapt, silent, recognizing in her a desirable madness, one they are also proud to possess—and she goes on, telling them how stunned she was to see a handful of students turn up from the École des Beaux-Arts, hired by the set decorator as backup, broke and talented, maybe, but liable to totally botch the job, and that night she was the one who prepared their palettes, kneeling on the plastic drop sheets on the floor, working by the light of an iPhone flashlight that one of them held over the tubes of colors as she mixed them in proportion, after which she assigned a section of the set to each of them and showed them which finish to use, moving from one to the next to refine a stroke, deepen a shadow, glaze a white, her movements at once precise and furtive, as though her galvanized body was carrying her instinctually toward the person who was hesitating, veering off course, and finally around midnight each one was at their spot and painting in silence, concentrating, the atmosphere of the set stretched tight as a trampoline, coiled, unreal, faces in motion lit by candlelight, eyes gleaming, pupils jet black; all you could hear was the rasp of brushes against the wood panels, the whisper of the soles of shoes against drop sheets, and breathing of all sorts, including that of a torpid dog curled up in the middle of it all and then a voice burst out from who knows where, an exclamation—Бля, смотри, смотри, как здесь красиво! Look, would you look at that! It's fucking beautiful!—and if you listened closely, you could hear the beat of a Russian rap song playing softly; the studio hummed, filled with pure human presence, and the tension was palpable until dawn. Paula worked tirelessly—the deeper into the night, the more her movements were loose, free, sure; and then around six in the morning the electricians made their entrance, solemn, bringing the generators they'd gone to fetch downtown, someone shouted *Fiat lux!* in a tenor voice and everything was lit up again—powerful bulbs projected a very white light on the set and Anna Karenina's grand sitting room appeared in the silvered light of a winter morning: there it was, it existed; the high windows were covered with frost and the street with snow, but inside it was warm, cozy, a majestic flame crackling in the hearth and the scent of coffee floating through the room; the producers were back now, too, showered, shaved, all smiles—they opened bottles of vodka and cardboard boxes containing piles of warm blini sprinkled with cinnamon and cardamom, handed out cash to the students, grabbed them by the scruff of the neck with the virile connivance of mafia godfathers or yelled English words into voicemail boxes that vibrated in Los Angeles, London, or Berlin; the pressure fell but the fever didn't pass just yet, each of them looked around and blinked, dazzled by the thousands of photons that now formed the texture of the air, astonished by what they had accomplished, more than a little dazed; Paula turned toward the tricky seams, worried, but no, it was okay, the colors were good, and then there were shouts, high-fives, hugs, and a few tears of exhaustion, some fell to the ground with their arms flung wide while others did a dance step, Paula kissed one of the extras for a little longer than necessary (the one with the dark eyes and strong build), slipped a hand under his sweater onto his searing hot skin, lingered in his mouth while phones started to ring again, everyone gathering their things, doing up their coats, wrapping scarves around their necks, pulling on gloves or taking out a cigarette; the world outside fired up again, but somewhere on this planet, in one of the large Mosfilm studios, they were waiting for Anna, now, Anna of the gray eyes, Anna who was madly in love, yes, it was all ready, cinema could arrive now, with life along for the ride.

⁂

Lashes of cold air, the bar door opens and closes like a pair of bellows in a forge, renewing the smokers on the sidewalk, and Paula shivers. She lowers her head, thrusts her hands into her pockets, scrapes at the ground with the toe of her boot while Kate and Jonas watch her in silence, pensive, envious of that burning night, so like the ones they had lived together at the Institut de Peinture, a night she told them about precisely so they would remember them all. Because the all-nighters spent painting side by side in order to hand in their projects at dawn on Madame la Directrice's large desk, like a tribute and an offering, these nights were their common good, the cornerstone of their friendship, a stock of images and sensations they returned to and dove into with obvious pleasure each time they were together again, exaggerating the urgency in the retelling, the exhaustion and the doubt, amplifying the smallest incident—the missing tube of color, the jar that was knocked over, the mineral spirits that caught fire or, worse, the error in perspective that they'd missed—replaying the scenes and delighting in appearing ridiculous, ignorant, insignificant specks before the work, anti-heroes of a gripping and comical epic from which they emerged all the more victorious for having brushed up against catastrophe, all the more valiant for having erred in the shadows, all the more ingenious for having nearly butchered everything; and these retellings had become a ritual: they were the required route of the reunion, functioning like an embrace.

They're sitting down inside again, Paula and Kate on the bench and Jonas facing them, heads tucked down, rubbing their hands together. What are you working on now? Kate asks him straight up, glass to her lips, eyes like a low-angle shot beneath turquoise lids, and it's startling to hear her reedy voice, no relation to her robust physique, as though her voice were dissociated from her body. Jonas leans back in his chair, amused, and then says with arms crossed high on his chest and hands tucked into his armpits: I'm working on Heaven, a tropical Eden, three and a half by eight meters. Silence. Paula and Kate feel the effect, and take it in. Kate drinks in slow gulps, eyes on the ceiling—she calculates the surface, evaluates the salary, quick—while Paula, unfolding her fingers one by one, lists the litany of color names they all know by heart, enunciating the syllables as though she were bursting capsules of pure sensation one by one: zinc white, vine black, chrome orange, cobalt blue, alizarin crimson, sap green and cadmium yellow for the greens? Jonas smiles, and goes on in the same rhythm, looking her straight in the eye: topaz, avocado, apricot, and bitumen—these two sit face to face and play off each other, it's a gorgeous movement—and then Paula takes a long inhalation and says softly: I'd like you to paint a spot for our big ape in your jungle, will you do that? Jonas nods without releasing her gaze, I will, and Paula lowers her eyes.

⁂

It's crowded in here, no one can hear anyone although everyone is talking, as though the din was filled with alveoli—a hive—as though every table built an acoustic space around itself to hold each clandestine conversation. Jonas rests his chin in his hand and looks at the women, one after the other, sardonic: the same, completely the same, both of them. Kate laughs and continues, curious: who are you doing this jungle of yours for? He suppresses a laugh, his shoulders shake, his chest palpitates under his arms, and he shoots back: no way, I'm not telling you anything, you little mole. He challenges her with his eyes, a smile on his lips, and Kate tries again, on the offensive, stepping into the role of the pragmatic young woman who keeps both feet firmly on the ground, compares the benefits of mutual funds, makes contributions to her RRSP, and keeps tabs on the salaries of the company of set painters: does it pay well, at least? How much per square meter? Eight hundred, a thousand? Jonas rolls his eyes and his smile grows wider, revealing crooked teeth, keep going, sweetheart, the guy's loaded. So Kate guesses again, Jonas indicates that she can keep going, and both women join in, one after the other, tossing out more and more astronomical numbers, rates that only the stars of the business would ever get, and soon they're playing hard, it's heating up, and then suddenly he pulls back: okay, okay, it's a special project. He pauses and his eyes ferret around them. It's an original fresco. Ah. He sits up straight and drives in the nail: it's my own work. In the silence that follows, the volume of the room seems to go up a notch, but

Jonas can still hear Kate's voice perfectly as it lays into him: oh so that's it, you're an *artist* now! He turns to Paula and, shaking his head, indicating Kate with the corner of his eye, says: you hear this jerk? They find their speed again, talking fast, and here comes that cutting vivacity that is the punching bag for tenderness. A server passing the table trips on Kate's helmet and drops his tray. Clatter, silence, applause. And then the racket starts up again, a racket that Paula plumbs with her eyes to find the industrial clock hanging above the bar and remembers that yesterday, at exactly the same time, she was running across Red Square. Her eyes sweep once around the clock face and come back to settle on Jonas, and in a single breath she utters: a kingdom for the great apes, Jonas, that's what you're going to paint.

⁂

The glasses are empty, Jonas grabs his pack of smokes from the table and says: and you, ladies, what's coming up for you in 2015? They go outside. Again the icy street, the gutter jammed with cigarette butts, and the crowd they have to extricate themselves from so they can move. Once they're out in the open, Kate pulls her phone from her inside pocket and jabs it into the space between them, saying solemnly: alright, enough bullshit, the time has come to show you some real professional work! Paula and Jonas lean in, their temples touching now.

⁂

An image gleams, very dark. Marble. The patina of the entrance hall on avenue Foch that she's been painting for eight days. Unfathomable black, veined with liquid gold, shadowy and ostentatious, majestic. The August sun dripping through trees to the underbrush, a Japanese lacquer veiled with gold pigment, the funerary chamber of a pharaoh. Are you doing a Portor marble for them? Paula lifts her head toward her friend who nods, turning her face away with regal slowness, blowing smoke out her nostrils. Yes. Damn, you're good, murmurs Jonas, struck by the fluidity of the veining, by the ambiguous luminosity of the painting, by the impression of depth he sees in it. Kate puffs up but plays it cool: I graduated with a Portor, you know, I like doing them. The photo is hypnotizing. Are you going to do all four walls? Paula is surprised—Portor is rarely chosen for large surfaces, she knows—it's too black, too difficult to do, too expensive. Kate's cigarette lands in the gutter with a quick flick: I'm doing the ceiling too.

※

A slick of pure oil. Kate had presented her sample of Portor to the building's management in these terms—at least that's what she tells her friends now, having stepped down from the sidewalk to the middle of the narrow street to replay the scene, playing herself and also the man she had to convince—a pale, thirty-something guy with a double-barreled name and disproportionate signet ring, narrow shoulders and round belly, swimming in his pearl-gray suit; he caressed his own head slowly as he studied the sample, unable to lift his eyes to this tall woman standing in front of him, unable to form a clear idea of her body: statuesque or mannish? Kate showed up to the meeting wearing a navy-blue suit and heels, she'd forgotten to take off her ankle bracelet with the skull and crossbones clasp, but she had combed and parted her hair to the side and eased up on her makeup: she wanted this job. Indeed, she had taken pains over her palette—titanium white, yellow ocher, cadmium orange, raw sienna, smoky ombré, Van Dyke brown, vermilion, a little black—and added two coats of glaze to obtain a surface that was simultaneously dark and transparent—obscurity, transparency: the secret of a good Portor. And her pitch had a good chance: the owners of the building were rich families from the golfe du Lion who spent three nights a year in the city. They wanted this marble, wanted it to be like a mirror of their wealth, to pander to their power, evoke the fossil manna sprung from lands where herds used to wander while people dozed inside the steaming tents. To land the job, Kate had expounded on the rareness of Portor, described the scorching marble quarries on Palmaria and those in Porto Venere on the Gulf of Genoa, quarries suspended a hundred and fifty meters above the ocean; she had talked about the boats that would draw up alongside the base of the cliffs where blocks of stone would be slid onboard, up to one hundred *carrate* per ship—the unit of measure, the *carrata*, is the load of a cart pulled by two steer, or three quarters of a ton. The ships would unload the raw marble onto the wharves of Ripa Maris and immediately be reloaded with blocks of marble set to dazzle—sawed, polished, sometimes stamped with the royal lily—before hoisting the sails and setting a course for Toulon, Marseille, Cádiz, passing Gibraltar and sailing up the Atlantic coast toward Saint-Malo, the route of the marble forking at Le Havre, becoming fluvial, and arriving at Paris; and finally, the last shot, Kate had extolled the royal aura of the stone, a stone valued by the Sun King himself, stone that could be found in the walls of Versailles and definitely not in the washrooms of hip restaurants—shall I show you some photos? And now she was imitating the postures of the property management exec, the way he'd held out a limp hand after introducing himself, drawing out his name, hot potato rolling around in his mouth; she mimics his evasive lechery, his awkward chic, but above all she includes herself in the scene, an actress, parodying her own cupidity, her adulation, foxlike, exaggerating the curves of her body and her Scottish accent, and all so beautifully that she takes up the whole street, immense and whirling, haloed by her movie-star hair, and people are starting to stir, to take notice in front of the café, getting intrigued, shifting to find a better view, heads are turning toward this young woman and her theatrical number. The manager had finally settled his skittish gaze on her, hired her for a trial, and then spent every evening taking stock of the progress of the painting, captivated; he was already hinting at other lobbies, other stairwells, other apartments to restore—he managed a significant amount of real estate in the west of Paris, pure and simple Haussmannian through and through, hundreds of square meters on which he intended to turn a profit. Rich at last! Kate's gums glow red as she laughs. And then she bows, like an actor at the end of a play, one hand on her heart, declares that she's buying a round, and everyone crams back into the bar behind her.

⁂

What are you going to do next? Jonas looks at Paula, the whites of his eyes yellow and pupils enormous beneath the brim of his hat. She shifts in her seat, I don't know, I just got back from Moscow this morning, remember. Beside them Kate deteriorates, starts to show signs of fatigue, tipsiness, or both—slouching, mouth open, eyes blurry—and it's a surprise when she finds enough energy for a jab: you must have made a mint with the Russians, they're rolling in it over there, aren't they? Paula smiles: I did alright. And then a cricket chirps from the bottom of a pocket and Jonas jumps up, phone to his ear, rushing out to the street without a glance at Paula and Kate, who stay on the bench. He walks past the window of the bar and sits down on the curb across the street, takes off his cap—a rare gesture—and throws his head back so the light from the streetlamp pours over his face, and then we see him close his eyes and move his lips while shadows form at his temples and in the hollows of his cheeks, and no one could have failed to see that he lifts his lids from time to time to look at Paula behind the pane of glass, Paula who has turned her back. At that moment he has the look of someone seized by love, a being gripped by the subterranean movement of love, and this was likely why the two women kept themselves turned away—it would never have occurred to them to come too close, or ask him about it, never, that wasn't how they worked, the three of them. Their love lives played out off-camera, they never talked about them, were reserved, aside from romantic disasters (Jonas) or head-on laconicism (Kate), carving a vein in these registers where love stories were always exalted and tragic, sex awkward or merely technical, and they were funny at this game; Paula would laugh as she watched them, squinting and wrinkling her nose, replying: tons! when they asked her: and you? Are you getting some? And when it came down to it, all of them kept quiet about love. When he gets back to the table, Jonas's cheeks are burning and his voice is buried, he doesn't sit down, just says flat out: I'm going to a party on rue Sorbier, want to come? Kate shakes her head, I'm exhausted, and I'm working tomorrow, but Paula stands up and says she'll go with him, she wants to walk for a bit.

Later, long after Kate had slowed down to pass them, sitting tall on her scooter, arm raised like a charioteer saluting the emperor at the start of the race, when the time of night made a whole other city emerge, Paula and Jonas walk up avenue Gambetta, alongside the wall of the Père-Lachaise cemetery. She puts her arm through his and with her free hand holds her collar around her freezing neck, he lowers his cap, reties his scarf, shoves his hands into his pockets, and they walk along together like that. You're not wearing enough, it's ridiculous. Jonas's gaze trails over the cemetery, drifting across the sepulchers that stand taller than the wall—stone crosses and statues, covered in lichen, glimpses of temples, slivers of cupolas, mausoleums of rock resembling cave dwellings. Paula presses closer to him in response and they continue on shoulder to shoulder. What kind of ape are you going to paint? Her voice is low. The steam that comes out of her mouth tears apart as they pass through it, and otherwise not a breath of air, the façades of the buildings are dark, cold vitrifies the city, and the sky, high above, is hard and sparkling. I'll do Wounda—Jonas answers softly, nose in his scarf, and at these words Paula's face grows radiant.

They reach the small square. It's midnight, the bars are closing, rows of bottles gleam at the back of darkened spaces, bay windows frame little shadow-puppet theaters where silhouettes are still in motion, carrying out the gestures of work, rinsing carafes, drying glasses, wiping down zinc countertops. Jonas has taken his arm out of Paula's, a firm gesture, I have to go, I'm off, and as he's turning away from her, she holds on, turns his collar up, you're not bad, but you stink of turpentine, you know? Jonas sniffs the sleeve of his coat, and Paula goes on, curious, trying to make the moment last, you might even say you're inflammable. Is someone expecting you? A jogger passes, glancing at his stopwatch, a guy in a fur coat walks his dog, an old woman smokes a cigarette on her balcony, bundled in a fringed shawl. It's quiet. What are you gonna do—are you coming or not? Jonas paces, eyes aimed at her.

Then he takes a step back, takes out his hands and places them under the streetlamp. Lit up like this, they seem to be detached from his body, emerging from the darkness, floating, whitish, vaguely monstrous, with long fingers, bulging joints, the lifeline carved into the palm like a knife swipe in a plank of wood, the pads at the base of his fingers peeled off by old lightbulbs, and the skin encrusted with various substances—oils, pigments, paint dryer, solvents, varnish, gouache, glue. Now yours. He gestures with his chin toward Paula, who shows her short, square hands: dorsal side, same thick skin, phalanges creased like walnut shells and short nails set with a line of black; palms up, the same signs. They stand for a long while forehead to forehead above their open palms that are the palest surfaces in the night, stencils, stamps, transfers—from far away you would have imagined you were seeing two hikers leaning over a topographical map, staring at the paper and deciphering the legend in order to find their way. Suddenly Jonas takes Paula by the waist, holds her close, and murmurs in a rush into her neck, I'll call you tomorrow.

Imbricata

NOW LET'S TALK A LITTLE ABOUT THE RUE
du Métal. Let us see Paula arriving in front of Number 30 *bis*
that September day in 2007, stepping back onto the sidewalk
to cast her eyes up and take in the façade—this is an important
moment. What stands there, in this street in Brussels at the
edge of the quartier Saint-Gilles (just a street, an insignificant
street, a street mended like an old woolen sock), is a fairy-tale
house: crimson, venerable, at once fantastical and folded away.
And already, thinks Paula, whose cervical vertebrae hurt from
holding her head so far back, already it's a house of painting,
a house whose façade seems to have been lifted from a canvas by a Dutch master: bourgeois brick, rows of gables, rich
metal hinges at the windows, a monumental door, elaborate
metalwork, and wisteria that entwines around the building
like a jeweled belt. Then, exactly as though she were stepping
into a fairy tale, Paula pulls the handle and the bell emits a
cracked ring, the door opens, and she steps inside the Institut
de Peinture; she disappears into the decor.

※

Paula is twenty, has a maroon Adidas bag slung over her shoulder, a sketch pad under her arm, and sunglasses on her face
behind which she hides her strabismus, so that the lobby she's
walking through now becomes darker and darker through
her lenses, dark but fabulous, thick, unplaceable. Scents of
temples and construction sites. The air, teeming with suspended
particles of dust, takes on the thickness of fog in places, the

heaviness of incense, and the smallest movement, the lightest breath, creates thousands of microscopic whirlwinds. She makes out a door on the left, a stairwell, and the opening of a hallway at the far end on the right. She begins to wait.

She puts down her things and lets her eyes trail over the room, across the floor, the ceiling, and the walls. She wonders where she's landed: on every side, and becoming more and more clear as the seconds pass and her eyes adjust to the dimness, the walls show a sampling of large marble facing and wood panelling, fluted columns, capitals with acanthus leaves, and a window open to the branch of a cherry tree in flower, a chickadee, a delicate sky. Suddenly she steps over her bag and walks toward the marble slabs—Breche Violet, she will later learn—placing her hand flat against the surface. But instead of the cold touch of stone, it's the texture of paint she feels. She leans in close: it really is a picture. Amazed, she turns to the woodwork and repeats the motions, stepping back and then leaning in closer, touching it, as though she were playing at making the initial illusion disappear and then reappear, moving along the wall, growing more and more stirred up as she passes the stone columns, the sculpted arches, the capitals and the moldings, the stucco; she reaches the window, ready to lean out, certain that another world stands right there, just past the casement, within reach—and at every point her fumbling only reveals more painting. Even so, she stops once she's in front of the chickadee paused on its branch, reaches her arm out to the rosy dawn, opens her hand to slide her fingers between the bird's feathers, and tilts an ear to the foliage.

❧

The appointment time, which she checks on her phone, suddenly seems as cryptic as the secret code of a safe—four impenetrable, solitary numbers, disconnected from earthly temporality. A light vertigo comes over Paula as she stares at them, her head spins, inside and outside get mixed up, she doesn't know anymore how to catch hold of the present. But at the appointed time, the door swings open silently and Paula steps over the threshold of a huge room bathed in stained-glass light.

A woman is there, behind a desk. Paula doesn't immediately distinguish her from the surroundings, she seems to be so much a part of them, to belong to them, fitted into space like the last piece of a puzzle. She's bent over a notebook, turning the pages with a slow hand, and she lifts her head to rest her gaze on Paula with the sureness of a trapeze artist landing on a narrow platform. We can see her clearly now, we receive full-on this face, neutral as a mask, and this poise—nothing strains, nothing wobbles. Economy and rigor emanate from this body, and Paula quickly feels ungainly, slovenly. The woman's blouse seems sculpted to her body, like a decorative panel, a breastplate, and her turtleneck, at once setting and pedestal, exhibits her head like an Elizabethan ruff, emphasizing the paleness of the skin, the curve of the jaw, the strong chin. She may be only a meter away from Paula, but her voice seems to arrive from far away, from within the walls, and carries with it an echo when she says, without preamble: Miss Karst, becoming a decorative painter requires learning depth of observation and a mastery of the stroke; in other words, developing one's eye (at this moment Paula remembers that she is still wearing her sunglasses)—and hand—the woman opens a palm, marking her words. Silence. The air is dry, metallic, frenetic, as though the room had been rubbed with chiffon and now electrostatic forces fill it to the brim. Paula is sitting still on her chair, back straight, neck stiff. Maybe it's over already, she thinks, maybe it's all been said, nothing more to add, the eye and the hand, there you go, that's it, I understand, I'll get up and go. But the woman continues in her deep voice—a voice of supple bronze that seems to be forming in her thorax and not in her throat—trompe-l'œil is the meeting of a painting and a gaze, conceived for a particular point of view, and defined by the effect it is supposed to produce. Students at the Institut have access to archival documents and samples taken from nature for their work, but the most important parts of the training are the in-studio demonstrations, the benefit of learning by example. Her words are so perfectly strung, slow, weighted, each sentence imbued with a strike so clear, each intonation so serene, that Paula grows agitated, as though the scene were surreal, as though she had stepped onto a proscenium to take the place waiting for her, to take on her role. The voice again: we teach traditional painting techniques, oil painting, watercolor, and our method consists—at this point the woman slows down, suspends her sentence, takes it up again after a moment, abrupt—our method consists of an intensive practical training. Attendance is mandatory, absence will result in being thrown out of the Institut and each project must be handed in on time. A lock of black hair, escaped from a quick chignon, disrupts her face now: the Institut's reputation is based upon the painting of woods and marbles. We delve into the very matter of nature, exploring its form in order to grasp its structure. Forests, undergrowth, soil, rifts, chasms—it entails patient work of appropriation (a dumbstruck Paula concentrates on the movement of the hands that twist and turn in the air—she holds to them, because everything else is going over her head). Any questions? The desk that separates them is a jumble of papers where the Institut's administration stretches out in piles beneath a dusting of iron. Between the crumpled invoices and the boxes of invitations, Paula glimpses the sketch of an impressive diving suit on the back of a kraft envelope and stutters an inaudible syllable, preparing to open her drawing folder, when the woman stops her: close it—an eloquent gesture with the flat of her hand. Pink and gold rays filtering in through the windows carve translucent diagonal lines through the space, creating aureoles on the oak wainscot-ting—*chef-d'œuvre* of trompe-l'œil—and on the faded carpet, on Paula's hair, which changes color, and on her face, where astonishment now creates a whole other light.

The current program—the voice has risen a notch, the eyes shine, aniline black, lacquered—lasts from October to March, the six months considered off-peak for house painters. Starting from the first week, we paint wood. Oaks, which are by no means the easiest, and also elm, for example, or ash, Macassar ebony, Congo mahogany, the crown of the poplar, the pear tree, the walnut—whatever species I judge important to know how to paint. In mid-November, we start on marble. Carrara, Grand Antique, Labrador, Henriette Blonde, Fleur de Pêcher, Red Griotte—and here again I will decide in due course—the enumeration of these names is more than just a table of contents, and the woman takes a visible pleasure in pronouncing them; her voice undulates through the room like a shamanic chant, and Paula understands nothing but the rhythm. In mid-January, it's the semi-precious stones, lapis and citrine, topaz and jade, amethyst, clear quartz; in February, drawing: perspective first, then moldings and friezes, ceilings and patinas. In March, we do gilding and silver plating, sten-ciling and commercial lettering, and then, finally, the diploma. All this is fairly dense, fairly substantial. Still speaking, she steps out from behind the desk and moves slowly toward the door, places a hand on the handle, indicating to Paula, who is thrown off guard, that the interview has come to an end, all while holding out a list of the required materials in the other hand. Don't forget to get a smock. Then, just when she's turning back to her desk, she changes her mind and whips around: one last thing—in the beginning, turpentine can cause dizziness and nausea, all the more so because we work standing up. You'll see, it's all quite physical.

※

Back on the sidewalk, the pale September sky blinds Paula and she squints and stumbles, just like every time she comes out of a movie theater and finds herself back in real life. The scene that just took place—the lobby, the wait, the interview—extends and changes shape as she walks down the rue du Métal, enfolded in the echo of the woods, marbles, and gemstones, the marvelous names. There is more to this world, she muses, more ways of seeing it and speaking of it. Her step lengthens and the sidewalk beneath her feet seems to speed up and carry her along like a moving walkway in an airport terminal. She heads toward the trees with leaves turning brown, there, on the square, and at the same moment, a flight of crows rushes into formation at the top of the street behind her. Paula pivots, alerted by the sound. The birds plunge in her direction—perhaps a dozen of them and some with a wingspan of nearly a meter, the sound of their croaking reverberating down the street, a wild, unreadable flight, only a haruspex trained in the best temples of antiquity could see in it a manifestation of the gods, could decipher in it an omen. The flock comes nearer, swells, fans out from one façade to the next along the street which has become a massive aviary, and Paula dives instinctually between two cars, crouches down with outstretched fingers covering the top of her head, sure that the crows are going to peck her with their beaks, their claws, shining like the skin of an orange, and hooked, hard,

hard as wood. She feels them pass above her head, feels the disturbance in the air, waits, and then slowly stands again. Something hits her on the back of the head just then, a little tap, a flick, and she sways forward, catches herself against the side of a car, and looks around—but there's nothing there, it's over, the birds have disappeared, silence has returned and the sky is empty over the rue du Métal.

⁂

Paula catches her breath and starts walking again. Around her, the cobbled street, the rooftops, the low buildings—all of it is shiny, sharp, revived, as though the energies buried in the stones had been whipped up. She blinks and touches the spot on her head where she was hit, says to herself, I'm alive, and starts to run, cutting across the square on the diagonal, gaining the opening to the metro nestled against the side of the Église Saint-Gilles, reaches the Bruxelles-Midi station, an aisle seat in a jam-packed Thalys hurtling toward Paris, the glass roof of the Gare du Nord beaten by a storm, the stairwell in the building on rue de Paradis, the old Roux-Combaluzier elevator, the family apartment that she rushes straight through, her room where she tosses her bag and sketch pad on the floor and then heads back along the hallway toward the kitchen, where her parents, Guillaume and Marie Karst, are making dinner together as they do every evening—beets with vinaigrette, shepherd's pie, crème caramel—and it seems that something has taken shape within her, an intuition has firmed up, because we hear her announcing: okay, it's decided, I'm going to the Institut on the rue du Métal to study decorative painting. Silence. Her parents don't put down their graters, their knives, their peelers, but slow a little and then grow tense: decorative painting? Well then. They both turn toward their daughter at the same time, flustered: so you're finished being an artist?

Paula looks out the window. She's been dawdling for two years, she knows it. There was the dullness of the bac, then enrollment in legal studies in Nanterre, on the pretext that it could lead to anything and she would have time to find her way, a wasted year. She was quickly out of her depth in a difficult, dense curriculum, at once meticulous and technical, horrified by the cramming—at the end of the winter, she discovered an artistic sensibility and switched streams the next September to take a foundation course for art school. The Karst parents had been silent witnesses to this movement, hoping for the solid ground of a vocation, but their daughter had turned out once again to be indecisive and something of a follower, choosing the film option so she could stay close to the boy she was in love with, beginning several documentaries only to abandon them (including a rather promising one about a grain of sand filmed through a microscope); and at the end of the year, the art school entry exams (it had to be admitted) had yielded nothing.

The parents begin to pace between the stove and the sink. Decorative painting. It sounds less magical and more arts and crafts—you want to do decor? Relieved at the thought that their daughter is enrolling in a solid training course, through which she will be more likely to find work, they are ready to believe in her again. But disappointed, too, without really understanding why. Surprised by Paula's aplomb as she sprawls on a wicker chair, bites into a crust of bread, and declares: I'm going to learn the techniques of trompe-l'œil, the art of illusion.

YOU MIGHT WONDER HOW PAULA KARST, this average young woman, sheltered and predictable (and a little on the lazy side)—someone who spends most of her time sitting in a café booth in the company of others like her, every ounce of existence frothing in the espresso with this mix of grace and vacuity that grazes genius; how this impetuous dabbler, for whom the future was invariably and comfortably concealed in a *sfumato*, ended up plunging headlong into the large studio on the rue du Métal. Even more surprising: she rushed there. You might wonder how she managed, in the space of three days, to find a two-bedroom apartment nearby, number 27, rue de Parme, and a fellow student enrolled at the Institut to share it with her, Jonas Roetjens; how she heartlessly dumped her boyfriend—a fashion plate with a perfect little beard, a perfect little tattoo, and perfect little jeans rolled up above his sneakers (he must have hardened his lips in bitterness when he read her brief breakup text, straddled his ridiculously hip bike, and ridden toward the Bois de Vincennes, stomach twisted in pain, forehead red); and it's even harder to fathom how she managed to find herself in Brussels on September 30, in front of the door to her new building, she and her father emptying the trunk of a Volvo wagon where the usual student furniture jostled, the kind that gets set up with a sense of responsibility: bedding, coffee maker, desk lamp, a few dishes, chair, table, bookshelf, two garbage bags full of clothes, vacuum, mop, computer; how she carried everything up three floors, hardy, some trips taken at a jog—this young woman who objects to all physical effort (long arms and long legs, though, and a slender build that makes her appear taller than she actually is); this young woman who is always the first to twist her ankle, to bump her head, to complain of a cramp. But the fact is that this young woman's move was finished in a snap, lightbulbs screwed in, bed assembled, computer and Wi-Fi set up chop-chop! Is she on fire or something? murmurs Guillaume Karst at each landing, out of breath, hands on his hips, leaning against the wall.

⁂

On fire? No, not yet. Maybe it's just the idea of shaking up her life. And Paula approaches what comes next with nonchalance, without reflection. Wasn't it written right there on the Institut's website that it was not necessary to have strong drawing skills to get in? Wasn't it a matter of following a purely technical training program, acquiring knowledge that was accessible to whoever was willing to do the work? Wasn't it simply about learning to copy? Copying. Child's play, Paula, her father had said over coffee in a gas station near Valenciennes, their eyes drifting past the lips of the paper cups toward the line of trucks rushing along the highway. Paula had dug in her heels: copying, yes, exactly. She fancies herself already as an apprentice, sleeves rolled up, ready to rip into it; an industrious artisan who's chosen a modest route to get to the heart of painting—learning drawing, acquiring a perfect understanding of the techniques and materials, starting at the beginning; she likes to tell herself that you have to begin with all this before you stand in front of a canvas, a wall, any surface, and what matters will come later, elsewhere, in another world, the world of true artists—and that's where she's utterly mistaken.

This first evening, standing in the middle of her room, hands on her ribs, belly out, Paula breathes deeply. A gust of heat warms her temples and makes her salivate. She did it, she finally did it—she left home, it's happening, she's going to live her life; but the ardor she imagined feeling as she uttered these words is nowhere to be found. However hard she plays the moment, strikes the pose, evokes an inaugural scene (young hero poised on the brink of the future and squinting toward a horizon full of promise), she's still on edge. Anxiety suffocates her, crushes her chest. Something rises before her, right there, something she will have to confront. She suddenly mistrusts the ease with which she turned this leaf—not a single obstacle appeared, not even her lousy drawing skills, not her reticence, her proud timidity, not even the cost of the tuition (high), a price her parents had agreed to pay without batting an eye—she overheard whispers in their room after she told them about the fees, and then nothing more. At the moment, the more she looks at the new furniture (the curtains with their impeccable drape, the green power light of the computer, the dishes and the bath towel full of the heady scent of starch, this material panoply she had so loved picking out, these things that ushered her into the world of adulthood), the more she senses that something isn't quite right. She thinks back to her father's last gesture, which he made just as he was getting back into his car, one leg in, one leg out, belly pressed against the open door, and that hand lifted toward the window where he knew she was watching, bye-bye, she couldn't hear anything but she saw his mouth moving and his head tilted back, bye-bye, he was smiling at her, his face was relaxed, he seemed happy, satisfied most likely for having done his job as a father—because that hand that was waving at her, that little sweeping movement in the atmosphere, also signified that he was sending her away, clear off, clear off, yes; and then the more the light declines, the more she tells herself that her parents saw this school in Brussels as a golden opportunity to get her out of the apartment on the rue de Paradis. She sits down on her bed, emptied out, elbows digging into her thighs, head heavy, and doesn't hear her phone as her father calls, over and over, from a rest stop in La Sentinelle.

DAZZLED FROM THE MOMENT SHE STEPS
through the studio doorway on the first day, entering a rect-
angular room of fifteen by ten meters, cement floor and glass
roof, with a mezzanine running along all four walls used for
storing hundreds of rollers and drawing pads, samples, and
small tools. Paula immediately likes the light of beginnings
that bathes the place, a white, matte light, made that much
clearer by the dimness of the lobby and the hallway, as though
it were necessary to pass through an airlock of opacity in
order to be able to see clearly, and then get to work. Twenty-
odd easels are positioned throughout the room. She threads
her way toward one at the back, sets her paint box down
on a wooden stool and puts on her smock. The other students spread out through the room, she hears English being
spoken a few meters ahead, stands at the ready, and then the
woman in the black turtleneck makes her entrance, small
here, smaller than in Paula's memory of her, but immediately
occupying a significant volume of space. Then the inventory:
the director calls out the name of each paintbrush and the
students verify that it's in their box, and Paula's are lovely
and clean, the ferrule sparkling, the bristles soft; here, an
ink brush, an angled brush with hog bristles, a veinette, a script
brush, a slender brush with a wooden handle and Kolinsky
sable, and the one she would consider her lucky brush, a
lacquer brush with Alaskan bear bristles, a gift from Marie,
her mother, given to her the day before she left. There are
many whose functions Paula doesn't really know (she placed
them in the box the way you might assemble a gang before a

break-in, assuring yourself of their silent and loyal presence), and which she examines now with curiosity: these are the tools for remaking the world.

Pain arrives soon after. Studio practice is indeed *quite physical*—a laughable euphemism—and the workload that slams into this student is all the more violent because she has, up until now, never really exhausted her young self. Headache, pain in her nose (sinuses stripped), backache (the twenty-year-old curve is nothing but a fire in the lumbar spine), sore feet (her heels grow blistered from pacing in front of her easel all day, and on the third day she decides to order a pair of sneakers online with soles specially designed for marathon runners), and there's this tension from lifting the brush and keeping it horizontal that inflames her shoulder, weighs on the shoulder blade. Paula makes the acquaintance of this body into which she was born—it's high time. What surprises her, though, are her eyes—sore from the first night onward, like bruises you press with a finger.

※

October is the woods. Sensation of entering a dim zone pierced here and there by shafts of light, in an acoustic space penetrated by other bodies and other voices, harmonious or dissonant. Other languages too, and the one spoken in the studio is a foreign language that Paula must learn, that she decodes, leaning over anatomical diagrams portraying a transverse, tangential, or radial cut, slabs of wood cut length-wise or quartered, revealing the flaws, the iridescence, or the silver grain, the fiber, the parenchyma, and the vessels. She keeps a little notebook in her shirt pocket with a black cover and a graphite pencil, she reaps the words like spoils of war, overwhelmed by the profusion—like a hand plunged blindly into a bag without ever feeling the bottom—learning to name the trees and stones, the roots and types of soil, the pigments and powders, the pollens, the dusts, and learning to distinguish, to specify and then to use these words for herself, so that the notebook gains value as crutch and compass: as the world slides, doubles, reproduces itself, as the creation of the illusion is accomplished, it is in language that Paula finds her bearings, her points of contact with reality.

It's hard. She wonders each morning whether she'll make it through, six months, a fall and a winter, tells herself over and over that it's all going to work out, it's a matter of days, that she'll find her footing. But she struggles to find a rhythm. Once past the initial shock (which she will happily recount later with the showy delight of those who've received a baptism by fire), and believing that she's found a kind of tempo, she lets herself sleep longer, ambling around social media, leaving posts for her followers, her friends—the scatterbrain! One brief moment of inattention that gets her a rap on the knuckles so hard she immediately reverts to her initial practices: up at six, bed at midnight, disconnect from the internet, bye guys, ciao chitchat. They laugh at her online: is this school a convent or something? And Paula smiles, oddly proud of this allusion to the life of an ascetic. She then takes her silence to the extreme, taking longer and longer to answer friends' messages asking for photos of the guys at the school, erasing texts from her ex-boyfriend without even reading them, her ex who has still not admitted to himself, it seems, that it's over for good between them, and who harasses her with over-the-top sexual insinuations that bear no relation to the rather chaste content of their relationship. The messages she sends to those outside the Institut grow fewer and fewer until they evaporate completely, and she only answers the phone when it rings from the rue de

Paradis. She becomes intoxicated, fascinated by what she's imposing on her body, which she never would have believed she could bear, and by the feeling of discerning in the work an unknown expenditure, something that burns.

The rooms, though, lose her and abuse her. Impression each morning of arriving at a former world, a world situated in the shadows of time, or more precisely a world where time had been dismantled in slabs and reassembled in the chaos, rebuilt. She's lost. She twists her ankles on a regular basis as she crosses the lobby of 30 *bis*, rue du Métal, disoriented in the dimness and the scent of cold wall hangings, and every time she perceives the pale light of the studio at the end of the hallway, its odor of hydrocarbon and its rustle of the jungle, she can't help but slow her step, feel her heart hit the ground running and her stomach in knots. Once she's inside, in the brightness, it gets more complicated. Painting in the middle of a group destabilizes her and makes her anxious. Consenting to be seen, to give access to what happens inside her in the act of painting, injures her reserve—as though she were naked. But the configuration of the studio (and in particular the storage mezzanine above the lower theater) gives her no possibility of finding a corner: people can watch her work from any angle. She is someone who's proud, and she withdraws into her shell. Never lingers in the studio, goes straight home after class, the way you'd head for shelter, walking fast, in a hurry to remove herself from the eyes behind her, the feedback spoken over her shoulder, the encouragements in which she hears only condescension and the criticisms that make her want to spin around and shove her brush into mouths that are open too wide, stop stressing me out! Sensitive, as they all are, the shy ones who retreat, touchy, bristling. Every day she can be seen gathering her things in a rush and beating it out of there with her head down, forehead aimed at the ground, never looking around her—and yet, this is her tactical mistake and this is how she gets hurt: withdrawn behind her easel at the back of the room, casting sidelong glances, swallowed up, Paula can't see those who are painting all around her, similarly blind, stumbling, and since Jonas never shows himself in the rue de Parme, her life amounts to this large piece of paper in *double raisin* format (100 cm × 65 cm) affixed to a wooden frame.

※

She sticks to it. Listens, makes notes, works, but still doesn't lift her head enough, except during the demonstrations given each morning at the appointed hour by the woman in the black turtleneck, skin bare and hair up, gaze translucent, turning in a circle without a word, one hand flat on her belly, fingers spread, the other holding the brush, the rag, the sponge, or passing around a piece of wood, a veined Zebrano, a moiré *Nauclea diderrichii*, as she would pass around a fragment of metamorphic rock a month later, Tuscan ruin marble or limestone with stromatolites from Britain, to demonstrate the antediluvian beauty, spontaneous, enigmatic—an innocent beauty, she specifies, impenetrable, while in her open hand the piece of wood or the shard of stone becomes the center of a magnetic field whose concentric rings stretch out across the room: a nonhuman beauty. And then she gives her lesson standing up, three quarters before the easel, without ever turning her back completely to her students—she paints in front of them, gives them an example, alternating on certain days with two other teachers whose appearance also imposes silence on the room, causes spines to straighten, makes eyes turn to the front. You can hear their skating steps from the entrance hall, soles that slide over the ground at a good clip, and suddenly there they are in the studio doorway, corpulent, historical, as though the past had regurgitated them here with a jolt, and in these moments Paula tends to freeze, panic-stricken. They look like brothers, both with big scholarly heads, long stone-setter's hands, a wealth of sarcasm when they address the class, paunch tucked into pairs of saffron or raspberry crushed velour pants, rough canvas aprons protecting their ensembles, and they sport (like prelates from the Roman Curia) blood red socks knitted from Scottish wool over ankles of a surprising delicacy. They give their lectures slowly, in cracked, guttural voices, but express themselves haughtily, with aristocratic, calibrated malice, constantly wiping the corners of their mouths with massive handkerchiefs they pull from their pockets with a flourish and cause to disappear like illusionists on stage, their body language precise, their sources documented. Paula lies low during their lessons, tries to become transparent, the thought that they might call on her, or worse, that they might use her work as a counterexample—here we have precisely the worst, the most spineless and unoriginal example, they'd say, as their eyes rolled behind their lorgnettes and their thin fingers, crooked as talons, moved forward to tear everything from her easel, reduce the paper to a sphere the size of a tennis ball which they'd toss over their shoulder with a moist smile, causing the rest of the class to go cold—start over, mademoiselle, start everything over from scratch. Each evening she works hard to review the day's lesson, recording each step, isolating each movement, unfolding the whole process until she can say it out loud, recite it like a poem by heart, and then she falls backwards, breathless, into bed.

She learns to see. Her eyes burn. Fried, worked like never before, open eighteen hours a day; an average that will soon include the sleepless nights spent slogging, and other nights of partying. In the morning, her eyes blink incessantly as though she'd been plopped down in full sun, lashes vibrating, butterfly wings, but after sunset she feels them weakening, her left eye limps, it slips to the side like someone sinking onto a bank of fresh grass at the edge of the path. She rinses her lids with blueberry water, places frozen teabags on them, tries gels and eyewashes, but nothing eases the sensation of tired, dry eyes, rigid pupils, nothing can stop the formation of persistent dark circles under them—her face has been branded, the stigmata of this rite of passage, of metamorphosis. Because *to see*, under the glass roof of the studio on the rue du Métal, high on fumes from paint and solvents, muscles sore and forehead burning, doesn't just mean keeping your eyes open to the world—*to see* is to engage in a pure action, create an image on a sheet of paper, an image that resembles the one the eyes have created in the brain. And it's not enough to see in detail—that's the least of it, thinks Paula, and later she'll be exasperated to hear her parents boast about her *expert precision*—it's not just about reproducing reality, giving a reflection of it, copying it. *To see*, here, is something else.

৵

Paula doesn't know what, not yet, but she instinctually understands that she has underestimated what would be required of her. And Saturday morning, in the zenithal light of the big studio, when the time has come for the tour of the easels, the students step aside to clear a passage for the woman in the black turtleneck so she can look at their work up close and say something about it, directions that are concrete, simple, words that some might foolishly take as empty or anodyne but which, in the silence, take on an exact shape, a weight that is just, a meaning that is right—try painting with your inner glaciers, with your own volcanoes, with your underbrush and your deserts, your abandoned villas, and your high, high plateaus—we can see Paula in the midst of the group, eyes shining, and in the same moment this thought is opening inside her: trompe-l'œil is something very different from a technical exercise, completely other than a simple optical experience—it's a sensory adventure that shakes up our thinking, challenges the nature of illusion, and maybe even—this is the school's credo—the very essence of painting. In her ebullient but tangled brain, the instruction she receives is resorbed as an elementary principle that she takes a while to claim for herself: trompe-l'œil has to make us see at the same time that it obscures, and this involves two distinct and successive moments: one in which the eye is deceived, and one in which it is undeceived; if the reveal of *l'impostura* doesn't occur—the woman in the black turtleneck concludes, shrugs, shoots her cold gaze over the group like a solitary bird—then all that stands before us is nonsense, a process, a fraud; and so the virtuosity, the intelligence of the painter's eye, the beauty of the tableau, all this cannot be recognized, all this remains out of reach. And you see, she says, this wrecks the pleasure, this kills the work—and that was the worst thing she could say, an incontrovertible condemnation; she makes the plosive explode and spits out these words with disgust: *kills the work.*

Learning to imitate wood is *to become one with the forest*—the woman in the black turtleneck also says *establish a relationship, engage with*—and Paula turns this phrase over in her head for a long time, allowing it to decant. She waits. A plant kingdom quivers in the studio, stretching out across the easels, proliferating on the palettes where the colors nuance yellows, layer browns, harbor a little red for the acacias and that absolute black you find in the heart of the purest ebony. The trees split open, revealing pale sapwood, darker heartwood, teaching a repertory of forms, an interlacing of threads, straight, undulating or spiraling, a seeding of pores and burls that add up to a world within reach. A forest rises in the studio, woven of stories, blending the woods of childhood—those of fairy tales, of the wolf and the nymph, of white stones and foxes, those we walk through holding fast to the hand of the escaped convict—with country woods and political jungles, each student bringing their own version, and Paula's is a forest from a movie, a reel of memory with holes burned through in parts, but where each detail of her mother Marie's face can still be seen, mouth open wide, eye in the viewfinder of a Super 8 camera with a Zeiss lens, neck grazed by beautiful gold chains that capture shatterings of sunlight and make a covenant with the vast underbrush where, in this month of August, she's shooting a short film—*L'enfant des fougères*, the story of a wild child inspired by Victor de l'Aveyron, a story of a child without parents, without siblings, the epitome of strangeness for Paula, who's always a little discombobulated, come summer, when vacation time gathers an abundant family around her; her mother requisitions the kids from the house, the oldest who need to be coaxed out in front of the lens, tracked down in their rooms or in front of the TV, and the littlest ones, excited, who have to be directed, and among them a nine-year-old Paula, who—at the exact moment when her mother shouts action!—enters the film, moves through the familiar forest which transforms as the camera rolls, becoming an unknown territory where both the faraway and the nearby disappear, where the temperature drops, where the volume rises—each sound bursts out and then lives its life of noise—the long take goes on, the child Paula walks in deep mystery, the familiar path becomes unfamiliar and she recognizes none of it, not the dry earth notched and scarred, rutted by agricultural machines, not the holes made by cows' hooves, not the play area where each stump has a name, where firecracker wrappers and cigarette butts are churned in with the earth, where neon yellow tennis balls forgotten under a barrel have gone grayish, spongy, and she feels herself becoming a different person. The half-dark is riddled with light, perforated by rays skewed in every direction, she stays inside the story with each step, reaches the hut of the wild child where, sitting on a stone and smoking a Gitane, a bare-chested boy waits, wearing a leather ushanka and aviator glasses—the eldest of her cousins. She doesn't even recognize him.

Oak, pine, eucalyptus, rosewood, mottled mahogany, thuja burl, Virginia tulip tree, or catalpa, October passes and Paula gets through, she's flustered, sweating, disheveled, dreams one night that her skin has become deeply lined, but manages to produce images, even if her painting stands out from the others as laborious and always a little weak. Until the day when she hears, for the first time, about the speed of the ash, the melancholy of the elm, the laziness of the white willow, and she is overcome with emotion: everything is alive.

JONAS ROETJENS. WHO IS THIS GUY? Guillaume Karst had shouted over the mixing bowl where he was beating egg whites until they formed peaks—a meringue?—the night his daughter asked him to sign a security deposit for the apartment she was going to take in Brussels. The radio was blaring so it could be heard above the noise of the electric mixer, an infernal racket reigned in the kitchen, and finally she had written the word *roommate* in chalk on a slate hanging from the knob of a cupboard. Her father had glanced up without stopping what he was doing, then leaned again over whatever was whitening in the mixing bowl, shoulders high, and jeans too, he was cooking with aggression that day, tip of his tongue pressed between his lips. You've met him? He had raised his voice again—probably taking advantage of the situation, he who never spoke to anyone with anything but moderation. Paula had shaken her head no and he'd turned his back to her and stood gripping the mixer as it busted their eardrums along with the molecules couched in the egg whites.

※

Jonas rang the doorbell of the apartment three days late, appearing under the shadow of a backpack shaped like a menhir, sketch pad pressed to his thigh, mattress held against the wall with one finger, a single mattress, grayish and stained. Handshake. Paula. Jonas.

Paula had been friendly from the outset, careful to make a good impression on this stranger with whom she was about to start sharing seventy square meters for the next six months. Want help bringing your stuff up? Cheery, but he shook his head, answered quietly, thanks, it's okay, everything's here already, grabbed his sketch pad and stepped through the door. Paula moved aside to let him through, flattening herself against the wall and pointing to a door: that's your room, I took the other one at the end of the hall. He nodded, okay. From the kitchen Paula watched him set his pack down with a rotation of his shoulders, scan the place with a circular sweep of his eyes, and then go back for the mattress—the top part of his face consumed by the brim of a baseball cap, the rest lit up in contrast, cheeks hollowed as though sucked in from the inside, straight nose, full lips, traces of recent acne on his temples. He moved in silence, slipped through the apartment, thin, supple, narrow hips, bare ankles, arms seeming extendable as he juggled the mattress and dropped it on the floor with a muffled sound—same arms as me, thought Paula. She did her best to smile when she handed him his set of keys, a complicated smile that had nothing very warm about it but mixed together shyness, calculation, and disappointment, because Jonas's look, more than his physical self, had disconcerted her—his shiny tracksuit jacket zipped all the way up under a black raincoat, his too-short jeans, white sneakers, gold hoop and beaded bracelets on his wrists, and beyond all this, something else that was undetectable. She would have liked to see him without his hat, now, for him to lift his brim a little, she would have liked to see his eyes, but no, his pupils remained hidden, they pierced through from the shadows, an animal with night vision, a cat, she thought, as she read out the Wi-Fi password, showed him the fridge, the cupboards, the vacuum, a little housewife suddenly ready to set out the rules of a future flatshare, but then, as though he had realized this might take a while, he interrupted her with a furtive hand on her forearm: I'm off. Paula nodded quickly, cheeks blazing, okay, see you tomorrow, and stepped back against the sink as Jonas shoved the keys into his pocket, yep, see you tomorrow—voice at minimum volume, succinct nod of his head. Then acrobatics down the stairwell, the sound of light-footed leaps that faded out until they disappeared.

⁂

Paula glanced at the bottle of wine and two glasses placed on the table, a get-to-know-you drink meant to mark the start of their cohabitation, a little mimicry of adulthood from which he must have fled, but a moment she still clung to, as she tended to cling to rituals, everything that allows us to punctuate time, to give it shape, and she picked up the shiny new corkscrew, grabbed the bottle by the neck, opened it and poured herself a glass that she downed in one gulp, eyes closed; and in that long swallow of alcohol, the second when she had first seen Jonas on the landing came back: he stood before her, seeming to contain a very condensed destiny, a nucleus of compressed energy that we could imagine would split open in time and consume itself to the end.

BUT A MONTH LATER, WHEN THE SKY OVER
Brussels takes on the color of porridge and the time of the
marbles has arrived, Paula falls out of step. The marvelous
names harden, they impose strict codes of representation, a
system of conventions, a syntax and a vocabulary as rigorous as
those of an entire language. The intransigence of the woman in
the black turtleneck intensifies, obdurate about the structuring
of emptiness and form, draconian about colors, hammer-
ing on about how nothing will be possible without mastering
this alphabet, without memorizing these names—Polcevera
green, San Siro mischio, Monte Gazzo alabaster. Painting
marble means giving oneself a geography, she declares during
the first class, and orders each of them to consult a list of
works, including a manual of geomorphology (referred to
as *Le Derruau*), a basic catalogue of antique marbles, the
memoir of a shipowner from Saint-Malo, and a few articles
on ideas of metamorphic facies, and, frankly, Paula flounders.

❧

It's November, it's cold, her skin is rough and her nose runs,
the corners of her lips are chapped and cracked, face like an
unmade bed. So tired she falls asleep more and more often
without even getting undressed: she sits down on the edge
of the mattress, kicks off her sneakers, pressing the toe of
one foot against the heel of the other, keeps her sweater on
but reaches behind for her bra clasp, slides the elastic straps
along her arms inside the sleeves, pulls the whole thing out

the front and tosses it into a corner, then topples onto her side under the covers and falls asleep immediately—and you might wonder what has become of her, the young woman who used to shower each night, cleansing her skin with Japanese clay and vitamin-fortified foaming soap, the young, spontaneous woman who would never have sacrificed her nighttime ritual, no matter how tired, the boxwood toothbrush and mint tooth-paste. Her room becomes an extension of the school studio, similarly north-facing and just as poorly heated: her sheets stink of turpentine, her pajamas are spotted with paint, dirty jars invade the window ledge and failed attempts at Sea Green marble are strewn across the floor—she thought this marble would be easy to paint because it's simple, monochrome, the sea at night, the thick, basaltic sea, an emerald-black shot through with filaments of a lighter green (serpentine) or white (talc) forming a supple, fibrous net on the surface, like shredded cotton wool—but on the contrary, it's a type that only experienced painters attempt, which she doesn't realize. You have to give depth to the stone, and for that you need to enter into it, descend to its center, but she isn't capable, she's drowning. So exhausted that she becomes slow, heavy, in pain. Are you eating, at least? her father asks one night when she phones at dinnertime. Paula is eating, sure, but very little, convinced that her slimmed-down body is stronger, harder, her gaze more lucid without sugar in her blood—not very smart. This same night, she announces flatly that she's dropping out, wants to get out of here, the best thing, in fact, would be for them to come get her right now, tomorrow morning at the latest, for them to pack up all the student paraphernalia just as easily as they'd unpacked and presto, è finita la commedia. Her father chews slowly. Paula imagines the looks he throws her mother, eyebrows in little circumflexes and shoulders shrugging, the palm of the hand that covers the mouthpiece while he whispers, what do I tell her? They consult each other, and then her mother takes the phone—her soft and indisputable voice saying the words *partner, roommate*, but Paula hears these words without believing them, eyes glued to the tip of her shoe as it rubs at a spot of paint on the floor, she hears that her mother is speaking for herself and for her father at once, in the name of this fused couple they've been for so long, this mysterious organism they form, in the presence of which it was so hard to grow up. Besides, Jonas is the star of the studio and does just fine on his own, this is what she replies in a hard tone; he is ethereal, indifferent, feral, eats out for every meal and only comes home to sleep, so that Paula barely sees him except at school where it's been a long time since someone so talented walked through the door. Easy to live with, then, never there. Paula keeps to herself, and exhaustion spreads through her body like a poison, cutting her off from the outside world.

NOVEMBER STILL, AND IT'S RAINING. PAULA toils over a Cerfontaine, a fairly technical marble, probably a little too difficult for her—two applications with oil, a third to glaze the grooves, you might wonder what went through her mind for her to choose this one—and Jonas, as it happens, comes into the kitchen. How's it going? She jumps, turns—papier-mâché complexion. I set up in here, it's freezing in my room. Jonas takes off his raincoat but keeps his hat on, and against all odds here he is, lingering, taking a mug from the cupboard and pouring himself some tea. Looking at his roommate's painting—it's the first time he has done so. His eyes slowly move over the image and Paula stands frozen, brush aloft. The rain intensifies against the window, a quick, pebbled rain—drumroll. What kind of marble is that? he asks. She takes a step back and answers without taking her eyes off it, it's a Cerfontaine. The name is tossed out confidently. But Jonas asks again: ah, a Cerfontaine, and where's that from? Paula spins toward him, surprised, shrugging her shoulders: where's it from? No idea. Again, the voice that falls, the sentence that closes. Wind sends the rain against the window in torrents, hard little drops, the panes shake and rattle, you'd think you were in a shack made of sheet metal. Jonas keeps his eyes on the painting as he takes his computer out of his knapsack, come, let's check it out, he murmurs, relaxed, while Paula, edgy, hesitates before placing her brush on the edge of the sink, sits down but looks at her watch, thinking it will be dark in an hour, she'll have to turn on the lamps to keep working, there will be shadows,

49

the colors will be off, everything will get complicated, I'll never have time to finish for tomorrow morning. Jonas starts reading out loud: *during the Late Devonian, 370 million years ago*—370 million years, Paula, three, hundred, and, seventy, he leans on each syllable—*the European climate was tropical and coral reefs formed along a band stretching from Maubeuge-Trélon in the west to Chaudfontaine in the east, reaching their strongest development and concentration in the region of Philippeville*—that's not far from here, Paula, we could go see it if you want—*the limestone formed from these reefs is gray in its medial section, red at the base and the top. The limestones richest in fossil remains have a gray-blue coloration, due to the carbonaceous material. The red coloration is linked to the presence of iron-oxidizing fossil bacteria. This marble is said to be a "dry rose" color, but is also called Rouge de Flandre, or fromage de cochon*—like charcuterie, Paula, have you ever eaten fromage de cochon?—*it is common in appearance and betrays no richness.* There. Jonas detaches himself from the screen and Paula opens her eyes again. The Late Devonian, millions of years, metamorphic rocks, coral reefs and the jungle in place of the Ardennes, limestones and fossils, breaches, fractures and pressure high enough to break the earth's crust, all that, she had never thought about it, didn't know the names or the images, considered the ground and everything that composes it to be simply a mess of time, randomness, and forces upon which our entire existence rests. She's speechless.

The pebbles of rain grow softer, everything slows, drops fall outside and the sun bathes the kitchen in a grapefruit light, almost Californian. Jonas drops three sugars in his cup, plop plop plop, stirs the tea, and it seems he's hedging. Paula gets up, picks up her palette and brush again, but before starting to paint she turns to him: and you? What kind of marble did you choose? Jonas drinks his tea slowly, Adam's apple sliding along the length of his throat. A Skyros. The two syllables screech in the room, then he explains: not really fromage de cochon, more like a windswept Greek temple, a distinguished old English gentleman on a Sporades island, a near-sighted little donkey climbing the village path, you know? Paula nods, then, quietly, facing her painting again: I can see them clearly, those steps between whitewashed houses, the old man's panama hat, the long lashes on the donkey, the sea all around. Jonas looks at her from the corner of his eye, really looks at her—this is also the first time he has done so, and you have to wonder what he's been doing all these long weeks, you think to yourself it's high time—hearing her distinctly when a little later on she murmurs as she dabs a bit of English red on her palette, I do like fromage de cochon, and in the silence that forms again, he gets up, shuts the computer in a sign of departure as the legs of the chair move away from the table, scrape the ground. Then Paula tosses him a smile over her shoulder, a smile that no one has seen from her before, simple and with a confidence so clear that he stands frozen, surprised—before him stands someone else, not the same person, the woman with the stony jawline, panic-stricken and tense, but a stranger whose face stirs—their eyes meet above the table, stay locked until Jonas says, leaning against the doorframe: we should get out, Paula, we should get some air. He scans the worn-out sky past the window—rubber tire pierced with coral—and they go outside. And later, when Paula thinks back to that first moment with Jonas, the moment when he would finally say her name, the fromage de cochon moment, she would remember having understood that the first element of painting is not painting, but going out in the world and having a beer.

THE NEXT DAY HER EXHAUSTION DOES AN about-face to become the scaffolding for her days, and Paula gains momentum. The end of the marbles project straightens her up, spine, head, shoulders, and something more seasoned emanates from her, which is nothing more than an aptitude for failure, a consent to the fall, and a desire to start over. She lifts her nose, unclenches her teeth, feels better. A feeling of finally gathering a little speed, a sensation that the outside air whips her forehead better and that her body is becoming taut, stomach and back gaining strength, shoulders and arms unleashed, movement of the wrists surer, lighter, and quite simply more lovely. Observing the stigmata the work leaves on her body brings her an inexpressible sense of well-being, of delight.

From that point on, she enters the studio with less apprehension, more boldness. Sure, she still has trouble controlling her emotions as she slaloms through the room to reach her corner, zigzagging between easels and keeping a mask of composure that doesn't fool anyone—her earlobes burn red and bright as two coals—but this emotion also signals that she has entered an agitated zone, one of whispers and friction, which is always a quiver of pure excitement, an electric shock.

The other students take shape in her field of vision. They begin to exist for Paula and she takes her place among them. There aren't too many of them—about twenty—and they, too, have shining eyes, blackened nails, arm hairs that reek of mineral spirits—this is how you recognize them around the neighborhood once their smocks are off; and they, too, are distributed in twos and threes in large, poorly heated apartments a stone's throw from the school, they too work like dogs and get together on rare occasions for a party fueled by alcohol that drags on until dawn after reaching, around midnight, the respectable ratio of thirty people in a ten-square-meter kitchen—a density designed to encourage carnal collision with someone, even if just for the night. Paula often stays at the studio late into the evening, working, walking around slowly, arms loose at her sides and hair down, stopping before the others' easels, daring to watch them as they paint, and even to form an opinion of their painting, and soon the shrieks she used to let out when she felt a presence behind her, those strident, ear-splitting shrieks—soon these disappear, and her eyes finally meet theirs, the others, in this big woolly web of gazes intertwined.

⁂

When she gives an overview of the students at the Institut, which she does more than once during this period, for her parents or a few others (a scant few) to whom she talks about Brussels, Paula always begins at the back of the room and proceeds in the direction of the hands on a watch—and as she does so, she's probably visualizing each face turning toward her, looking her in the eye and giving her a nod, like an actor in the opening credits of a series from the eighties. This mental circuit puts Jonas in the spotlight first, though she doesn't linger over him, thus reserving for him a special fate, an exceptional provision, Jonas is Jonas, is all she says, quickening her phrase and batting her hand in the air, as though, here again, all you had to do was open your eyes to understand what's different about him—this mix of gentility and crass egotism?—and then she points out, among others, the theater decorator from Boulder, Colorado (dead ringer for Buster Keaton, identically clad in a black tie and white wing collar shirt); and further on, with white, veiny skin and bluish eyes, the baroque chapel restorer, graduate of the Fine Arts Academy in Florence, who paints half-naked under a raw linen shirt, wearing a loose, Gentileschi-style turban; beside her, head like a Borzoi's atop a long narrow torso and short fat legs, the young banker from London on sabbatical who chews gum nonstop and always wears his Sex Pistols T-shirt; next we have, to Paula's right, hair razed to the skin and wrestler's build, the only working artist in the studio, a guy from Hamburg with mucoid vocal cords, hands like washing paddles—in Hamburg, he made tableaux out of scrap iron, zinc, and corrugated sheet metal (oxidized remainders meant to represent the wear and tear of capitalism and the melancholy of globalization); he gathered these materials at the docks beside the river, jumping into workboats to head up the river, passing the sluices, heading farther and farther toward the estuary, toward the open, and would do this every day, rain or gale; continuing on, to Paula's left we find a young Flemish man with curly hair like a Greek shepherd's, son of a wheat grower near Ghent, who smokes Player's and pays for his studies by shooting pool in the backrooms of bars in the quartier Saint-Gilles; next, the Spanish students, Alba and Inés, cousins whose relatives are scattered throughout the world of the elite, multiple intertwined families of the sort that grace the cover of *HELLO!* magazine at baptisms and marriages, and they too were probably photographed as children, chubby-cheeked and white-gloved, holding the blonde lace train of a woman from their tribe; when she gets to them, Paula takes her time—Alba and Inés's presence at the Institut illustrate the socioeconomic diversity in the student body, the studio polarized between penniless students and these blue-blooded young women, raised by nuns in private schools, having hit the road pronto, always together, not having done much in the way of studies but with a good handle on languages, enrolled at the Institut so they might repaint all the family castles scattered across the old country, where the paneling has decayed, where the marble is missing, where the flower baskets have faded in the depths of the alcoves; they laugh the same husky laugh when they say they have a closed market, and they tell the story of how they fled marriages so they could live out their single life in style; and indeed they are party animals, with legs like posts and generous hearts, who swear a blue streak, creators of multicolored cocktails and sensational rollers of joints; and finally, less than a meter from these last, painting chickadees on rose petals while she listens to heavy metal with her earbuds deep in her ears, stands Kate Malone—the real deal, strong head and foul temper, always on her guard.

⁂

These beings who paint together forty-four hours a week and who would likely be described by their close friends as self-absorbed, scorning all form of community practice, accumulating narcissism and megalomania in interesting proportions and only accepting the humility of artisans so they might better boast about painting as artists, these beings, strangely, always end up forming a group around Christmastime. The beginnings of a structure that appeared in October become the rule, establishing customs, sedimenting a customary law that includes, for example, the cleaning and replacement of common materials (ordering, receiving, distributing), the starting of a pot for studio drinks, and the obligation to help each other—they gather in groups to finish the painting of anyone who's stuck. From then on, the students of the rue du Métal make up a little society unto themselves, connected to the material of the world but closed off into a few of the city's streets and isolated, schoolwork leaving little room for leisure time, when they might make friendships beyond the school's walls (and by now each of them has understood the advantage of seeking resources on site rather than losing time combing the countryside). So clandestine connections form within the school, romantic, friendly, sexual connections, and enmities as well, connections that grow tighter and tighter as the weeks roll by, forming a network that grows more and more dense, more and more active, such that the school finds its organic form and begins to function as its own ecosystem—it's a moment that the woman in the black turtleneck waits for with a certain impatience each year—she finds herself then face to face with a unified force, and this is what she likes.

But very quickly, in a pendulum swing that she anticipates mischievously, these same students start to worry about their originality, they squirm, stand on tiptoe to stick their heads above the pack, and stake their claim to *their* way of doing things, their unique brushstroke. This thirst for distinction that torments them surfaces again after the shock treatment of their training in woods and marbles—it reappears like the lump in the batter, and soon the students make it clear that they see the required exercises as straitjackets, rigid, narrow, stifling their movements, suffocating their personalities, drying up their desire—this is how they express themselves, incensed. The woman in the black turtleneck pretends not to have heard, continues to dispense her impenetrable smile left and right, rubbing her hands together—she knows the students well, it's the same each year, yes, she knows them by heart. She knows that the reference to the Renaissance atelier, this image of creative fluidity and collective fermentation in which they like to see themselves reflected, always begins by stroking their egos—shared space and techniques, influences and knowledge, a sense of service and order, values of the artisan, respect for the hierarchy of experience, abdication of self for the good of the group, continuity of life and work—before becoming a kind of melting pot they need to tear themselves away from in order to exist in their own right. Bingo! That's when she counters them, rubs them the wrong way. Recites the rules in a voice so calm she's almost goading them, demanding, for example, that the proportions of colors on the palette and in the jars be respected to the milliliter, harping on about method, this is how it's done, this way and no other, self-caricatured as the henchman of a narrow-minded academicism, as a tyrant of the formula. If she sees the least sign of a gesture toward interpretation on a painting, she sends the student back to the canon, the model, keeps them on the side of trompe-l'œil, the side of total illusion; she tracks the brushstrokes on the canvas, the emotion in the hatching, the overly gloomy feel of a shading or the over-the-top elation of a glazing, she works at erasing the young painter, erasing the painting in favor of the image. Of course, she justifies this harassment by championing technique, the beauty of the technique, but she's clearly also a little sadistic. And yet, Saturday morning, once the paintings are displayed side by side on the studio wall—twenty-odd images of the same format, that reel off the same splinter of wood, the same slab of marble, twenty-odd trompe-l'œil done following the same process—she stands before the wall in silence; you can feel that she's taking her time, working her audience's attention like the magician who sets up the delay, manipulates the suspense—then, slowly, she names the author of each work, without making a single mistake (each painting is then lifted, so the name of the forger can be read on the back). They can distinguish the excess of water in the work of Buster Keaton, the heaviness of Gentileschi's, the excessive use of China White by the Greek shepherd, or the off-centeredness of the image typical of Paula. While some would have confused the work of one for that of another, the woman in the black turtleneck restores to each student his or her singularity.

⁂

When Paula lifts her head, then, after the episode of the Cerfontaine, she realizes that the paint-spattered smocks surrounding her contain people, that the paintbrushes are held by hands, linked to bodies, faces, temperaments, and histories. And finally, having claimed in early December to have embraced chastity, forsworn all relationships—no time for that, she proclaimed online, a ridiculous, solitary cowgirl squinting on the prairie and striking a match on the sole of her boot—she drops this resolution the way you'd let a shawl slip from your shoulders on a summer night.

She becomes close to Kate, who pounces on her after class one day and asks her point-blank: are you the one who lives with Jonas Roetjens? Kate is one of those young women who enlarge any space they move through, smile rarely but laugh loudly, make constant snide remarks, curse out loud when it's their turn to receive delivery of paper palettes for the studio, sit down solo at the café each day for a real meaty lunch, and are so concerned about distinguishing themselves from the Daddy's girls at the Institut that they never miss an opportunity to say they paid for the tuition themselves—in Kate's case, by working as a bouncer at a Glasgow nightclub, the Nautilus; she also has fish tattooed on her arms, fish that she shows Paula, pulling up her sleeves in the middle of the street, and whose fins move when she flexes her muscles.

༜

There's a party the night before Christmas vacation at Buster Keaton's place, and in the general euphoria Paula finds herself frenching an umpteenth cousin of the Spanish girls at the back of the bedroom-cum-coatroom, and then, an hour later, she's naked with him in another bedroom, a hundred meters from the first and nearly a carbon copy of her own. The guy is passing through Brussels for a tennis tournament and has slender legs and a sense of timing, the skin of his back covered in beauty marks—you could take advantage of his sleep to lean in, armed with a pen and a ruler to trace the constellations visible in the Milky Way. They capsize against each other and stay intertwined till morning. Later, he falls asleep on his stomach, profile crushed against the mattress, and when Paula, clothed again, comes to lean over him, grazing his face with her tousled hair, he opens an eye, smiles, and then turns on his side—and later still, she will be surprised by the ease with which she slipped into this night, she who used to find sex so intimidating.

SNOW-WHITE SKY, NEARLY NOON. PAULA goes in to the building on rue de Parme wearing an oversized sheepskin coat and Doc Martens with midnight blue laces, she's got dove-gray shadow on her lids, revolution red on her lips, and climbs the stairs with her heart rushing—so pretty today that she would have wounded the eyes of Jean Valjean. Over the break in Paris, her memory of life in Brussels was drained of color, but she had barely begun to make her way through the compact crowd in the Gare du Nord when these visions came back in full force, and with them, impatience for the warm kitchen and the scent of paint, impatience for the acoustic foliation with its superposed tracks of kettle rumbling, fridge vibrating, brushes scraping, canvas, rags, the wind that rushes in between the windowpanes, the flush valve that leaks, the floor that creaks, and voices, steps, breathing; impatience for Jonas, too.

The apartment is dirty, the kitchen floor strewn with crumbs that crunch underfoot, the table greasy, dishes piled in the sink, spaghetti stuck to the bottom of the pot, paintings drying in the bathroom, a bundle of dirty laundry lying in the middle of the hallway, cigarette butts festering in cups of cold coffee, garbage cans overflowing. But when Jonas steps out of his room with a smoke between his lips, in a baseball cap and dubious robe, she turns toward him with her face shining. He grabs a clementine out of a plastic bag hanging from a chair, leans one shoulder against the doorframe and nods, glad to see you again, Paulette. Hey, Jonas. She heads toward her room, stops for a moment before the door, then opens it in a rush—I'm back, I'm home. A roll of paper has been placed on her bed with a fortune cookie in shiny paper tucked under the elastic. Paula opens the roll. It's her—a portrait of her, painted by Jonas, with her different colored eyes and her strabismus. She sits on the edge of the bed without taking off her coat, stunned to be holding, in her two hands, the image he has of her. He's drawn a medial line in pencil through the oval of the face, an axis that divides her face into two distinct sides, both captioned with an arrow—on the right: black, obsidian eye, the one that probes; on the left: green eye, broccoli side, the eye that drifts. At the bottom of the page, he sums it up: The Two Paulas. Thin lips, aquiline nose, eyebrows arching under brown bangs, almond-shaped eyes of women from Siena, high cheekbones and a dimpled chin. She takes her gloves off, the paper vibrating between her fingers. When she comes back to the kitchen, Jonas turns his back to her and moves the sponge over the table with excessive diligence. She starts to unwrap the rest of the Christmas feast, listing the contents of each package: chocolate, dried fruit, prosciutto, bottarga, gingerbread, and so on until she finally blurts out: thank you, Jonas. They look at each other, then Jonas stubs out his cigarette in an empty yogurt jar: I like your face a lot, Paulette.

They've grown close, now, haven't stopped growing closer since the Sunday of the fromage de cochon, and from that moment on what they share is much more than an apartment where the windows are poorly caulked, where the bath towels reek of mildew, where bits of diluted paint swirl around the drains. They've learned to glaze, to score, to soften, to stipple, to moiré, to lighten, to create a little iridescence with a polecat-hair round brush or an eyelet in the glaze with the brush handle, to draw short veins, to speckle, to wield the palette knife, the squirrel-hair two-headed marbling brush and the pitch pine brush, the large and the small spalter, the flat brush, the billiard cloth, and the burlap; they've learned to recognize Cassel earth and Conté, light cadmium yellow and cadmium orange; they've painted these same Renaissance ceiling angles with pudgy little cherubs, these same raspberry crushed silk draperies plunging from the cornices of Regency giltwood beds, these same Carrara columns, these same Roman mosaic friezes, same granite Nefertitis, and this apprenticeship has transformed them together, has shifted their language, marked their bodies, fed their imaginations, stirred their memories. They've also lent each other sweaters, washed with the same soap, dipped into the same packs of cigarettes, same plates of fries, have munched from the same bags of McDonald's late at night, same kebabs, have shared the same toothpaste, and that January night when Kate came over needing help to finish a Japanese-inspired set—pleated parasol, hanging lantern, little macaque on the branch of an apple tree in flower—and then collapsed around three in the morning across Paula's bed, they slept side by side. They've seen each other dazed with tiredness, bitchy, self-centered, stressed out, but also exhilarated, joking, proud of their paintings, they've seen each other drunk, sick, with bad breath and greasy hair, they've shown each other things we tend to hide—I have this thing behind my ear, can you take a look?, seen each other in pajamas, in bra and panties, in boxers, and they've seen each other naked—a bedroom door half open, a sudden irruption into the bathroom, a hallway where a naked bum runs past. Everyone wonders what their relationship really is, if they're sleeping together or not, or just sometimes, if they are lovers, and they themselves wouldn't know how to answer, prefer to dodge the issue rather than formulate a hesitant, muddled phrase, riddled with paradoxes, but one thing is certain—they don't like it when others get between them: the morning after her night with the tennis player, Jonas says coldly, you should see your face, and goes on to harass her about her last painting, which was weak, about jerks who play tennis, about that paintbrush he lent her and which he suddenly needs urgently, all this while she brushes her teeth showily, turning on the taps, Jonas, she finally says in a singsong voice, drying her mouth with the back of her hand, Jonas, she repeats, changing her T-shirt, re-appearing fresh and laughing, Jonas, look at me, but he had just slammed the door behind him. And Paula gets worried on the nights when he disappears, waits up late, falls asleep on the kitchen table, head rested on her crossed arms, the way kids used to take a nap after lunch in primary school.

And yet, for all that, they've never really revealed themselves to each other—social background, past, family. As though they'd skipped right over the required step of telling the story of oneself, of confession, and gone directly into the next phase, where we enter into the heart of a relationship, straight to the brass tacks, the phase where one makes himself known through the fact that he's left-handed, knows how to fix a scooter, takes sugar in his coffee, swims in cold water, hates perfume, loves Westerns and listens to rap, and where the other shows herself in the fact that she knows how to mend a shirt, washes her hands twenty times a day, sleeps with the window open, binges on the internet, doesn't have her driver's license, is allergic to eggs, stingy, gets up at the head of the table to recite "La mort du loup" at the end of a wedding banquet, cries at the movies, has a phobia of pear-shaped breasts, and dyes her hair. One might imagine they've opted for autobiographical ellipses out of decorum, out of distaste for banality, out of pride, because this way they can evade determinisms—they reduce themselves to silence, they come from nowhere, unmoored, unencumbered, the sole captains of their lives: no father, no mother, voila! People mock this illusion—right, no father, no mother, sure! Their life together incorporates silences, absences, and evasions; it doesn't require that everything be seen, everything be known about the other, be scratched, scraped—it makes do instead with that which holds itself back inside, unshareable. Some would go so far as to say that they don't even talk to each other, miscalculating the density of their reserve, the intimacy that spawns beneath language, the infraverbal intelligence that circulates between those who do things side by side, which Paula and Jonas do every evening when they get back from the studio, set up in their hallway, cobbling together a DIY lighting arrangement so they can see clearly, spreading newspaper on the floor, channel surfing until they find a good station on the radio, some music they both like, or reheating coffee on the stove before entering into the night with brush in hand, without exchanging more than murmurs, rumblings, a you alright? which elicits only a nod, sometimes a glance, Jonas saying you dreamer, I wonder how you see the world when you have two eyes that look in different directions, and Paula, amused, hairpin between her teeth and hands lifted behind her head to pin up her hair again, shoots back, you wondering which of my eyes you're supposed to look at? Jonas lighting a smoke that Paula will smoke too, pinching the filter from between his lips to bring it to her own, as though the content of all conversation had become accessory and all that mattered was living together in the same place in the world.

The night they slept side by side, Paula lay down behind Jonas, surprised to see him without his ball cap, and plunged her face into his fine, fluffy hair, which was probably thinning because of being constantly stuffed under a hat; she slotted her knees behind his and put a hand over his hip, and he, adjusting his body to hers, took her hand and brought it against his sternum, as though wanting to feel her body even closer to his own. Their skin was soft, they had a scent of earth and water. Later, Paula freed herself, turned onto her other side, and then it was he who nestled in behind her, lips at the height of her neck, and she who took his hand, brought his arm over her shoulder to wind it around her, wrapping herself in him. They stayed pressed together like that the rest of the night, she felt the steady gust of his breath against her neck—cold air when he inhaled, hot when he exhaled—and in the morning, in the empty bed, stirred up, Paula listened to the voices in the kitchen, Kate and Jonas, the crackle of eggs in the pan and BBC announcers on the radio.

THEY EVEN GO TOGETHER TO SENZEILLES
to see the Beauchâteau quarry and find the Cerfontaine.
Get up early that morning, another Sunday, put on warm
clothes—Jonas, a fur-lined army jacket, bought in a surplus
store in Schaerbeek, and Paula, the sheepskin coat—then take
the first train for Philippeville, facing each other on chocolate-
brown moleskin bench seats worn thin with use, cups of
burning hot coffee held between their thighs. The train car
is empty except for a trio of young women coming back from
a night of clubbing in Brussels, party girls in miniskirts and
leather jackets who talk loudly for the first few kilometers,
all wound up still, then collapse abruptly against each other,
features drooping, lids lowered, stilettos dangling, a heap of
torn tights and vague cleavage, the makeup starting to form
lumps on their skin sprinkled with glitter. Jonas dozes, hat
brim pulled down over his face, but Paula is far too restless
to sleep. In Philippeville the station is empty. They cross
the concourse and knock on the window of the only taxi
in the station—a taxi that seems preordained, waiting for
them. The driver stirs inside, he was asleep, and looks at
them, taken aback. He has a birthmark around his left eye,
almost as though someone had crushed a black tulip there,
sports ostentatious whiskers and a synthetic mustard-colored
turtleneck under a sheepskin vest. After drumming on the
steering wheel a moment he agrees to take them, okay get
in, but warns them they'll have to hitchhike back, he won't
wait for them, it's Sunday, he gets off at noon and will be
headed home to tuck into a plate of shepherd's pie. The car

carves through the winter landscape, the sleepy villages, the bare fields, passing cyclists and hunters. The driver knows the quarry well—it's a popular spot for school trips because of the fossils, he says, grandiose, and the fact that two young students would have come all the way from Brussels just to see it brings about a feeling of pride in him, as though the quarry were his personal possession. Two kilometers south of the village, he parks at the side of the road, Paula and Jonas get out, the doors slam like gunshots. It's almost eleven o'clock and the sky is heavy, gray, near-bursting with rain. A sign indicates a path where they set off in single file through the undergrowth until the space opens up before them and they come out onto an embankment, facing a cliff with a perfectly smooth face above an artificial lake. The sizeable front face of the quarry. A wall so disproportionate in the landscape, so incongruous, it seems to have emerged from another world. Thickets of ferns, copses, frame the base of the vertical wall—bare, and of a purplish red resembling bruised human skin, or an ancient wound that time has cauterized, dried, faded. Here it is—Cerfontaine! Jonas's words reverberate as he moves toward the wall, and this flash of a voice, this movement highlights the silence and stillness of the site, emphasizes the character of the place, at once monumental and fallen into disuse. They come together at the edge of the stagnant water, side by side, facing the cliff, and lift their heads. Come see.

❧

What stands before them is an impressively high wall, maybe thirty meters tall, as unexpected as the ramparts of a pre-Columbian city glimpsed through the foliage. A wall striated with lines, notches, marks. The most visible of them show evidence of the quarry, old sectional plans for the exploitation of the rock, while others, further up, more difficult to make out, show the history of the formation of the ground. The beauty of a slice of fromage de cochon! With a finger Jonas lifts the brim of his hat and places his hands on his hips, playing up his amazement.

A slice of time. The wall has the look of a frontal cut and reveals, distinct from the neighboring geology, the shape of a domed coral reef, an incredibly beautiful structure created by colonies of coral that ended up knitting themselves together here, embracing each other and convulsing to form mountains, to form bedrock, all of this in a tropical climate, in warm, clear, shallow water, millions of years ago. Three hundred and seventy million, Paula, remember? He's not looking at her, but opens out his arms as though he could contain the entire site, and declares that this type of structure, bioherms, numerous in the area, can be as large as two hundred meters in diameter and ninety meters thick, and if you look closely, each moment of the formation of the reef, visible on the wall, shows the force of the waters that bathed the area successively: calm waters at the base of the bioherm, and then rougher and rougher until they are flat-out turbulent in the middle of the reefal mass, turbulent and pure, oxygenated, whirling, mixing billions of shells, brachiopods, and stromatoporoids, billions of tiny living organisms.

❦

Paula, who was disappointed on first seeing the place—what the hell are we doing here?—follows her friend's gaze and places her own there, exactly as though she were walking in his footsteps, in sand or snow, and makes out the beautiful cupola shape, the terracing, the different colorations of the rock, and now the wall stirs, it shakes itself like an old body, no longer an inert vestige marked out in a manicured circuit for geologists and earth science hobbyists, nor a cliff that human industry has chiseled over and over to exploit the mineral substance. Now all at once it is a story. As Jonas speaks, the striations on the wall are lines that become sentences, forming little by little this far-off tale that she meditates on, even as she moves about the site, trailing a hand along the rock face, scaling the schists, collecting the pebbles.

It's the story of the jungle from before, of the primitive mangrove, the barriers of coral and transparent lagoons that saturated the place in the Devonian period, the tale of the lagoon that lay here before the great upheaval ravaged the earth in the Paleozoic era, before those phenomena of an incredible violence that provoked the catastrophe: extreme climatic oscillations, lowering of water levels, thickening soil, trees and plants that appear and take root, anoxia of oceans, asteroids crashing, glaciations! Jonas chants the names of the phenomena and suddenly they spring forth from the rock, like a wizard causing diamonds to spurt from a toad's mouth. High pressure, Paula, very high pressure! He concludes with a grimace: the end of the Devonian was the Apocalypse! She looks at him, wonders whether he's just making shit up, picks up a stone, examines it, and then tosses it, watches it skip over the flat water, and Jonas picks up again too: after all that, a long time after—his voice is slower now, he's telling a story, he has never spoken this much and Paula knows something is shifting, something is opening up, widening—once the area was dry, the coral fossilized, and people had set up encampments, once they had sown seeds, built villages, conceived children they had to feed; once they had invented gods, priests, and lords and built temples for them, churches and castles with sonorous floors, stairwells where one might make one's cape fly and fireplaces in which to burn secret pacts and compromising love letters, after all this time (which was nothing but the blink of an eye in terms of the age of the cliff), there was the advent of the quarry. The exploitation of the marble and the exploitation of the men hired to extract it and place it in the hands of whoever had declared himself owner of the land—and how this guy managed to make the others believe that he owned the rock, this rock produced by the action of time, to the point of making them climb rickety ladders to whack the cliff with picks, I still don't know. The continuous exploitation of the cliff over the span of a century and a half erased the old traces of extraction, but we can imagine that hundreds of mustachioed men climbed these ladders, these wooden rungs, that some of them grew dizzy and clung on for dear life, that others were scared to fall backwards and smash their heads seven or eight meters below, and that all of them screamed in fright, the wall echoing their voices, as between the walls of a canyon. The first blow to the rock at the end of the eighteenth century must have resounded like a warning shot, the start of a revolution, but at the time no one took it that way: the marble was pierced with iron shims and wedges, as the small puncture marks suggest—then the holes were filled with dark gray powder, the explosive injecting just enough force into the rock to break off blocks of it. The workers are innumerable, they handle the metal and the powder, and strangely enough, they don't flinch, even when the frost burns, the sun hammers, or the rain pours down. The quarry owner comes only rarely and always without warning, the hedges quiver along the little path and suddenly there he is perched on horseback in front of the high wall, the workers turn without taking off their caps, lips pressed together, the foreman rushes over, the owner asks a question or two about the yield of the cliff without giving him a glance, and then, with a kick of his heels, makes a half turn in a cloud of dust and heads off at a gallop bareheaded into the countryside he loves more than anything in the world, and those who remain perched on the ladders, hands dirty and eyes dull, are no longer so sure this is all as it should be. The marble workers' job changes in 1874 when the helicoidal saw is introduced in the quarry—three steel cables spun into a helix that cuts the rock through continuous friction. The cliff becomes smooth, softened, it shines like mother-of-pearl in the sun and takes on its current physiognomy, its singular profile. Once extracted, the marble is brought to workshops where it is cut, polished, and then driven to Parisian apartment buildings, bourgeois provincial houses, and certain rooms in the castle of Versailles, where it joins other marble, from Flanders and Hainaut, popular in this palace from the beginning. Soon the quarry workers win the right to smoke on their breaks, to form a union, to have one day off a week and then one month a year, and the owners are no longer young heirs—now they are capitalist societies held by shareholders who scurry off to the Côte d'Azur from May to October, where they like to stroll in braided leather loafers with no socks, sporting white linen pants and straw boaters. The high wall recedes with each progressive cut, and each new slice reveals more fossil shapes in the stone, more traces of life caught in the rock. After the First World War the activity declines: woodstoves and radiators replace fireplaces, decorators recommend wood, glass, polymers, everything that can be moved by a child's hand; and now marble, connoting as it does the conservatism and weight of a certain staid pomp, slowly stops being extracted. The Second World War passes over the quarry without changing the trend—the place may have been used as a hiding place for men, weapons, and rolled-up parachutes tossed into the night by Allied planes. A few more years and in 1950 the Beauchâteau cliff finally returned to silence. The abandoned quarry now became the realm of fossil collectors and teachers besotted with hands-on lessons, one of those natural alcoves that the most considerate landscapes provide for lovers, a site of pagan pilgrimage for those who wish to cure a severe case of eczema, autoimmune alopecia, or erythrodermic psoriasis, and soon it's the hideout for the youth of the canton, one of those notorious places where kids make fires, where drugs circulate, where used condoms can be found in the bushes along with pages ripped from porn magazines, and from which no one comes out a virgin—at the time, saying that a girl *goes to the quarry* means she's easy. When night falls, the cliff—standing like a gigantic city wall behind the undergrowth—reverberates with the bass thump of satanic music, wild barking and strident shrieks, terrifying those who hear it from the road. There's a crowd at the quarry, they think, revving their motorbikes and hurrying past. And today, it's become something else again—Jonas gears up for his conclusion, Paula holds her breath—scientists come to take samples and measurements, to test-drill the rock. The wall is considered to be like a photographic slab, a piece of blotting paper where graffiti has become epigraphy, where everything that has happened since the beginning of time has left its mark, a palimpsest.

And now Jonas falls silent. He has used up his words, and his features relax. The quarry is frozen again, like a set piece from the theater after the show, after the story has unfolded, after everything's been said, lived, and language has cleared out. Paula walks toward the artificial lake feeling like she's crossing the plateau one last time and leans over, watching her shadow as it floats over the murky, rippled surface, wonders if a placoderm from the Devonian period might suddenly break through the water with a roar and shoot

72

up into the air, jaws gaping, scales dripping, and at the same time she remembers the hundred-year-old carp that sleep in the ornamental ponds at Versailles and the balls of bread crumbs she used to throw when she was a child, trying to attract them, to make them appear, while her parents beside her also peered into the cloudy water and whispered to her all the things these carp must have seen—some may have even greeted Louis XIV in his coruscant jewels, his flounces, his wig, and his white boots with red heels; they must have been there, kept awake by the elaborate tricks that caused fire to appear on the water just to please this king, the king everyone wished to please, and the carp had likely remained hidden away at the bottom of the pond all these long years, scared or sly, concealed in the algae, indistinguishable from the weeds, and Paula, leaning over the water, begins now to imagine sea creatures far older than her, enormous, silent mammals that breach before primitive boats, water streaming down their sides, that show their white bellies in a spray of foam, creatures hunted down across the ocean until the hunter goes mad, ones that swim along Kate's tattooed arms in the Glasgow night as she stands guard at the Nautilus door, and Paula reaches out her hand toward the fin that emerges before her eyes, beneath the leather sleeve, at the surface of the water, and then black spots, dizziness, vertigo, and Jonas's hand holds her back by the shoulder just as she's about to plunge into the water.

ONE DAY IN FEBRUARY, KATE RUNS INTO
Paula in a cinematic rainfall by the cigarette machine at the
corner of the square. A pack tumbles down, Paula picks it
up and stands aside as Kate begins the operation in turn
for a pack of strong Pueblos. Want to come dry off at the
bar? Kate looks at her, hair streaming, indifferent to the
rain—Scotland—squeezed into a tight mauve sweater that
doesn't do anything for her.

It's a weekday, work is waiting, looming, and yet five
minutes later there they are, seated face to face with a beer
in front of them in one of the bars on the square, and Kate's
bust takes up a disproportionate amount of space between
them. I'm dropping out, I'm quitting, I'm going home. Paula
doesn't bat an eye, but examines the face of the woman who
is also called *big Kate*: strawberry-blonde hair, thick line of
eye pencil beneath her lashes, milky flesh, a vague resemblance
to Anita Ekberg when she puts her hands on her hips and
thrusts her shoulders back saying: types of wood, trees, moldings, drapery—I don't give a shit, finito! She claps her hands
together, then adds in a louder tone: I am an artist. The guy
behind the bar throws her a glance, curious, and Kate offsets
the outrageousness of this declaration with a burst of laughter.
We might imagine that she'd follow through, that she would
get up, take a few small damp bills from her pocket, put her
hat on, and take off into the night, but no, she stays sitting,
quiet now. Paula waits. Her almond-shaped eyes give off a
serious flash: we learn how to paint the grain of a ten-year-
old walnut and that of a hundred-year-old walnut, that's it,

that's the deal. Kate grinds her teeth: awesome! It may not be awesome, Paula continues, suddenly bridling, but the thing is that copying them still involves getting an idea of them, wanting to know them, which is not so bad. She puts a hand to the back of her neck, pulls her hair to one side with an automatic gesture and begins to twist it, pressing the end against the table like she was blotting a Japanese paintbrush. Then says gently: having a nap under a walnut tree makes you go crazy, they're delicate and give off a cool shade, did you know that? Kate shrugs. The bar is empty, night is falling in long thin threads, and suddenly we can tell Paula's no longer so sure Kate is bluffing. You're going to quit *now*? You're not going to leave two thirds of the way through the semester, are you?? Kate doesn't answer. She leans back against the booth and then picks up again, slowly: we'll all end up camouflaging ruins for cheap, covering cruddy walls with flowered façades or decorating themed rooms in shitty hotels. That's not the world, and I know you know it too. Dark water swells in the gutters outside, the cornices and trees trickle, but it's over now, the rain has stopped, the square is a puddle where reality's distorted, and Kate's voice rings out as she speeds up: I'm sick of copying, imitating, reproducing, what's the point of that? Go ahead, I'm listening. She's shoved her hands into her pockets, bending her elbows so her shirt sleeves rise up on her forearms, uncovering her square wrists, and higher, peeking out from under the leather, the edge of a tattoo, a gorgeous tail fin. Paula would like to push the sleeve up even higher to see the fish that swims silently on the skin of her arm, this one and the others, she knows they're there, super-powerful—the shaded shark, the secret whale, the friendly dolphin—she'd like to place a hand on their skin, she'd like to swim alongside this fauna from the deep, lean against their necks and be carried along in their wake. Instead she murmurs: the point is to imagine. Kate goes still. For a few seconds, she gazes out at the street, at the people stepping out from under doorways and awnings to start walking again, avoiding the gutters and stepping over the streams. Then she finishes her beer, gets up, and leans across the table to place a kiss on Paula's forehead. The point is to imagine.

THEY MEET UP ON RUE DE PARME EVERY weekday evening. Kate, Jonas, and Paula. They go in, turn on the lamps, tack sheets of paper up in the hallway, arrange the models, the reference photos, and sometimes a natural sample they've borrowed from the school's collection; they start the playlist they've made for this final rush and from the sound of the first chords of the first song, they begin—they've omitted harrowing sounds and heavy lyrics in favor of ballads with a perfect structure, cosmic cavalcades, and a few bouncy hits to warm up on their breaks. They've told the others that they'll turn out this goddamn painting on the double, that they'll whip it up fast, that frankly they don't give a shit about the diploma, and that all this has gone on long enough; but once they're at their stations, I know they slow down, take their time, as though the whole challenge of painting was to wring the last drop from these final nights, to sift through them in order to isolate each sensation, to hold onto each second, to gather up each atom, and soon these nights roll together into one single night, and the sentence begun between them on the first night has come to form one single sentence, shared, confident, one of those phrases where silence is never a rupture, but instead a continuity. A sentence like a branch drifting down the length of the river.

❧

The painting for the final project. One per student, one and one only, that will not only display their technical skill, but also sum up the entirety of their experience at the school. A sort of *panneau libre*, since it's left up to each of them to choose. Jonas will paint a type of wood—the heart grain of oak, with its characteristic medullary rays—Kate, a type of marble—Portor—and Paula, tortoiseshell. A mineral, a vegetable, and an animal: together we three can create the world! Kate calls out these first words as she pulls off her sweater, crossing and then uncrossing her arms toward the ceiling—and here as ever is her robust beauty, stocky (though she has lost weight), hair pulled back to reveal her protruding forehead, strong nose, prominent eye teeth, ruby-red gums. She stands in front of her paper, opens a jar of pure black, picks up a spalter brush and begins to cover the entire background, which sets to shining in the lamplight. In the kitchen, Paula drinks water from the tap, standing on tiptoe and holding her hair back so as not to dip it in the dirty dregs at the bottom of the sink. She lifts her face, dripping, and asks them loudly: but who will do humankind? Aren't we forgetting humans? She too begins to prepare her background—cadmium orange and vermilion—while Jonas starts his glazing and murmurs, distant: humans? What humans? Who wants more humans? Who would be dumb enough to want more humans? You, Paula? Shouts can be heard, stampedes. Groups of students come up the road from the square in droves, it's going to be like this all night. Kate turns to the other two to ask for some cadmium orange and Jonas hands her the tube. Paula lights a cigarette.

※

Tortoiseshell. You're not being a bit of a show-off? This is how Jonas responds to Paula's decision, ironic, as though he were unmasking her suppressed narcissism, her prissy megalomania, her strategies to stand out, and then he puts on an expert voice to add: oak is something entirely other, less sophisticated but more complex. Kate, dismayed by her choice and trying to convince her to change her mind had gone one further, pragmatic: you'll never paint one, there's no use, you're wasting your time. Then they had looked at her slant, half-joking and half-serious, neither of them aware that Paula had started the process fifteen years earlier when she crouched down in an old garden with a handful of lettuce leaves, a gift for an ancient creature—the reptile's rare appearances, sometimes with a space of several summers between them, setting off screams from the vacationing children that caused the tortoise to flee behind a large rock—shut up, ordered the eldest of the cousins authoritatively, then granted herself the right to advance toward the stone, armed with a stick to drive the tortoise out, but then there was insurgence, protest, no, get out of here, you're the one scaring it, there was pushing and shoving and elbowing, little Paula standing her ground to watch the show just like all the others until the marvelous moment when the tortoise finally reappeared, forehead low to the ground, neck stretched out so far it showed the supple, elastic skin that joined its head and limbs to its shell; it moved along a sure course, determined (if slow) and indifferent to the chatter of the kids who stepped aside to let it pass, fascinated, disgusted, excited, timing it with a watch and a tape measure, attempting to establish its age by reading the shell, the most knowledgeable among them arguing thousands of centuries and pronouncing the word prehistoric, while Paula, deaf to all this, escorted the tortoise toward the bed of lettuce, crawled alongside it with her knees in the dirt, murmuring encouragements and sweet nothings in its ear, until she fell into the black and lachrymal eye of the animal, a little girl from the end of the twentieth century caught in

79

its gaze as though in a spatial-temporal rift that was far too deep for her, because all at once, gone was the tortoise of nursery rhymes and fables, of seven-in-the-morning cartoons, all other tortoises were erased at the sight of this one, here, this beast, a monster in miniature but very real, emerging all at once from the shadow of a stone as though from a fold in time, just to make contact with Paula.

⁂

Kate is hot under the lamp. She's working on her black. Soon she'll take off her tank top to paint in her bra, and her skin, pearled with sweat, will reflect the shadowy gleam of the Portor. For the moment, she takes possession of her painting and something voracious emanates from her movements, a desire for theatricality and the exaggerated life that goes along with it. She turns toward the other two and she's aglow, horse-like, bottom lip swollen from being scraped by large upper incisors: a luxury stone, a stone for the rich! Beside her, Jonas fights with his pride as he concentrates on his oak—we can see he'd like to strip his painting of its anecdotic quality, rid it of this feeling of an exercise, which he finds degrading: what he wants is to give the painting itself a value equal to that which it must depict—to paint the painting, in short—nothing else matters. Twenty more minutes and he takes a step back to mutter: easy, Milady!—and it's not clear whether he's addressing Kate—maybe he's not addressing anyone, but rather speaking to his painting, the way you'd try to slow down a mare that had set off at a gallop, whoa, precious, whoa. Paula and Kate, on either side, don't even hear, they've entered the space situated precisely between the hand and the painting, between the end of the brush and the surface of the painting, and maybe it's here, in this interval, that the gesture takes form, that painting takes place. Kate anticipates the moment when she'll drop the web of gold on her background, when she'll inject the light, knowing that her hand will need to measure out energy to the millimeter, while Paula looks at her paper, tracks the way her imagination seizes the elements of the world, bit by bit, and then composes the materials of her dreams, works at the slow and prodigious magnetization of images.

※

In the Institut's library, she had begun by opening the atlases, had located the hawksbill sea turtle (*Eretmochelys imbricata*) in the Caribbean Sea, along the coasts of the West Indies, or farther south, along the coast of Brazil, never far from the shore, and usually swimming in the surface waters among the seaweed, plankton, and little fish; on maps, she had noted the hot spots for egg laying across the surface of the globe, and among them, little Cousin Island in the Seychelles—that confetti of earth scattered in the Indian Ocean—rare birds, palm trees, rare and controlled human incursions, mostly scientific, biologists and ethologists coated in high SPF sunblock wearing khaki Bermuda shorts and boat shoes with leather laces—where it's easy to tally a thousand nests buried in the sand; she listened to the egg breaking, the shell cracking, fracturing slowly—sometimes over the course of three or four days—and finally freeing the sticky little creature; she imagined the little one's progression toward the shore, its first steps on the beach, its way of rushing slowly, the shell that bobs along and the movement so full of grace; she visualized its first strokes in the little waves, feet becoming powerful oars, and then the swim toward the open ocean where it would soon be in danger, would have no more than one chance in a thousand of surviving, gulped down by a shark (shell shattered with a single snap of its jaws), caught by a fisherman with a striped suckerfish at the end of his line (this protector fish, whom the turtle would have trusted completely), and Paula imagined all of this so clearly she could see the streaming scales in the hull of the boat, their sparkle, and the toothless smile of the old fisherman. She ran to the museum immediately after, stood before the body of the *E. imbricata*, leaned over its carapace, awed by the ingenuity of its design—the thirteen scutes, the layering of the central ridge and the four lateral pairs, the two holes in the plating, one for the head, one for the tail—she turned the animal over to stroke its breast plate, there where the blonde tortoiseshell can be found, the rarest type of all. Bone, horn, nail, beak, claw, cartilage—she tried to distinguish the materials these words encompassed, paused on the keratin that linked them, a living protein, the very substance of the shell. The very substance of hair! exclaimed her hairdresser one Saturday afternoon while Paula's mane streamed foam, shampooed, and the hairdresser held out a color chart with combed and carefully laid out locks aligned in rows like erotic fetishes. Paula's eyes widen and she points to a lock of hair labeled *tortoiseshell*. That's the one you want? That's a very popular highlight in Hollywood, I'd call it honey brown verging on golden blonde, lots of elegance and depth, soft contrast, the stars are crazy for it, Julia Roberts, Sarah Jessica Parker, Blake Lively—do you like Blake Lively? Paula nods and leans her head back again into the basin, the hairdresser's hands massage her scalp, and three days later we see her running home along the rue de Parme, taking the stairs four at a time and rushing straight into her room where books are piled up in a corner. She's looking for a specific one, doesn't know which but knows it's there, knows she'll recognize the title or the cover, kneels down on the floor, sifts through the piles, turns each book over one by one, and finally sees it, grabs it, and holds it to her chest. *The Old Man and the Sea.* She stays there for a long while, stock still, patellas pressed into the floor, sore, and in the silence of the empty apartment, by the light of a bedside lamp, she finds the passage where Santiago, the old fisherman, tells the boy who bought him a beer that fishing for sea turtles will make you go blind, that you'll end up burning your eyes—Paula's heart leaps as she rubs her own, burning too.

⁂

Almost midnight. Kate has just left the room to make a phone call. They can hear her speaking English in the next room. Is it her boyfriend? Jonas asks softly. He's starting the rays of his oak now, working with the billiard cloth in the still-fresh glazing. Paula nods, he's in Glasgow, he's starting to feel like it's been too long, he wishes she would come home. Then she moves closer and asks: you're doing the wipeout method? You're not going to paint it? Jonas shakes his head: I'm doing it this way, it's quick, precise, light, I love this technique. Paula presses: but won't it be a bit soft, a bit *liquid*? Just then Kate's laughter bursts out from the other side of the wall and Jonas says louder, okay, I'm taking a break, I'm hungry, I'll go pick something up, what do you feel like? He looks at his watch and adds: at this time of night it'll have to be McDonald's or kebabs. Get me some fries then. Paula heads for her room to grab some cash, slips in soundlessly, furtive, and hurries even more at the sight of Kate lying stretched out in the dim light on her bed, topless, jeans unbuttoned, caressing her breasts with one hand while the other holds the phone screen a good distance away. Sorry, says Kate, I'm on Skype. The door slams, Jonas's steps ring out in the stairwell and Paula goes back to her painting.

❧

She's preparing her palette: one part imperial black and one part Van Dyke brown that the brush mixes in with little touches as she works on the coalescence of the images. She slowly calls up the two giant turtles caught along the coast of Borneo around 1521, whose flesh alone weighed twenty-six and forty-four pounds—Paula had consulted the account of Pigafetta, read the story of the crossing of the Pacific, the anguish of the ocean, the days that piled up, scant water and food, mice being sold for thirty ducats, rats that pissed on the biscuits, leather and wood shavings boiled for soup, scurvy and beriberi, first contact with the Indigenous peoples, wary diplomatic missions, the pearls of the Indigenous leaders large as chicken's eggs, ambuscades, and flurry of flummeries—spears against arquebuses, Magellan killed by a poison arrow in the Bay of Mactan; she calls up a marquetry in tortoiseshell worked in gold leaf at the back of a studio on rue de Reims by André-Charles Boulle, a piece of such virtuosity that Louis stiffened as he looked at it, raised an eyebrow—such insolence!—and named the artist Royal Cabinetmaker in order to keep his entire production for himself. She summons the cradle of Henry IV, the legendary bassinet fashioned from the varnished brown shell of a sea turtle—she can easily picture the royal infant, the pleated ruff below the double chin and the lids with their long lashes closed; and finally, she synchronizes everything with this pair of glasses in the window of the optometrist on rue de Paradis, an article whose exorbitant price he had justified by reminding Paula that natural tortoiseshell possesses an extraordinary quality: autograft—it's indestructible, it's forever.

⁂

Jonas returns while she's stuck in a rut, shifting from foot to foot in front of her paper. He's surprised by the blast of heat, you'd think you were in the engine room of a cargo ship at full steam. He hands her a dazzlingly yellow box of fries, points to the six-pack of beer he's brought back. Kate still on the phone? Sounds can be heard from the other side of the wall, small cries, heavy breathing that Jonas comments on quietly, imperturbable, I leave for one minute and everything here goes to the dogs, and Paula smiles without turning from her work. She still hasn't started painting, she's slowly picking up the fries and eating them in silence; she wipes her hands on her shirt, picks up her palette and brush again, takes her stance—nothing beyond the edges of the paper could make her turn her head at the moment. The shell is there, within reach—it stirs at the surface of things, tangible. It would suffice to open her palm to cause it to come forward, the way we do with a wild animal, to call it over and caress it, but Paula has barely begun this gesture when the shell pulls back into a space where its materiality vanishes and where, veiled and even more desirable, its cloudy light can be glimpsed. It's a question of patience, she thinks, I must lie in wait. Sitting in the kitchen, Jonas gulps down his hamburger and watches her, struck by her pale, almost translucent skin stretched tight, skin of a tambourine, by the dark shadows like spoons under her eyes and her liquid pupils: women are only interested in substance, he says out loud, without letting his eyes leave her. It would be nice to joke, to relax the atmosphere, even more so because in the next room comes the creak of bedsprings now, stirring, moaning, sounds rising, lengthening, bursting out, the hallway resonating like a well of desire. Kate is having an orgasm, Jonas puts down his burger: how can we possibly work in peace here? and in the clamor, Paula begins to paint, condenses the sum of the stories and the images into a single gesture, a movement sweeping as a lasso and precise as an arrow, since her painting contains at the moment something quite other than itself, gathers up the grazed knees of a five-year-old girl, the danger, an island in the far reaches of the Pacific, the sound of an egg hatching, the vanity of a king, a Portuguese sailor who bites into a rat, the rippling hair of a movie star, a writer gone fishing, the mass of time, and beneath embroidered swaddling clothes, a royal baby asleep, as if in a mythical nest, at the bottom of a shell.

꘎

So, is everyone hard at work? Kate reappears all smiles, loose, cheeks red, and takes a deep breath before grabbing a beer and popping it open, takes a long drink straight from the bottle, then begins the veining of the Portor with the two-headed marbling brush, the golden netting, the web of light, the time has come. She moves fluidly, the brush light, working fast, as Jonas softens his canvas with gentle touches and Paula starts on her wipeouts, skimming the sponge over her painting. The night has become malleable, extendable, they paint as if the past and the future had disintegrated and the present had been replaced by the act of painting. Right up until Paula stretches sometime around four o'clock in the morning, arms extended out to the sides, says I'm going to bed, and goes into her room, closes the door, leaves her clothes crumpled in a ball on the floor, and falls into a deep sleep.

It's summer. The sun creates moving shadows on the river bottom, diamonds that form and deform, undulate, making ringlets in the sand, the stones, the mosses. Paula enters the cool water, pushing aside long fibrous grasses combed sideways by the current. A living animal is moving beneath the surface, a khaki-colored animal flecked with black, gray, and gold. Its skin has taken on the aspect of the river, the movement and light; the creature moves through the water, camouflaged. Paula lifts her eyes above the surface to follow the flight of a metallic blue dragonfly that disappears into the furze, then peers back down into the water, but the creature has disappeared. May never have existed. It's a trompe-l'œil, thinks Paula, tilting her head back in the sun. Nothing is happening here but the river itself. Then she pushes off in a sidestroke toward the mangrove, turns over onto her back, floats in the current, coming close to the far bank soon, water up to her waist, feet sliding on the stones. Suddenly the creature reappears, less than a meter away. Paula shivers: a turtle—but isn't the river the site of all reflections, all mirages? She dives under and it's no illusion: it's well and truly an *E. imbricata* with changing scales, swimming with her, its eyes wide open.

IT'S BUSY THIS NINETEENTH OF MARCH ON the rue du Métal, lines have formed on the sidewalks, people are rushing, they have the determined gait of those who are going somewhere, moving forward heads down into the wind, and some of them recognize each other, wave to each other, then slow as they near 30 *bis* where a crowd is gathering. The hushed clamor of the wait. Some of them extricate themselves from the crowd to finish a call, while others, backs resting against cars, smoke a cigarette; the sky is a toned-down blue, and rain threatens. There are a few familiar faces in the crowd, and among them Paula's parents, catching their breath. Guillaume Karst looks at his watch, lifts himself up on tiptoe to glance over the heads jammed together in front of the door, it's time, he says, soles back on the ground, it's going to open soon.

They were afraid of being late even though they were up at dawn in the room their daughter had reserved for them in a nearby hotel—just as they were leaving, a doubt before the mirror—clutched by a fear of showing up in their Sunday best, they reviewed their outfits, Guillaume taking off his tie in the end, Marie choosing a simple black sweater over the pale-blue silk shirt with its swallow print. They had lost time. Now, they wait hand in hand, attentive, conscious that on this special day, the day of Paula's graduation, they also have a certain role to play, and they must not make too big a deal when their daughter is called forward to receive her scrolled paper tied with a red satin ribbon, when she pauses to seek out their faces in the audience, or, on the contrary, when she rushes the moment with boastful reserve—they must remain even-keeled.

⁂

The day before, having arrived too early at their daughter's apartment building, they had circled the block—must above all not be early, must above all not seem impatient or antsy—and then, too, they were holding hands. Jonas was the one who opened the door for them, impassive, hands dirty, as Paula shouted from the bathroom that she'd be ready in two minutes. They paced in the kitchen, silhouettes swallowed up in their winter coats—puffer for Guillaume, a blue pelerine for Marie—awkward, out of place, careful not to touch anything and forcing themselves to cover up their surprise at the sight of these surroundings, Guillaume especially, stunned to see how the little student apartment so nicely set up in September has become this cesspit. The different rooms—bedrooms, kitchen, bathroom, hallway—have lost their particular function, now forming nothing but a blurry continuity, the final frontiers having been crossed only recently, maybe even in the last three days, just as dikes give way before the river in spate, and now it's all painting, painting everywhere. A proliferation. The paintings are drying, spread out on the floor or hung up on the walls—the doors, too narrow for more, hold only color charts, color tests—the sinks in both the kitchen and bathroom have been transformed into tubs of dirty water where brushes are soaking, and every last bit of flat surface is cluttered with bottles of solvent, overflowing ashtrays, concoctions mixed in bowls, powdered pigments in cups. And then there are the open books, dog-eared magazines, images, postcards with reproductions of paintings—Poussin, Rembrandt, de Chirico—dirty rags and crumpled up pieces of paper towel, chip bags and empty yogurt containers, tins of condensed milk (Jonas), Coke cans, Yop bottles, here and there a glove, a cable, a lighter; the rare remaining sacred spaces are dedicated to computers (even the beds are overrun, Jonas's was finally lifted up against the wall where the slats could serve as a drying rack for paintings and a few items of clothing, a sock, a pair of boxers, a sweater). The smell surprises them, too, so strong it seems to have taken on solid form, and Jonas, seeing them go pale, hastily opens the window. Then he clears a corner of the table by transferring the clutter to one of the remaining free chairs—so they still couldn't sit down—and invites the parents to put down their bottle and their cakes. Thank you, young man. Paula's father now has his arms free to embrace his daughter who's emerging from the bathroom at that moment, damp and pink, hair wet, I was in the shower, we were up late, while Marie hugs her from behind, leaning her cheek between her shoulder blades. Their child. They hold her for a few moments in this sandwich, in front of the boy who doesn't know what to do with himself anymore, zips up his jacket while looking away, judging this little choreography of a reunion to be quite excessive, and then moves slowly toward the door, okay, I'm off, I have to go—his favorite phrase.

Wait, one moment, let's have a drink together first, a glass of champagne to celebrate! Guillaume Karst is already picking up the bottle as his daughter grimaces, here, now? are you sure? embarrassed that he wants to mark the moment so formally, yes, now! You like champagne, don't you, Paula, and he immediately pops the cork, while Marie, still a bit stunned, lays out shortbread cookies on the lid of a metal biscuit tin with pictures of little Bretons in folkloric costumes. Paula looks at Jonas as if to say, stay, and a few moments later they're drinking champagne in the kitchen, meeting eyes above hurriedly rinsed juice glasses—a new complicity is being woven between them, Jonas knows her parents now, and Paula has allowed this scene to happen, she's letting herself be revealed.

⁂

They had agreed that Paula would do what she needed to do, as though they weren't there, don't worry about us, we'll take care of ourselves, we're grown up, but now they are lingering, not knowing how to leave, setting their glasses down with a decisive gesture, knotting their scarves again, then pouring themselves one more, go on, one last glass and then we'll be off. And then suddenly Paula's mother says she'd like to see what they've done this year, their paintings, and Paula twists her mouth and shakes her head as if to say oh no, not possible, but Jonas preempts her, with pleasure, and guides them through the tiny apartment that has suddenly grown immense, deep, hiding ever more images of marble, of wood, more cloudy skies, more golden forms, the space divulging its treasures the way a coat might turn out its pockets. Paula follows, complaining continuously that they don't have enough space to look properly, that it's not dry yet, that they can't see anything, can't understand, but they can't hear her, this is all happening without her, it's Jonas who's leading the tour. He positions Paula's parents before the paintings and tells them the names of the woods and marbles, the types of decor, holds out the brushes, exhibits the palettes, and they, hands crossed behind their backs, lean their faces toward the paintings murmuring, it's astonishing, it's incredible, what a lot of work! In grand conclusion, standing before the painting of Skyros, he asks the couple theatrically: so, do you believe in it or not? Guillaume and Marie nod, laughing, yes, we believe in it, we'd certainly like to believe in it, in any case, that's Greece, one of the Sporades islands, summer, the light of reason, Guillaume gets carried away, his face hums with pleasure, while Marie goes one further, the light of myth! Are they drunk or something? thinks Paula, irritated, and in fact, drunk is exactly what they are, merry, tipsy, enthralled. Jonas leaps about like a mountain goat in the hallway, as though the response of Paula's parents affirms his work, and then suddenly cuts the scene short—he shakes their hands and says, we'll see you tomorrow, index finger in the air, officious: here it comes, the big day! What a phony, thinks Paula as he steps out the door.

The light dims all at once after Jonas leaves, dulling the angles, drowning the details, and the apartment is soon steeping in a lusterless liquid, like the kind you'd find at the bottom of a painter's pot, the colors all mixed together. I'll walk you back. Paula closes the kitchen window and pulls on a coat, and the three of them leave together. In the street, she slips between them—back into her place—and they walk arm in arm in the cold all the way to the hotel. Your friend is nice, Guillaume Karst says, in the careful way he has with language, and with his daughter, and a hundred meters further on Marie adds, yes, very nice, you're so lucky to have found him.

※

Paula hugs them in front of the hotel entrance, see you tomorrow, the big day, but she doesn't leave right away, stays there watching them through the glass, not letting her eyes leave them as they cross the lobby to the elevator, slow and calm; and then her eyes progressively frame them in a reality that has finally detached from her own in order to become theirs, as if they suddenly belonged to another world, as if they were characters in a film, moving inside a story from which she was absent. She never feels as close to them as when she stands like this, hidden away in the darkness while they move farther off into the distance, in full light. What she feels then, and what gradually tears at her heart until it becomes so painful she turns and flees, is the sensation of perceiving them as strangers, of touching their mystery, a feeling that brings back the canary-yellow pajamas that itched her bum and the sound of her plump little heels against the floor, evenings when she'd get out of bed after the ritual kiss and totter down the hall to hide behind the kitchen door and discover what her parents' life was like when she was asleep—or rather, that they had their own life when she wasn't there, a life from which she wasn't missing; standing there in the half dark, peering through the crack, she watched the meal unfold, fascinated by what took place in the kitchen, the total calm, the cutlery scraping and the glasses refilled, the sounds of mouths chewing, intrigued by the conversation that had no end, that accompanied their movements—Marie's hand that pulls the skin off a chicken wing, peels an apple, brings her wine glass to her lips, and Guillaume's hand that dips a spoon into a dessert bowl, elbows on the table, that reaches for the mustard, the brown sugar, or turns toward the sink to fill the water jug from the tap—riveted by the way they listened to each other, drank each other in with their eyes, these two who had already lived together for ten years and hadn't spent a single night apart in all that time. In those moments her mother became a different woman, her father a different man, and little Paula no longer knew who they were at all, faraway beings caught up in professional lives that took them elsewhere (Marie to Paris, for internal communications at Air Liquide, Guillaume to Aubervilliers, to the research and development department of Saint-Gobain), but they shared the slings and arrows of these other lives with detachment, minimizing impact and detail so as to better sequester themselves inside love. The child stood in the slim ray of light and spied on them until one or the other, aware of her presence for a long time already, turned toward the door, becoming her father or her mother again in that instant, and said, there's a little girl who'd best be going to bed right now.

⁂

The students' pieces are displayed in the large studio, which has been cleaned up for the occasion, and is well lit. Art gallery, display window, the visitors move through it as if in a cortège, spreading out, and one by one greet the woman in the black turtleneck for whom today is the worst day of the year. Tailored dove-gray flannel pants and flat-black waxed derbys, courteous and neutral, she welcomes them nonstop, mistress of the house. At times we can see her grow weary, no longer able to calibrate her words according to her inter-locutor—curt when she should be affable, distant when she would like to be warm. The crowded rooms, the excessive noise, the interminable parade, the faces streaming with pride, the fatuous excitement, all this weighs on her and annoys her, she would have preferred a hundred times over (this year once again) that the school skip this event and remain a secret lair housing a few young forgers, as they work at carving holes in reality, passageways, tunnels, galleries, and she along with them, setting an example, teaching them the game. Still, when she sees Guillaume and Marie coming toward her, quiet, attentive, she opens up instantly and extends a hand.

We're Paula Karst's parents. The noise diminishes all at once. Paula chose a turtle shell, she tells them quietly, leading them through the commotion to their daughter's easel, which holds her painting. It's a wise choice, she continues: turtles are protected, the trading of natural shell is prohibited, so this material, prized by decorators, has slowly disappeared, and rare are those who know how to paint it as well as Paula does. The parents are moved, they gaze at the painting, standing for the first time before this unknown part of their daughter, stunned by what she has produced: this radiant image, impossible to describe, this surface that captures river pebbles, underwater plants and reptiles, and the idea of placing a hand on the paper to feel the shell goes through them both at exactly the same moment. They thank her and move away calmly, against the flow of the procession, and soon a few of us can see them lift a hand, waving to Paula, who has appeared up there on the mezzanine, a hollyhock on its stem, diploma rolled like a spyglass, scanning the crowd, stopping on the two of them, hey you two down there, she murmurs, I'm here, I see you.

ON THEIR LAST NIGHT, THE STUDENTS FROM
the rue du Métal all get drunk together because it's the last
chance, the last big one—they get completely blitzed before
separating, allow themselves pledges, declarations, promises,
and tears, they drown their sorrows and give in to a certain
sentimentality without a fuss, leaning against the bar, each
one pronouncing their farewells before the group, glass lifted
high. But sometime around midnight, Jonas disappears. Paula,
tipsy, goes out into the street without a coat to look for him,
walks through the neighborhood with arms bare, her steps
clacking in the cold streets, and reaches the Institut, thinking
the studio lights might be on, maybe Jonas is inside with the
woman in the black turtleneck—they meet up some nights
now, everyone knows, and work together, assessing a pigment,
testing the composition of a varnish, modifying a technique
or simply having a conversation about painting, leaning over
rare books, catalogues of exhibitions in Amsterdam, London,
or Madrid, over stupidly lavish design magazines; people say
she would have liked to recruit this talented young man for
her school, even though she hated his hoodies and permanent
baseball cap, this guy who calls her by her first name, for
whom she pours a glass of cognac or Chartreuse, something
strong and burning, before they get down to it, and whose
cigarette she takes from time to time to have a drag or two,
suddenly cheerful, light, a young woman, but he eludes the
silent question, won't let himself be pinned down, and instead
wonders aloud whether this *world specialist in Carrara marble*
wouldn't have preferred to be a painter rather than a master

forger and respected director of a world-renowned painting school—you mean a *real* painter? she asks, teasing him,
shrewd as a marten, a lock of hair over her left eye. But no,
all the lights are off at 30 *bis* rue du Métal, and Paula goes
shivering back to the party, finds herself squished between
the ex-banker from London (in a pale pink sweatshirt with
fuck written across it, crying hot tears into his beer), and the
painter from Hamburg who, quite drunk, is pestering her to
sleep with him, reminding Paula of a promise she is no longer
quite certain she hadn't made, come on, let's go, he puts his
hot heavy hand on the small of her back and licks her neck,
laying out his arguments thickly, it's tonight or never, they
will never see each other again, it will be too late, and Paula
dodges him, keeping watch out of the corner of her eye for
Jonas to come back, but he doesn't. Around five in the morning she walks Kate back to her place. The two women kiss
on the mouth and hold each other for a long time on the
doorstep, and then Kate agrees to make her fish swim one
last time on the skin of her arm—and for this she takes off
her jacket and sweater and steps out under the streetlight,
where she appears like a magical creature in the night, her
full flesh haloed in a cold, milky light. Back on rue de Parme,
Paula climbs the stairs while outside dawn creeps over the
city, the first day of spring, she thinks, visualizing in a flash
all the types of wood they have learned to paint, and on the
landing, even before she opens the door, she can sense Jonas's
presence. He's here, he came home. Hard little tears suddenly
spurt from her eyes, spouting horizontally, and she wouldn't
be able to say whether they are tears of rage, exhaustion, relief,
or powerlessness, but in any case, they won't stop—a veritable
fountain. Jonas is standing before the sink in the kitchen,
doing the dishes, shoulder blades and line of vertebrae like a
row of buttons protruding beneath his T-shirt, pink rubber

gloves dripping water onto the floor. He stares at her for a few seconds, lips pressed tight together, as though he's waiting for the explosion. You okay? His question is accompanied by a movement of his head, and Paula freezes—a tornado held in check—then pulls herself together, looks at her watch and asks what time the woman from the agency is coming to do the walk-through of the apartment. He turns back to the sink: at five o'clock, we've gotta get a move on.

⁂

Because they've got to tidy up now, roll up the paintings or place them into drawing folders, clean the brushes, put the lids on the tubes, file away the documents, take apart the furniture, fold, sort, pack the bags, and take out the garbage. And once the apartment is empty: scrape the paint stains off the tiles and floor, scrub the bathtub, scour the sink, strip the grime off the walls and vacuum the floors—they've got their work cut out for them if they want their deposit back. They clean all day without exchanging a single glance, a single word, except for a few sullen questions—what do I do with this? Paula asks, brandishing one of Jonas's socks; whatever you want, I don't care—and when everything is sparkling, the floor shined, the windows clear, when there's no longer a single trace of their passage through this place, once the woman from the agency has left, after handing them their check with coarse formality, they do something strange: they lie down side by side on the floor and stay there in silence until night falls, staring at the ceiling—and maybe they both try then to gather up into themselves all that has happened between them during the six months of their training, what they have been for each other since the Sunday of the Cerfontaine, filling themselves up with this apartment so it might become as elementary as the landscapes of childhood, those we discover over and over as if for the first time, and which bring back in an instant everything we've forgotten; maybe, too, they think of those who would move in after them, students from the Institut who would resemble them, and whom they envied for their beginnings, rib cages puffed up with promise and mouths agape; or, maybe, they simply rested, because they've racked up quite a few sleepless nights, and they are exhausted.

⁂

Still, late that night, they could be seen sitting cross-legged on the ground in front of the computer screen, looking up sites with charter flights to paradise islands—the Seychelles! the Seychelles! sings Paula, shimmying her shoulders—they surf for a long time, faces chiseled in the artificial light, compare flight times and prices as though they're going to leave the next morning at dawn, and Jonas happens to click on the face of a monkey, launching a video they watch pressed tightly against each other, hypnotized by the strength of what they feel, because it is the film of a release, but also of a goodbye—which complicates everything: at the moment of being reintroduced into the wild, after having been saved and treated at the Tchimpounga Sanctuary in the Republic of the Congo, Wounda, a female chimp, suddenly turns back toward Jane Goodall, world-class primatologist (with the physique of an English poet), places an enormous hand on her slender shoulder, rests her head on Jane's neck and embraces her, while Jane hugs her back. The music is awful and Jonas puts it on mute. Silent, now, the scene suspends time, pierces the tropical forest to create a clearing where the woman and the monkey hold each other, alone in the world, in communion. Paula and Jonas burst into tears. Something hits them, together:

the rediscovered pact between humans and animals, the idea that to live free means having to separate, the gratitude for what has been lived, given, or the heartbreak of love, I don't know exactly what, but this night, their last night on the rue de Parme, Paula and Jonas watch this video dozens of times and cry, while onscreen the woman and the chimpanzee close their eyes, holding each other, and emotion electrifies this edge of the jungle.

Tomorrow, they will close the apartment door behind them, they too will hold each other, and then each one will set off into their life. No tears! they'll urge each other, laughing at a little decorum, saying they aren't altogether sad for it to be over—it's okay, I've had enough of you, now I'll finally get a break—and will do their best to hasten the sticky temporality of goodbyes. But even though they have trust, even though they have no doubt they'll become singular to one another, unique in the world, loved, something is still coming to an end here, and they take note: the time of the Institut de Peinture and of the apartment on rue de Parme, this time of their youth and their training, this time has passed. Paula closes her eyes and hammers out these phrases in her mind, she wants to feel their violence, as though suffering will allow her to prolong the time, to scrape out a few more minutes. They have to leave the studio now, the way we leave childhood, and reacquaint themselves with the outside, return to a world they had abandoned without even realizing it. Everything is altered, forever. And when they watch Wounda turning one last time toward Jane before disappearing into the jungle, this is what they're thinking: each one is the monkey for the other, by turns or at the same time, monkeys on the brink of something.

Time Returns

A FIRST JOB TURNS UP AS SOON AS PAULA gets back to the rue de Paradis, less than a month after graduation, while she's brooding in the apartment, disoriented, as though there were a time change between Brussels and Paris too brutal to be quaffed in a few nights, as though she were returning from a faraway land, a time out of sync with earthly clocks, and as though there was nothing left of her time in Belgium but a great fatigue. She keeps the blinds in her bedroom lowered, the slats angled to keep the room in semi-darkness—do her eyes need to rest from all they've seen out there, do they need to return, to recover from all that?—and doesn't go outside; meanwhile it's April, the regreening, skin of shoulders and ankles reappearing on the sidewalks, the air tart, sparkling, a mouthful of chlorophyll, the sky crystalline, the colors of the city reignited, and if she would just go out even for a little, Paula would see these colors as she has never seen them before, would know how to name them properly—nacarat, Great Maiden's Blush, paprika, aquamarine, baise-moi-ma-mignonne, Naples yellow, chartreuse, after-the-rain green, pomelo. But she's emptied out, her rhythm is broken. Is it idleness that weighs on her, or is the slow work of memory already pulling her down a narrow hallway, head thrown back? She can't quite manage to reassemble the pieces of her life from before. Her parents hover and gently encourage her to do something: you should see to the administrative details to convert your Belgian diploma, you should find out about that painting internship in Savoie in August, you should sign up to audit courses at the

Beaux-Arts. They encourage her to go out, go to the pool, see some friends—ironic, coming from them, who never go out and never have visitors, spend their free time studying and creating menus together that will honor the spring vegetables popping up in the market stalls—but she doesn't call anyone, not even her closest friends, the ones she left behind last September in that zone that's now out of reach, like a blurred and insubstantial shore from which she's distanced herself for good. In the first days she sends several texts to Kate, to Jonas, but their responses don't spark a conversation—skimpy, hurried, broken with exclamation marks—and the idea that she too could be compartmentalized now into a period of their past, this thought hurts her. From then on, she feels best in her room, on this hermetic islet where she can revisit at will the winter in Brussels, where she can bury herself with abandon in what she just lived, the same way we give ourselves over to debauchery.

⁂

One morning, the doorbell rings. Paula is alone in the apartment and finally goes to open it: it's the neighbor from the first floor, in a polar fleece robe, feet bare in her old slippers. Paula doesn't immediately notice the presence of a baby between the folds of the robe, sleeping in a carrier, and greets the neighbor distractedly, phone in hand, as though she were waiting for an urgent call. The skin of the neighbor's face is marked by sleepless nights, her hair stringy and teeth neglected, but the look she gives Paula is striking when she says: a sky—I want you to come paint a sky in my baby's room.

A sky in a bedroom. Paula doesn't know what to say, but immediately throws herself into this commission as if it were a matter of painting the ceiling of the Sistine Chapel—she is transported by the subject, a sky, primary and perennial at once—and I would have loved to have been inside her mind at the moment when the skies of painting coursed through, all of them, all at once, the roundup, the grand cupolas with gods passing by, the mechanical ballet of the planets, the cosmic orbs set to the tempo of rockets and flying saucers, the human sky of metaphysical emptiness and black storms, the fogs of estuaries, the Zen daybreaks, the blazes in Technicolor, the concrete blue where airplanes and drones converge along with a few high-flying birds, a balloon filled with hydrogen, and then the smoke, the ashes, the autumn leaf carried by the wind. She contemplates the work with the seriousness of a hotshot professional, immediately goes down to see the dim, cramped room, ceiling clean but bulging as if buckling under the weight of the building, and then listens intently as the young mother describes the fresh, light, ethereal sky she wants for her child, for her child's dreams, when he will lie here on his back, in his cradle, woolen covers pulled up under his chubby arms and kittens embroidered on the sheets. The deal is sealed on the doorstep—Paula doesn't bargain—and less than an hour later she's pushing a cart down the paint aisle of a hardware store on avenue de Flandre, buying different acrylic blues in half-liter jars, a tube of raw sienna and another of burnt umber, a roller, sponges, a paint tray, several meters of black plastic, and then, once she's through the checkout, she shoves everything into a backpack, takes the metro back to the rue de Paradis, drops her bags off in the baby's room and goes upstairs to get her brushes—spalter, rabbit foot, round brush—and a shaky ladder she hauls over her shoulder.

The room to be painted is on the first floor with a narrow window onto the courtyard, the view obscured at all hours of the day by a glistening black wall, and yet it's here, in this drab, confined place, that she finds her rhythm again, regulates her breathing, revisits her musculature, and those watching her at this moment—the large turtledove that has spiraled down the well of the back courtyard, the old bald woman glued to the opposite window, the high school girl leaning out to gauge the weather as she picks out a sweater—are struck by the expression on her face, by this face that remains imperturbable while the rest of her body springs into action as if she had set off a process that nothing could interrupt, not until the final touches have been added, each movement contained within the one that precedes it, each gesture flowing from the entire chain.

She begins by preparing the space, getting down onto her hands and knees to spread the plastic sheet on the floor, then climbing up and down the ladder, moving it meter by meter along the walls to unroll painter's tape around the edges of the ceiling—a fastidious operation meant to ensure a clean finish. Once everything is ready, she hangs the jar of white over the ladder steps with a piece of wire, pulls herself up onto the top step and begins to apply two base coats with the roller, head tipped back, thinking of this sky she's going to paint, this diaphanous, sparkling space, located at the edge of transparency, which will diffuse a radiant light, the source of which no one will be able to place; she imagines this sky, at once ethereal and palpable, and which she will punctuate with a prosaic, tender cloud—that's what I'm going to do for this little baby.

Later, in the middle of the afternoon, the white is dry, the ceiling ready for the second coat, and Paula kneels down. She casts a glance around her at the pallid walls, the window without direct light—she'd read somewhere that the walls of Paradise were made of sapphire, and yet, she smiles, I'm on the right street, rue de Paradis, tripling the elastic around her ponytail—and then she opens the jars, sliding the point of a knife under the lids; and as she uncovers these shining surfaces, these placid and unctuous textures like industrial cream—the creamy filling of a Mont Blanc, only blue—she thinks over the procedures that allowed people in other times to imitate the color of the sky, decoctions whose ingredients she liked to recite to Jonas to make him laugh, to impress him, to play the witch busy at her retorts, the alchemist who possessed the secrets of nature and the formulas for its metamorphosis, trying out new mixtures so he would look up, so he would ask her a question; she thinks again of that blue in the Middle Ages, vials filled with blueberry essence cut with vinegar and *the urine of a ten-year-old child who has drunk good wine,* and of that ultramarine they used instead of gold in the early Renaissance, more sparkling, indeed, than gold, and more worthy of painting, a blue that had to be gathered beyond the sea, behind the horizon, deep within ice-bound mountains devoid of humans where these cosmic droplets were hidden, celestial pearls, lapis lazuli brought back in fine cotton purses tucked under a shirt next to the skin, the stones pulverized against marble plates upon arrival, the powder poured into a mortar and then mixed, according to the recipe, with egg white, sugar water, gum Arabic, or plum or cherry tree resin—*merdaluna*, as they said then in Venice—and ground even finer with gray water, ash, ammonium salt, before finally being filtered through a piece of silk or linen; and, still leaning over these jars like an orant, Paula suddenly hears the voice of the woman in the black turtleneck the day she declared, leaning over the rail of the studio mezzanine, projecting her cutting shadow onto them, that the knowledge contained in these preparations, their skillful, confident production, all this gave a tableau its nobility, its valor, its moral energy—and on this last point, it was clear she wasn't kidding around.

Paula takes paint from each jar, mixes the three blues into the pure white, adds a drop of phthalocyanine, and slowly begins the search for her color. The skin of her face heats up and beads with sweat, she breathes with her mouth wide open as though she couldn't get enough air, and the paint tray is reflected in her eyes, which haven't blinked once, her brush stirring a blue as it forms, her wrist making her hand beat faster and faster, emulsifying a possible sky. She finally stabilizes a color, one awash with references, then gets up, stiff and a bit dizzy, knees cracking; she leans the paint tray against the ladder, climbs to the top step and, standing two meters above the floor, a scarf tied under her ponytail (peasant style, Girl-Guide style, fifties pinup style), with one hand steadying her and the other moving her brush—shoulder low, elbow at a forty-five degree angle to avoid tendinitis, capsulitis, *frozen shoulder*—she paints.

⁊₹

Outside noises have ceased, quiet reigns over the walls, and only Paula's breath as she works creates a rising vibration. Deaf to the susurration, she continues to propagate a vast and dreamy sky, taking care to lighten it at the corners and sides to create depth, leaving a reserve area to bring a cloud into being, the volume and mass of which she works with a sponge, embellishing the contours, and soon it floats on the ceiling like a small and very human blimp.

Evening has fallen, it's dark outside, and Paula plugs in a halogen lamp to continue her painting. Inside the room, the window has transformed into a mirror, while from outside it becomes a dormer lit up in the night, the diorama of a profession, the film of a small work site, and you can bet that the large turtledove, the bald old woman, and the high school girl, each at their various heights, have returned to their own windowpane to watch, eyes trained on the heroine's silhouette, perfectly framed, straight, sure, balanced on top of the ladder as though in the middle of a flaming hoop; they observe this something firm that crowns her, this determination perceptible even in her drop shadow, where the ponytail, enormous, seems hardly to move, where the head, in a play of perspective, seems to touch the ceiling, supporting the young sky like a caryatid; surely all three of them stay there until Paula stops abruptly, turns off the light, and closes the door behind her, engulfing the scene in darkness all at once.

The next morning, neck sore, shoulders aching, eyes burning, Paula hurtles down the four flights, anxious about what she'll find behind the door to the little room. She goes in, lifts her eyes: and she's underwhelmed. Sees none of the celestial splendor she thought she was painting in the final hours of the night—but she *was* high on paint fumes, does she need to be reminded?—instead, sees a sky that's too dark, multicolored, without depth. She paces for a few seconds, distraught, and then pours pure white into a small tray, picks up the spalter and climbs the ladder again, fights her own gravity—wobbly, not much sleep—and finally makes out a spherical bump in the ceiling, a flaw that her painting incorporates as the very shape of its sky, and now she paints at full tilt, it's beautiful to see, the ceiling transformed into a surface where she wouldn't be able to say whether it tended toward transparency or opacity, but which pleases her. The bedroom is converted into the basket of a hot air balloon, into a yurt on the plains, a rock shelter, and when Paula finally steps down to the floor, swaying, drained, and announces that she's finished, the young mother comes into the room and lets out a cry, bites her lips in amazement, and her hand flutters about in the air as if stung by a wasp. Paula, on the other hand, can't even look at her work anymore, lowers her eyes and turns away, embarrassed, then says she's thirsty and needs to wash her hands—and maybe something is already detaching from within her, maybe if she lifts her eyes toward the ceiling she won't be able to recognize herself as the author of that blue, and would be uneasy to observe an unknown presence within the same body as her: did I paint that? A second later, she's paid in cash, hand to hand; her fingers, burning from solvents, brush the fingers of the young mother and then crumple the bills into her pocket. Back upstairs, she joins her parents who are washing fingerling potatoes and grating radishes in the kitchen, brandishes the warm wad of bills, and announces that she's not enrolling anywhere in the fall, not going back to university: I'm going to find other jobs. Guillaume nods, places his knife on the counter, and retrieves a jar of duck rillettes, which he begins to spread on toast. I thought you wanted to be a painter. Paula turns. I want to paint, that's all.

SUMMER SHARPENS, THE CITY TAKES ON
another speed, puts on another soundtrack, voids appear,
flat, vacant, abandoned zones, the sun burns like a white-hot
disc, and Paula idles. She surfs social media, joins the Face-
book group for former students of the Institut, posts notices
in the neighborhood stores, cold calls a design studio for
department store shop windows, two interior design agen-
cies, some theater scenery repair studios in Saint-Denis and
Montreuil, but everywhere she goes, lips curl into a taciturn
pout, we have nothing for the moment, we're closing next
week, check back in September. Guillaume and Marie try to
trick their daughter, asking her to do a patina on a friend's
studio, another friend's chimney, to do a walnut burl veneer
for the elevator of the neighboring building, something that
will get her *foot in the door*, as they say, falsely cheery, but
Paula suspects secret dealings, even that they're paying for
these little jobs themselves, and, offended, she shuts herself
away. Jonas and Kate send little news, unless to compare their
respective salaries and keep each other informed of negotiation
margins—how high do you think I can go? Jonas has found
work on the set of *Rameau's Nephew* that will be mounted at
the Théâtre de la Monnaie in November, Kate is painting a
fresco of the Grand Canal in Venice at the back of a Glasgow
pizzeria and getting ready to touch up the ones that cover
the walls at the Nautilus, where she has picked up her old
position as a bouncer, sexy and uncompromising Cerberus
at the gate of the abyss. Paula doesn't have a dime, she joins
her parents for a few days in Charente, and otherwise withers

in her room, this summer sucks. Worse, September brings not even an ounce of contrast: the only difference is now it's autumn, not back-to-school—and she's stuck below the waterline, no projects or plans, out of the game.

⁂

Her phone screen lights up. It's Alba, one of the Spanish cousins from the rue du Métal. The offer is direct, shot straight as a rocket: the Museo Egizio in Turin is preparing an exhibit on the discovery of Kha and Merit's tomb in 1906, Ernesto Schiaparelli led the archaeological mission—you know? The scenery agency overseeing the thing is managed by a cousin of my mother's—she's tough, I warn you—who's recruiting an emergency team of painters for the wall panels. Paula knows nothing about Ancient Egypt—but remembers having seen, as a child, sarcophagi of pharaohs and the mummy of a cat during a family outing entitled *A Sunday at the Louvre*, the trace of which can be found in a photo album labeled *1997*—has never heard of Kha and Merit and has only a vague idea of where Turin is, but to hear Alba—rapid-fire delivery, husky voice, unfettered coarseness of an aristocrat—is to return to the rue du Métal, and Paula, who wants to keep this voice in her ear, borrows the money for a plane ticket from her parents, gets her gear together, and rushes to Orly.

⁂

Turin is austere, elegant, and has a cold splendor. Paula crosses the piazza Carlo Alberto on the diagonal, feet freezing in her canvas sneakers, impatient to find her friend at the Circolo dei Lettori restaurant on via Bogino. The two of them embrace with gusto—Alba overdoes it—but Paula must still swallow her pride: she will only be painting the backgrounds of panels that other artists will then cover with the cliffs of the Valley of the Kings and Deir el-Medina: Kha and Merit's village, as it was lit three thousand years ago in the powdery dawn of the New Kingdom of Egypt. Paula absorbs the blow, crosses her arms and nods her head, I get it, then makes her way to the museum for a little visit to the collections that has been organized for the technical team, which, though she's only doing backgrounds, she's nonetheless still part of. The curator is a young guy with a beard the color of rye, a walnut-sized bun, and a black velvet suit. He gets straight to the point: the largest collection of Egyptian artifacts in the world, outside of Egypt, is right here—his two index fingers point at the ground and Paula begins to take the measure of the place. Then he leads the little group at full sail into the room containing the objects found in Kha and Merit's tomb, that couple buried in the same mortuary chamber, and stops in front of the statue of a young man standing in front of a chair. The guide rubs his hands together, looks at his watch and says: I will only speak about one object—this one here—he indicates the statue and this gesture opens his narrative: in Ancient Egyptian times, those who, like Kha, a royal architect during the reign of Amenhotep II, were wealthy enough to have tombs constructed, often commissioned Deir el-Medina artisans to make a statue that would incarnate them as they wished to appear in the eyes of the Gods when they entered eternity. These statues were then buried with them—the young curator expresses himself pedantically, casting a hard eye on those who listen distractedly, eyes sliding toward smartphones—and the miniature double offered a refuge for the soul of the deceased, in case some misfortune were to befall his mummified body. But the statue was not a representation of him—it *was* him. Paula shivers, certain now that the voice is addressing her and her alone when it says: the double is blessed with life.

The curator tosses out these last words before slipping away, walking backwards, as if to say, there, I'll leave you to meditate on all this. The group breaks up in a disoriented rustling, disperses around the glass cases, but Paula doesn't move, frozen before the statuette of Kha, painted chair in the background, presented as the archaeologists found it in the funerary chamber on that February day in 1906, while workers continued to dig into the valley of Deir el-Medina, at work for over a month by then—and once the dirty work was done, Ernesto Schiaparelli, in a three-piece suit and off-white safari helmet, dusted off the entrance to a tomb amid the scree, a well of about four meters, sealed by a brick wall, behind which a tunnel led to another wall that had to be knocked down, and then a long antechamber containing a ceremonial bed, and finally the funerary chamber where, hidden from the world for three millennia, in the middle of a room where a human gaze could not even be imagined, lay the coveted bodies and treasures. And among them this figurine, depicted mid-step, chest banded with a garland of real flowers that had traveled intact across a mass of time and darkness so great that none could conceive of it. Paula plumbs the painted eyes of the statuette, contemplates the nose carved in wood, the closed mouth, the hands open beside the body and the feet separated as though halted mid-step, and soon, because she's looked at it so long, she's no longer so sure that everything is immobile behind the glass; and if the statue moved toward her and opened its mouth, now, she would believe it—and the young curator, peering at her from the corner of his eye, can tell she'll need some time to digest this tête-à-tête, convinced it will be more than enough to give inestimable value to any trip to Turin, although this particular trip will turn out to be difficult and barely lucrative for Paula.

⁊ᷓ

But Italy overall proves fruitful for her. It's like a thread you pull and lift, a necklace of opportunities, each job containing a fork in the path toward the next, holding a further chance. Paula grabs whatever shows up, sometimes at the last minute, sometimes without really believing it, says yes to large jobs, to modest and menial work, to quick remuneration, bills held out by a hand that's often diamond-encrusted and reticent, with pointy nails—a pincer. After the background of the scenery panels for the Turin exhibition, it was a buttercup-yellow patina in a hair salon in Milan, followed by a bathroom in faux marble at the house of the hairdresser—megalomaniacal and romantic, the client chose a Candoglia, the same stone as the Milan cathedral; next, Paula painted old-fashioned lettering on the storefront of a chocolatier in Brescia, the set for *Conversation en Sicile* put on by an amateur theater troupe from the parish of San Luca, made the column for *Le temps et la chambre* played by the same troupe six months later in the Avignon OFF, painted three panels of eucalyptus—a gray marble—for the bedrooms in a Provençal farmhouse in the Drôme converted into a hotel, a chimney in Sarrancolin that she has to start over, the client changing her mind to a bohemian pink that will match the fabric on her couch—a small, poorly paid job that lasted too long, a bad move—paints the walls of a pastry shop in Carrara marble as sparkling as rock candy, two columns in indigo blue and coves in faux boxwood for the choir stalls of the church in Mergozzo, in the Val d'Ossola, which she executes under the direction of a blind and persnickety priest—she sleeps in a Spartan room in the rectory. On the first night she climbs onto the bed, stands on tiptoe on the pillow and reaches up to unhook the crucifix nailed to the wall, an ugly cross with a silver-plated Jesus twisted in suffering, his face enucleated, ribs protruding, which she tucks into the back of a dresser drawer before lying down on her back, eyes on the ceiling; the last time she held a crucifix in her hands was when she'd found herself almost completely alone one August in a little countryside cemetery—a funeral had derailed, they had mistakenly unsealed the cousins' vault, hysterical laughter had broken out at the front of the procession and spread all the way to the end, the undertakers rested the coffin for a moment on the gravel and took a breath, drenched in sweat in thick black suits, while the children were already leaning over the edge of the hole, hoping to see skeletons, and then the gravedigger had turned up in the cemetery, scraggy, sideburns like sabers, work jacket open over a T-shirt, shit, half the tombs in here have the same name, he shouted, then ducked between the sepulchers to unseal the other tomb, the right one this time, but after so long waiting in the beastly heat, the men had taken off their jackets and loosened their ties, makeup was running, feet were swollen inside high heels, babies had woken up in the arms of big sisters, and the older folks had begun to sit down on the gravestones, scattered here and there like large crows, fanning themselves with the booklet from the mass, disapproving of the young couples who'd gone off to wait in air-conditioned cars; once the coffin was lowered into place, the oldest son of the deceased, who was very red in the face and stricken by this mess, had launched into a song to the Virgin, *Chez nous soyez Reine,* and a few frail voices had taken it up, but the priest, who had another mass to give ten kilometers away, rushed the ending and everyone crossed themselves in a hurry before dashing off to the reception; Paula, lingering near the tomb, had watched the gravedigger who was filling the hole, the odor of fresh cement in the pail went to her head, and then she placed the crucifix on the headstone; so you believe in that stuff? the gravedigger asked as he leaned on his shovel, the cemetery deserted, car doors slamming behind the wall, and then he downed a liter of warm Fanta, head tilted back, eyes closed.

❧

She joined the cohort of nomadic workers, those who move around all year long and sometimes travel great distances, depending on their gigs (quite distinct from the celebrities of Twitter and Instagram who are brought, all expenses paid, for the launch night of a cell phone, makeup line or shrimp sorbet—hairdressers and colorists, star-spangled pastry chefs, soccer players, surgeons with gleaming white teeth, agents of all kinds, cult columnists—and quite distinct also from the constant flux of workers hired for the jobs that proliferate over the surface of the globe, the inexhaustible and underpaid labor force that circulates in the baggage holds of globalization). Paula, for her part, moves in an intermediate category, that of the freelancers, and although she's been working in Italy since she got her diploma, on various jobs and always for Italian backers, she's still not registered with the Maison des Artistes. Freelancing is nebulous, there are the stars who move from one job to the next, sought after, the calendar blacked out several years ahead, and the others, who don't work enough, have nothing booked beyond three weeks. Those of Paula's caliber tend to say yes to everything for fear they'll be forgotten or blacklisted if they're not available—they buy their own plane and train tickets, invoice low-cost hotel rooms or furnished studio apartments-cum-high profit investments—functional rooms equipped with good Wi-Fi and hastily slapped together cupboards, rent increased for an extra pillowcase or dish-towel—and in a few hours at most, wherever they are, they reinvent the cozy cell they will inhabit for the length of their stay. They speak several second languages badly and none fluently but have a practiced ear, and in less than two weeks the timbre of their voices change, they take on the accent of the place where they are, new gestures accompany their stories and their skin begins to shimmer in unison with those around them. When in Rome . . . this is how they cheer themselves on. They are all-terrain and polyvalent, adapt themselves to all practices, all protocols, all rhythms, and this is exactly what makes them useful, this is why they're hired. And Paula among them begins to garner some experience, those who have worked with her recommend her gladly if they're asked: she's a reliable worker, skilled, works fast, known for her ability to improvise—indeed, she has stocked her memory with ways to face a certain situation by recalling another similar one solved in another time and place, always keeps rigorous notebooks where she records the chromatic references of rare tints and the composition of specific varnishes, a repertory of the vocabulary used in different trades, with definitions and translations included, as well as a progressive mapping of her network of clients.

※

These modest jobs follow one after the other, giving Paula a continuity of work that's enviable these days, and a material autonomy, fragile but real. Exhilarated, she rents a room near the train station in Turin, in a dreary apartment on via Giotto, learns Italian, gets by with more and more ease—so well that she can negotiate a salary, overtime, an advance. It's the language of the land of marble, right? she writes to Kate, who natters on about how mastering English would be more useful and this is what she should be working on.

She acquires the supple stride of resourceful, pragmatic women, those who hop on trains, take long-distance buses, put on their makeup in the reflection of windows and rear-view mirrors, drink from the tap and willingly strike up conversations with strangers, these savvy women who make their way easily through the crowd, never linger too long in one place, dash off smiling, not looking back, already at a distance, already somewhere else. But this new flurry of activity, which she likes to showcase perhaps a little too much, exaggerating the rush, giving herself airs, proclaiming left and right that she was *swamped*, embellishing the number of hours spent without sleep and the difficulty of her jobs, disturbs her lucidity: she's unable to see that precariousness has become the condition of her existence, instability her mode of life—she ignores the extent to which she has become vulnerable, and she's unaware of her solitude. Sure, she's meeting people, yes, lots of them, her list of contacts grows ever longer in her smartphone, her network thickens, but caught up in a relationship of economics where she's required to fulfill an order in exchange for a salary on one hand, hired on limited-time jobs on the other, she never creates relationships that last, she accumulates intense crushes that flame like straw fires without leaving a trace, disintegrating in a matter of weeks—heat and dust. For example: friends forever with a woman hired on the same job as her—a stairway in Golden Yellow Algerian Onyx, horribly difficult, for the head office of a Milan shipowner—both of them living in an apartment made available by the company director (a guy with a thin mustache in a straight cashmere camel coat who found it very charming to put up these two little French women in overalls), and they are super close in a heartbeat, telling each other everything, in considerable detail, sex included; and then once the stairs are painted, their paths diverge and they detach all at once, both of them—in three days it's over, and then nothing more, a smiley face from time to time, a text, and neither one misses the other. And Paula—who claims to be a nomad, a free spirit, perfectly adjusted to this way of life, dipping into short-term loves, disdaining premature conjugality and the sight of people of her age settled like old slippers—is destabilized bit by bit by the discontinuity of her emotional life, by these infatuations without a tomorrow, by the alternating current that currycombs her heart. She learns to measure her distances, to not get too involved, to always keep going; for the first two years of the Italian period she'll have three lovers and that's it, lightning conjunctions that always take shape in the interstices of the job, or the day before the job is done, as if it were only at the moment of leaving that Paula could consent to let herself go. And then one Sunday in March, she dissolves into sobs on a Frecciarossa train between Milan and Rome.

※

The news from Glasgow is grim. Kate is having a hard time. Soon it will be three months since she touched a paintbrush, and there's nothing on the horizon. Last time they Skyped, she was still working at the Nautilus but was so broke she'd taken a babysitting job—the little girl dreamed of trying out for *Britain's Got Talent*, turned on her karaoke machine the minute she got home from school and jumped around non-stop in the living room, a nightmare. The last job in particular had taken a bad turn: just as she was about to pay her for a simple frieze, the client, dressed in a little red leather jacket, had told Kate she'd be cutting her fee on the pretext that the floor was stained. Kate denied responsibility, demanded her money, and stood over the client, canines clenched, forehead so close that the other panicked, bleated out that she was *crazy*, and threw the money in her face; and Kate, white with rage, gathered up the wad and shoved it back into the client's hand, telling her to top it up and give it to her again nicely, with an apology, please, which the client had refused to do, backed up against a glass table, pulling out her phone to call her husband, repeating over and over you're completely insane, you're a menace; and then Kate grabbed her spalter, opened a jar of paint, and crossed out the elegant, seventeenth century—inspired foliage with great sweeps of the brush, the scene inspired by the Grand Siècle that had taken her three days to paint on the ceiling of the entryway. She'd shit on the whole thing, flinging drops of paint on the ground, indeed, and then walked out the door past the dumbstruck client and straddled her bike just as the nice silver Audi Q5 belonging to the husband rolled up. That's it, I'm *persona non grata* around here, Kate had joked, I should probably get out. Paula had cheered—come! and Kate had shot back, Are you gonna buy my ticket then? Bad-tempered, adding crossly, I have a boyfriend, remember? And it had been radio silence since then.

Jonas's silence is of another sort. Jonas is snowed under. Hyperactive and guarded, always somewhere else. His work on *Rameau's Nephew* in Brussels earned him a two-year contract with a prominent Slovenian set designer, and his professional sphere was Eurocentric right off the bat, prestigious productions he keeps mum about, superstitious and stingy. Paula is vexed to read his name by chance in a laudatory article about an adaptation of *Macbeth* at the Théâtre Royal in Namur, or later in a presentation of *Othello* at the Berlin Schaubühne, hurt to hear him minimizing his jobs in a detached voice when they Skype, his face pixelated on the screen: stop, Paula, all of this isn't even painting. Let's stop talking about work, tell me about you, that's more interesting, suddenly close, all distance banished, the world retracted, geography dispelled, are you meeting some people in the midst of all this? And then it's Paula's turn to play evasive, to create artificial gray areas; and as soon as the Skype window closes she feels empty, hands cold, wouldn't be able to say whether they had really talked, feels that they are growing apart from each other, wonders when she'll see him again, shadow over half his face, and the ember of the cigarette hovering at the height of his cheek.

PAULA OPENS HER EYES AND LOOKS AROUND. She recognizes the place but it takes her a moment—an unusual moment—to surface. She lets herself be swallowed up by consciousness and the rising day, slowly reconstituting the chain of events of the previous days. Everything happened very fast. A five-week job canceled at the last minute—the patina for a three-hundred-square-meter apartment in the center of Turin—and the series of arrangements that topple like a house of cards: she gives up her room on via Giotto, gathers up her few things, which barely fill two big duffel bags, the paint box, computer, chargers; leaves the keys and the rent in cash on the table in the hallway and then slings one bag over each shoulder, and, balanced like this, sets off for the station to wait for the bus that takes her to the airport—in the check-in line, she watches a woman her age for a long time, who shuffles forward, kicking her bag, eyes never leaving her phone. A few hours later, Paula pushes open the door of the building on rue de Paradis and then stops short in the lobby, attention caught by the fake marble patina on the walls—a Red Verona that's barely believable, nodules too thick and the ammonite fossils weirdly distributed—that she is really seeing for the first time.

※

Paula listens to the sounds of the apartment—her parents are up and the toaster pops in the kitchen. She'll have to play a tight, close game—listen, I'm not moving back in, it's just temporary—and hold her head high. Hey, you two, she calls out, party's over, I'm baaack!

This room is her room. The only bedroom she knew until she turned twenty. She slept here as a baby in a straw Moses basket with red gingham trim on a rattan stand, then in a child's bed beneath a wooden mobile depicting the extraordinary voyages of Nils Holgersson—a wild goose ridden by a little boy in a red vest and royal blue pants—then in a wrought iron bed repainted sky blue by her mother, and finally in this double bed which she'd had to fight for at the beginning of her last year in high school and which, it's true, takes up a lot of room. The room had been redone then, she remembers, the arrival of a new bed providing the occasion to repaint the walls white, to change the carpet, to replace the flowered curtains with shuttered blinds, and to chuck out everything that was a relic of the little girl she'd been: the small desk varnished white, the dozens of boxes of knickknacks, the glitter pens, the faded stuffed animals, the notebooks, the huge jumble of photos she'd spent so long arranging, disassembling, rearranging—photo booth shots of friends, three or four crammed onto the bench, postcards of paintings by Rousseau Le Douanier, ads for perfumes or fashion photos, *Le Baiser de l'hôtel de ville* by Doisneau, Leonardo DiCaprio. Paula had been ruthless with these trinkets, these artifacts of childhood—without batting an eye, she'd affirmed her control over this space, her fine taste and newfound maturity. The only things that had survived were a miniature kayak carved out of cork, a Tahitian necklace, a few books—including *Myths and Legends of Ancient Greece,* a white hardcover volume with gold edging—and Uma Thurman on the poster for *Kill Bill,* whetted katana and lemon yellow suit, sexy life-sized warrior. Other images and objects have infiltrated this room since she left, but nothing has altered the austerity of the decor, this starkness that was so desirable in the eyes of the radical high school girl, that determined seventeen-year-old who emptied the drawers, tore the photos and magazine pages from the walls and filled garbage bags while her mother folded the curtains into plastic bins and her father, standing on a ladder, unscrewed the curtain rod and tried not to think about the pull tab on the zipper between Uma's breasts.

Uninhabited like all the bedrooms of children who have left home, Paula's room had little by little become dissociated from the rest of the apartment, disconnected from its organic function. Without completely excluding it from their daily space, her parents had deactivated it: everything was in order, each thing in its place, and the carpet still had vacuum marks on it—but it had become inert, silent, withdrawn into a space where the lights were no longer turned on, where air didn't circulate anymore. It was clear to anyone who opened the door that no one came in here much, unless to get a raincoat or a pair of boots from the closet, a suitcase on wheels, a sleeping bag. Paula perceived all this the second she stepped into the hallway, home during a gap between two jobs, and it got her back up—she wanted to continue to occupy all her space, to revive the room that had been dedicated to her since her first day on earth. She stood in the doorway and shouted, this isn't a shrine, then went in, made noise, turned on the lamps, and threw open the window.

꘎

Paula stretches, turns onto her side, and her eyes stop on another face less than a meter away. It's a child of ten smiling in the sun, a little girl in sandals, skinny and tanned. She's standing in a field wearing orange terry cloth shorts and a T-shirt with a picture of the submarine *Le Triomphant*; around her the grass is brown, the sky empty, there's a necklace of watermelon seeds around her neck and her left eye is covered with a thick bandage. The photo is leaning up against the books on the shelf—it's a Polaroid whose colors have turned, and in the white margin under the image, someone has simply written: *Pola*. She's surprised that her parents would have chosen this photo to place here, the only one visible in the room, a shot in which she's not the cute little girl she knows she once was—a lively and loving kid, though too tall for her age and awkward, stumbling, a beanpole, they'd say, incapable of seeing her size as a physical asset—which might have allowed her, for example, to make an impression on those smaller than her—but a child whose face betrayed a problem and, if not a disability, a strangeness at least.

Standing naked in the middle of the room, Paula touches the old Polaroid, as though her fingers could gather up everything it emanates, restore the child who smiled for the camera, standing in a field scorched by the August heat wave. What could she have done to merit being photographed that morning? She brings it to her face now, her breath speeding up as the scene develops, that sky-blue cotton T-shirt with velour synthetic letters across her belly spelling out the name of a nuclear submarine, the power of it all the greater for being reserved, controlled, dissuasive: *Le Triomphant*. Her godfather, senior officer on the ship, had mailed it to her in a package at the end of a campaign—a mission in seas whose names he could not reveal, so that no one, not even his wife, knew which waters the craft had traveled through—it submerges one fine day in the harbor in Toulon, Brest, or Lorient, reappears after several weeks in a spray of foam, its Conning tower breaking the surface to become again a perch for birds, and the crew lined up on the bridge are pale, eyes blinking and bodies heavier by a few pounds. As the yellow delivery van did a U-turn in front of the door, Paula had unsealed the large envelope in the middle of a swarm of kids who'd come running to see, and had immediately pulled on this shirt from the bottom of the sea. Three of her cousins had showed up on bikes then and started to ride circles around her, watching her, mouths open and faces burning with covetousness—young coyotes—and Paula had paid them no mind, conscious of her privilege, happy to have the envy of these boys she venerated like demigods (while for them, she was nothing special—a girl), since this T-shirt couldn't be bought in shops, only in Navy outfitters, at the back of military arsenals, inside sparse rooms with controlled access where you could also find fisherman's sweaters and combat pants, caps, topcoats, boots, tin tumblers, and rank insignia. The average mortal could not possess such a shirt without being intimately related to the domain of submarines, and it was this that made little ten-year-old Paula swell with joy, chest puffed out above long skinny legs: to be seen in the eyes of the world as someone who was connected to clandestine seas, to dark depths, stakeholder of an invisible planetary order, shot through with torpedoes, teeming with threats.

Paula pulls on a pair of panties and a tank top, distantly surrounded by the black hulls of submarines patrolling atolls of Polynesia at this very moment, offshore from North Korea, at the bottom of the Black Sea and under the rail de Sein, thinks of all that circulates below the surface of the world, of secret, superpowerful passions—love—and oddly enough this is the precise moment that she receives a selfie from Jonas, bareheaded, serious and wearing a tie, encrusted like a gem in a dark green marble reminiscent of the majesty of antique Porphyry—Serpentinite, thinks Paula, startled. She immediately recognizes one of the most famous slabs of marble on the planet, the marble of the rostrum of the United Nations headquarters in New York City.

IT'S SUMMER AGAIN—BUT WHICH SUMMER?
2009? 2010? she loses track when she talks about it, only the
string of places she's been gives order to these last years, only
the seasons circumscribe her memory, and she can be seen
more and more frequently taking out her large black daybooks
to reconstruct her past—and Paula is painting a vestibule in
Paonazzo in an Art Deco villa in the heights of Portofino.
It's a difficult marble, statuary, a variety of Carrara with a
pure white background, scattered with purple flecks and shot
through with yellow veining along the cracks, as if a harbor
of rust sweated through the fissures in the stone. She's having a ball painting it in the first heat wave of July, the sea air
carrying away the scents of resin and dust that lie in burning
layers at the heart of the pine forest, her shoulders glisten, a
trickle of sweat runs down her spine and soaks her lower back,
her armpits drip onto the swimsuit she's wearing under the
smock, her feet stick to her tennis shoes splattered with paint,
she drinks iced tea from a thermos as the house murmurs,
languid conversations, the clinking of ice cubes at the bottom
of whisky glasses, and when evening comes, sticky, she heads
down a narrow path to the deserted beach; sleepy creatures
scurry off as she passes, lizards with blue bellies, scarabs black
as LPs, orange firebugs with their armor like human masks,
all of them making the underbrush rustle and the leaves hiss,
stiffened beneath a veil of dust; then, at the shore, she buries
her bare feet in the gray sand as the sea spreads out before
her, slow, thick, veering to a Majorelle blue into which she
walks with pleasure, entering without a splash, as if it were

simply a matter of splitting the water, of feeling the empire of it, full contact, and then she immerses herself slowly, first leaning her head into the dimness and then diving down to brush the furrowed ground, the bare skin of her stomach thrilling with pleasure. She rises toward the brightness, looks at herself for a long time on the underside of the sea, in her inward mirror, and then, at the surface again, she swims far out toward the open, stretches out on the peaceful swell and floats, eyes on the sky, thinking of these last rambling, lonely months, little leaps from place to place, skips of a flat stone; she recalls these places where she never stays longer than four or five weeks, these days melting together into a single movement, the movement of finding the next job without letting the intervals in Paris last too long, without having to ask her parents for a little more (which they willingly give her), she thinks of these painting jobs, one after the other, no downtime: is this her life? The sky slowly darkens above her, pulls back toward the east in a dying blue you'd think was applied in two coats of gouache, and Paula remembers the large glass ceiling of the rue du Métal, that light of the studio, so particular, as if it emerged from this image, as if it were the very continuity of it; and then Jonas appears, Rembrandt mouth, face half-hidden by the brim of his hat, secretive eyes, iguana skin, pupils of bluish-black, whites of his eyes with hints of pearl, ashy circles underneath. She floats at the surface of the water that has grown dark now, cobalt blue: he's not answering her messages anymore, three weeks since the last email, and she hears herself say, in the middle of the sea, Jonas, I love you.

☙

Paula finishes the Paonazzo on the appointed day, unknots the scarf from around her head, wipes her forehead with the back of her hand, and closes her eyes. The painting is remarkable, the marble so masterfully done that the owners immediately feel the mineral coolness of the stone, and they compliment Paula with words like *miracoloso, incredibile, magico*. A Campari Orange is poured for the young painter into a blown-glass tumbler, she's offered a gold-banded Dunhill cigar and seized by the waist, a swim suggested, in the pool tiled with stonework, studded with *tesselles d'or*, and then she's paid in cash. Soon after, the season is in full swing along the Ligurian coast, in Rapallo, Portofino, Savona, all along the craggy shorelines of the Golfo di Genova, the couple from the villa have visitors, the guests are amazed by the Paonazzo, they press their palms to it and their eyes grow wide. A producer laughs when he learns he's been fooled, and with a snap of his fingers asks for Paula: I want her to come to Rome. As soon as this pronouncement has been made, the guy forgets Paula and her Paonazzo, of course, pours himself another glass of white, runs his hand through his hair, brushes a laurel leaf off his linen pants—but the thing is already set in motion and the following week Paula is, indeed, in Rome.

AND THAT'S THE END OF SMALL PRIVATE
jobs, unpaid samples, delicate color charts that must be checked
with absent men, hesitant women who are falsely in a rush
and therefore all the more demanding: Paula is hired for
three months at the Cinecittà film studios where she becomes
signorina Karst—and with these words, she sees herself in
a lemon-yellow hoop skirt and ballerina flats. What awaits
her, though, is nothing like a pirouette: she has to paint the
façade of St. Peter's Basilica. Ah. Paula stands with her arms
crossed in the studio of the set dressers and is not quite sure
she heard him right, the guy who began by clapping his hands
and shouting *silenzio!* Around her, no one seems startled, the
men pat the pockets of their jeans and go out for some air,
placid—their hands, which have built bigger, crazier, more
complicated things than St. Peter's Basilica, are not easily
impressed. Some people even laugh silently to themselves,
bellies thrust forward, and stand around in circles smoking,
palms pressed to their mouths: their job is to realize the dreams
of directors, to satisfy their egotistical fury, materialize their
fantasies, it is exactly the reason they are here. *La fabbrica
dei sogni,* the dream factory, that's the real name of Cinecittà,
did you know that, *signorina*? A guy with terrible teeth leans
toward her, he has very deep-set navy blue eyes and there is
black hair on his wrists. He speaks right into her face and
recounts, by way of welcome, the anecdote of the set painter
who had hailed the director with these words: Maestro, you
can begin, the cosmos is ready! That's us, in a nutshell. Paula
laughs. The cosmos. No kidding.

They continue. The set decorator lays out the tasks in a heavier voice: they'll be doing the central section of the façade, the *loggia papale*, the two side windows, and four of the eight existing columns; about twenty-five of the 115 meters that make up the width of the Basilica. A fraction for the whole. Which will sum up the whole place as it appears to the world on election nights, lit up, the newly appointed sovereign pontiff come to bless the crowd, his old man voice murmuring into the microphone while cardinals with red biretta shuffle on side balconies. Vatican scarlet, then, and travertine! Then he announces with delectation: last thing, the Sistine Chapel will be reconstructed in its entirety in the studio. Upon hearing these words, a few voices burst out, and two young guys laugh as they imitate the scene of the *Creation of Adam*, the index fingers of the man and of God pointing toward each other, about to touch as two conductive bodies would touch, life coursing through them; they strike the pose between workbenches, slouch and straighten again, excited as kids—holy shit, the Sistine Chapel!—as Paula, at the word *Sistine*, sees again the studio at the Institut and the woman in the black turtleneck silently painting the famous trompe-l'œil that runs, repeated, along the side walls of the chapel, on the lower section, a damask drapery, acorns and oak leaves scattered, pontifical coats of arms, this is the sub-ordinate portion of the composition, she says devilishly, it's the cheap cut; she seems to paint with her mind elsewhere, eyes half-closed and barely looking at what she's doing, saying they'd be starting from the bottom, saying lots of fascinating things happen there; after that it will be time to raise their eyes toward the heights, toward the frescos; saying one should progress slowly and in stages, yes, I advise you to go slowly with the Sistine, she murmurs, almost threatening—and then the voice of the set decorator suddenly chills the atmosphere: okay, maestros, let's not get carried away, Big Image is taking care of Michelangelo's frescos! He's walking through the studio now to distribute a first duty sheet, shrugging his shoulders and explaining with a mocking air that the production company has opted for large-format digital printing: we're just making the finishing touches. And then he stops: one last thing—we're working on Nanni Moretti's film, *Habemus papam*.

%

Each morning at half past eight, Paula takes the metro to Cinecittà on the A line, walks through the tunnel that runs under via Tuscolana—odor of piss and garbage, she pulls her scarf up over her nose and speeds up—and then, back out in the open air, she heads toward the entrance to the studios, shows her badge, and then the vast lawn extends before her; she walks around it, headed for the workshops, hips swaying beneath the weight of a shoulder bag with brushes, rags, note-books, and a clean apron rolled up in a ball; her hair, in a thick side braid, bounces against her left breast, counterbalancing the bag. The day has come, the buildings lighten to ash gray then mauve, the air smells like the recent countryside, she's at Cinecittà for Pete's sake, and five minutes later she's in her smock and at her post.

Disconcerted in the first few days, though, and dis-appointed. She was expecting to enter a baroque castle, sparkling and messy, and instead walks into an architectural complex designed to meet the needs of filmmaking, the modular organization dividing up studios, dressing rooms, workshops, and warehouses according to the imperatives of industrial rationale. Geometry of forms and perspectives, sobriety of lines, orthogonal severity of the map, swathes of lawn and umbrella pines planted in straight lines—at first sight the setting is sober, homogenous, as if it had emerged from the earth in one block, born of the will of a single person, a demiurge, who would have tapped the ground three times (namely, Mussolini, Paula is aware, even if her knowledge of the site's creation and history are vague and incomplete). Alba the Spanish cousin—who regularly posts photos of her job sites on Instagram—warned her: there's not much happening there anymore, you won't see anything, you're wasting your time, and Paula's starting to think she was right. There's not much to see. The twenty-two soundstages on the site are giant crates as secret as coffers, as tightly closed as metal shipping containers piled up on guarded wharves, and the promised extravagance of *Fellinian* ground—ostentatious artificiality, fleshy, farcical, metaphysical creatures, stuccos and plastics, celebrations of poetry and masquerades—none of this is to be found. But it's precisely this tight weave between the visible and the invisible that begins to stimulate Paula's vision as she walks past the windowless buildings each day, trailing her fingertips along their walls until her scraped skin is covered with an orangey dust—she lifts it to her nose and breathes it in like the very scent of cinema. There's a hidden life behind these outer walls, a life she wants to reach. Pine needles crunch underfoot like a dry wood fire.

> ⸎

Parachuted here by a powerful hand and then immediately forgotten, Paula quickly realizes that they don't quite know what to do with her, and discovers what it means to be a mere adjustment variable, temporary and flexible, in the place where art and industry attempt to coexist. She learns the hierarchy of positions, familiarizes herself with the nuances of the labor aristocracy, colors her Italian with a few Roman inflections and assimilates the lexicon of film studios. The painters she works with are experienced, frank, and technical; the women in particular impress her, ingenious and hardy as they are, fast-talking, with dynamic egos, negotiating their overtime inch by inch. They've grown blasé about working for the movies, they're jaded, immune to the myth they're helping to bring to life, indifferent to the stars, the juicy anecdotes, rumors that circulate, and most of them look sardonically, mocking, at Paula's naïveté—for her everything here is desirable.

To begin, she's routinely sent off to fetch whatever's missing, a tool to verify a paint match, a letter from the courier, a cell phone left at the cafeteria—Kate, orange hair in a bob and turquoise sweater: that's bullshit, tell them to get tae fuck, you're not their lackey!—but Paula takes the opportunity to learn the terrain, map in hand and smock open, banana chignon held up with a paintbrush. Soon she can be seen taking shortcuts, sniffing out diagonals, finding slant ways, hanging out on the studio side where she stumbles upon scenes that prove the place has life in it still: a guy in a polka-dot suit carrying a resin Juno in his arms; gameshow hosts, high heels and breasts compressed, cheeks plastered with terracotta, shouting into the phone—*Grande Fratello*?—faces from sitcoms wearing gladiator sandals and Roman togas, smoking on their breaks—*The Borgias*?—the silhouette of a woman in a long white coat slipping into a limousine, golden hair cascading down her back—Julia Roberts for the Lavazza clip?—a trio of teenagers looking for the set from *U-571*—a "submarine movie," American destroyer against German U-boat, the Enigma machine to be seized, golden ears, torpedoes launched into the ultra-black of the abyss; and Paula, flattered to be taken for a native, for a studio insider, guides the three students to the set and into the control room of the ship, where she, too, leans close to the dials that blink in the dimness, near the sonar and the periscope, suddenly feeling it all: the atmosphere of the high-tech chamber launched at full speed into the wild ocean, the absence of light that cancels out temporal signposts—the intensity of neon, turning to red at nightfall, is the only thing that punctuates the time onboard—the reverberation of sounds, breath and silence, human perceptions that reconstruct a strange world, she holds her breath, plucked, strung with emotion—child of *Le Triomphant*.

अ

Life seeps out between the joints of the studios. Behind-the-scenes glimpses fill the doorways. The air quality is different here, frenetic, vibrating—the buzz of a hive, traffic teeming before the black orifice, bees hovering, waiting in line, coming and going—and the closer she gets, the more Paula snoops about, quick to intercept what goes in and out of these buildings like telltale traces of that which takes place inside; she keeps an eye out for provisions (water coolers and cartons of wine, junk food for the dressing rooms, sometimes a Parma ham delivered under plastic with its wooden plank, sometimes hot croissants); observes the delivery of materials (kilometers of cables, computers, crates of sound equipment in pieces) and can't stop herself from staring at the faces of those who've been in front of the camera (and who she can pick out now from among everyone else simply by the grain of their skin) when they re-emerge into the open air, eyes blinking, features heavy with makeup, simplified by the latest contouring techniques or simply overcome with the emotion of a scene, the adrenaline of an episode where they've been reunited with their mother, where they have forgiven an unfaithful husband, where they have spent themselves, or danced, sung, cried, where they've brushed up against big stars, and it's this transformation that troubles Paula, the idea that something inside these hangars has the power to change those who venture within, that these big parallele-pipeds contain something to spark such metamorphoses. She waits for a passage to open, for a crack to widen—similar in this way to speleologists who walk along the bases of cliffs, alert for a little breeze that could signal a thermal exchange and foretell the existence of a cavity in the rock, maybe a cave—but strangely she hasn't ventured to explore the back of the site yet, where, in juxtaposition, the large exterior sets are spread out—not yet.

Adaptable, constantly moved from one task to the next, and not only on the two sets for *Habemus papam*—the papal loggia and Sistine chapel—Paula is placed for a time on the team of painters doing the groundwork: sand, plaster, add a patina—shit, that's basic wall painting, you're trained for more than that! hollers Kate from Glasgow, face altered in the video chat, crude in this moment. But Paula is anxious to be accepted and complies without batting an eye, finds pleasure in painting out of frame, freed from her easel, in paint-ing these block colors, these vast monochromes. I'm feeling good, I'm returning to the foundation of painting: covering a surface!—she mimes using a roller with large movements before the screen where Kate is also painting—her nails—in the bathroom of the Nautilus, dismayed. Then one Sunday, Paula joins the emergency battalion come to turn a thousand square meters of wood into simulated concrete, and sits on the ground in the middle of all these men on lunch break, surprised to be placed here among them, her shoulders between theirs, to finally be an arm, a hand, a skill, a source of energy joined with that of others, untethered from the solitude of craftsmanship to join their circle—she refrains from telling them she would have preferred to paint wood on concrete, that this is in fact what she's qualified to do.

⁂

One morning she's sent to assist the painter on the set of a TV series, lighting touch-ups—a bourgeois living room, wall hangings with acorns and Versailles parquet, Knoll furniture—and Paula is made to understand that this is considered a promotion. She arrives early, but at the wrong *teatro*, goes into the next one over, peeks between the flaps, then shoulders it open all at once and stands in the doorway, legs like jelly: the set is plunged in darkness and the daylight behind her traces a ray the width of the door on the ground, in which her shadow is projected, clearly at the start, then blurring as the ray rushes toward darkness—a coastline lit up at night and the sea before her, this is the image that comes to mind. Paula lifts her eyes to the rows of spotlights crisscrossing the ceiling in a framework of metal girders. The dimensions of the space are impossible to guess, it must be enormous, maybe it's the decompression chamber that leads to another world. She takes a few steps inside, completely uncharted, listens to the space making her body resonate and thinks to herself how much she would like to live here.

THE WOMAN WHO SITS DOWN OPPOSITE
Paula in the metro car emanates a strong smell of stale tobacco.
Short, sturdy, a silver fox fur muffler, mouth thick and dark,
hair like steel wool. Paula recognizes her, squirms, and finally
leans toward her and blurts out: we get off at the same stop,
I work at Cinecittà too. The woman looks taken aback, then
smiles mechanically, and turns her gaze away without continuing the conversation, so Paula leans back against the seat,
holding her bag tight against her belly and turns her eyes to
the tunnel. A few minutes later, past the guard post at the
gate to the studios, the woman lights a cigarillo and waits for
Paula to catch up. Encouraged, Paula pounces: what do you
do here? In the raking light of dawn, the green of the large
central esplanade is a lake of brightness, the two women's
footsteps screech, the hum of the traffic is silenced, and it
seems as if the space is forming a listening chamber. I'm a
makeup artist, I've been working here for thirty years, my
name is Silvia—thirty years of makeup, thinks Paula, as the
image of Liz Taylor in *Cleopatra* springs forth, her violet
eyes lined with kohl, her exaggerated eyes that reached up
to her brows, swallowing her forehead, and suggested less the
Queen of Egypt than the movie actress, the Hollywood star
who mustn't be hidden—on the contrary, must be enhanced
beneath the makeup, this is what they paid for; and then
the two of them fall silent, walking on together past the
large head of a woman on the ground, a remnant of Fellini's
Casanova, frightening, her eyelids also painted, primitive and
totemic, goddess of cinema, and then they're in the studio

and workshop section. Paula throws quick sidelong glances at the woman's profile, somber, looking for a way out so she can continue on alone, but against all odds the makeup artist holds her back: and you, what did you come here to do? Paula's eyes widen, she answers: I'm a set dresser, I'm working on the next Nanni Moretti film, I have a three-month contract—proud to throw her cards down, to possess the titles that legitimize her presence. The woman lets out a sad little laugh, but this place is finished, my girl, the cinema has long since cleared out, the directors are leaving the studios to shoot their films for less money, the teams of craftspeople are diminishing, people who know how to do everything, people you can ask for anything, the moon, *anything*—she lands heavily on this last word. Studios today are all about reality TV and commercials, galas, massive shows for the launch of a brand of sunglasses or some band's latest album, and the magic of the studios is summoned back for one night through huge sound systems, naked ladies, and laser beams. It's not cinema anymore, it's events—Silvia coughs in anger, then slows down to take a drag of her cigarillo, which sets off her sentence again, speeds up her step, now it's a matter of a land transaction to take over the forty-four hectares of the area, the seventy-five kilometers of roads, the twenty-odd sets, to relocate the shoots, get rid of the two hundred salaried employees, transform Cinecittà into an amusement park, vitrify memory, sell the myth. A mass of rage, that's what it is now, a compact mass. The words *shame, Fellini,* and *pornography* roll out before them to land in the intersection where, a moment later, she crushes her cigarillo with a twist of her heel, picks it up and tucks it into her pocket which apparently serves as an ashtray, then lifts her head and says no one's a fool, here. But at the moment when their paths diverge, her face lights up and she catches Paula by the chin:

come and see me in makeup, I like different colored eyes, and you're walleyed, we'll see what we can do.

⁂

You're walleyed, you're walleyed. Paula watches the makeup artist walking away as these two words land firmly in her left temporal lobe, the place where voices from childhood are lodged, where familiar phrases resonate, transformed by time into riddles. You're walleyed. She lowers her head and continues down the path. The kid from the old Polaroid comes boomeranging back, fawn's legs, orange terry cloth shorts and hands on her hips, the summer of the *Triomphant*. You're walleyed. And, at the time of the photo, there really was something odd about the face of little ten-year-old Paula, something out of alignment. An anomaly. She has a lazy eye, she has one eye that tells the other to buzz off. When they sit down at the table, her cousins cross their eyes and burst out laughing: you look like Dalida. They spread their hands out as wide as they can before her: how many fingers? It doesn't make her laugh, she'd prefer a hundred times over to be consistent with the anatomical canon, with nice, parallel eyes and a straight gaze. Desperate attempts are made to correct this defect—exhausting ophthalmologist appointments during which the child sticks her little chin into a synoptophore and looks at all kinds of figures which she has to count, order, and describe. Just before the summer arrives, the ophthalmologist prescribes a permanent eye patch for her left eye, to reeducate once and for all this eye that has abandoned its axis, this unruly eye, in order to make it work, because it's been decreed lazy, a slacker, the kind that leaves all the work to the colleague—an expression that Paula hadn't understood. The child goes into a panic, but what should have been the summer of her disgrace becomes instead the summer of her triumph—the *Triomphant* summer. The eye patch gives her the air of a heroine. She becomes a singular child, Cyclops, pirate, one eye gouged out, attracting the attention of grown-ups, intriguing her cousins, frightening the younger ones. Preferential treatment allows her to stay with the adults after lunch and to collect little presents in compensation for the swims she can't take; anyone who teases her is scolded. When it's time to change her bandage, which must not be touched or get wet—do *not* get it wet!—Paula barricades herself in the bathroom grimacing like a capuchin monkey, followed by a little cousin, one she's chosen, a submissive spectator to whom she shows her treasure of gauze and sterile compresses, her rolls of bandage. She stands in front of the mirror and does the honors with care, first washing her hands conspicuously and then taking off the bandage, pinching it with her fingertips while the little witness holds her breath, excited at the thought that the sick eye will be revealed, leaking, lashes coagulated in a greenish paste, lid blistered like an old mushroom—and then is disappointed, in the end, to see nothing, nothing but a closed eye. Suddenly the witness is far less attentive to the spectacle of the great Paula, who continues her playacting, dabbing all around her eye with blue gel, then applying a new compress, taping it on gently, forming a star. Paula comes to cherish her eye patch, the questions it provokes, the precautions it demands, the way her face looks, and the more days go by, the more she shows it off with this affected swagger that ends up irritating those around her—God, she's annoying! A little before school starts up again, the bandage is taken off during an appointment meant to celebrate the victory of ophthalmic science and the eye-patch method. But instead, inside the medical office with the lowered blinds, beneath the white compresses and the closed eyelid, what is revealed is that the left eye still deviates, obstinate. The ophthalmologist is already opening her agenda to jot down more reeducation sessions—*a salve*, she says, battle-ready—when Paula's mother, against all odds, gets up from her chair, takes the little girl gently by the chin and, right in front of the stunned ophthalmologist (Paula remembers a fat, moist woman with quivering flesh, perched on little pumps that flared out on contact with the ground and seemed to suffer from holding her up all day long), murmurs, that's enough, we're going to leave it alone for a while, this little eye will do just fine. Paula pulls on her cardigan and follows her mother out of the office, disconcerted. As the years pass, she convinces herself that this exotropic eye—a word that swells her with importance, and which she loves to say—allows her to always have one eye that's looking elsewhere, while the other gazes straight ahead, and that there's even, yes, there's even something desirable in that, it's a kind of magic power and above all it has its charm—which is entirely her own.

Paula rubs her eyes. The makeup artist is just a speck now. She hurries, her steps stubborn, butt clenched tight, little muscular legs stuffed like sausages into acid-wash jeans. The sun squashes apricot pulp onto the walls of the studios and the scent of pine comes back to fill the atmosphere, tonic. Far off, the workshop is open, the supervisor's dog has settled in its usual place, lying in front of the door, and the moped motors cool down on the concrete.

SCUSI MISS! SAYS A VOICE BEHIND PAULA, leaning through the doorway of the plasterers' workshop. The guy pushes a dolly piled with bags of plaster through the door, and Paula leaps out of the way to let him through, a few heads turning without stopping their work. The man has eyes the shape of coffee beans, swollen and slitted, red hair, a stand collar jacket zipped over his shirt and a little seaman's hat rolled above his ears. Paula introduces herself: they told me to come see you, said you needed people this week. He looks her over, puts a hand on his hip, gestures with his badly shaven chin toward the plans of the loggia drawn on large sheets of paper and stuck on the wall like pieces of a puzzle, then looks at his watch: okay, well then you're late, we're doing the cornices of the loggia this morning, drop your stuff over there.

It's white in here—a space spattered with milk—and cold, and the voices ring out as they would in a train station. Butler sink and a handwashing station, long wooden boards set out on trestles, and, scattered about on all sides, galvanized tin buckets, troughs, containers of all sizes, and a few zinc plates. The tools appear next, suspended from nails. Varnished handles draw the eye, red or orange, blades glint and Paula moves closer, curious: brick trowels, chisels, planes, wood compasses, spatulas of all sorts, all of them waiting for the hand that will pierce their mystery as it grabs hold of them, will reveal their function, and Paula knows that their shape, their maneuverability, and their weight will lead to a singular action. The guy reappears bareheaded in a T-shirt and tosses Paula an apron which she puts on and ties at the back with a quick gesture, then he unrolls the silicone mold on the table—the negative of a sculpted cornice that will overhang the papal loggia. He looks at Paula and smiles, twisting his mouth: Cinecittà, realm of tradespeople, realm of charlatans! The others chuckle from their spots around the room—Paula hears them but remains impassive, and leans closer to the mold, intrigued. I'll show you, watch what I do, and then you can start.

He fills a trough from the tap and eyeballs the amount of plaster, as though he knew instinctively the correct ratio of water to powder, then stirs the surface until powdery little islands appear, at which point he plunges his forearm into the container and stirs it all together to form a smooth paste. The loggia for St. Peter's will be so light a ten-year-old child could carry it in her arms! Next, he picks up a large brush with long soft bristles, dips it in the bucket, and starts to walk slowly along the length of the table, throwing the plaster into the mold until it covers it completely. How long are you here for? He speaks as he daubs, distant, as if making small talk. Paula answers without lifting her head, I don't know yet, we'll see, and concentrates on what she sees, the casting, the concrete nature of his procedure; she wonders in reverse about the construction of the initial model and the silicone mold. There! He puts his brush down. And now, we'll reinforce the thing, we'll make an ultra-strong cornice! He picks up a hank of tow rope, swings the fibers, forms a thick bed that he spreads out in the mold, then picks up the brush again and the bucket of plaster to fill it, calm, coming and going along the table, head tilted back slightly in order to better see his work, movements precise but relaxed, almost nonchalant, as if he were going through the motions without thinking of anything, not even of Paula standing in front of him, her dancer's bun perfectly pinned and chin steady, enacting a gesture that comes from far away, and in the same tranquil tone he continues: you've left nothing behind? They exchange a look, Paula catches two glints of dark blue in the cracks between his eyelids: no, nothing. The workshop is so sonorous you can hear the conversations of the plasterers as if they were wearing tiny clip-on microphones, but Paula isn't listening to anything but the swish of the brush. He looks at her from time to time, measures her body with his internal compass, integrating her anatomical coordinates with a cartographer's precision but keeping the movements of his wrist so perfectly cadenced that the brush seems to work all on its own, all of this at once very simple and very enigmatic. You're like a bird on a wire, then? He puts down the brush to finish tamping the fibers with his bare hands, getting rid of every last trapped air bubble, kneading the creamy material that's already starting to harden. Then he rinses his hands for a long time under the cold water while Paula watches the cornice harden on the table, how long do we have to wait now? He takes out his pack of smokes. We're going to get a coffee. He adds, sparkle in his eye, you'll see, I'm a charlatan too.

INSTEAD OF HEADING STRAIGHT FOR THE metro, Paula leaves the ordered sector of the studios behind and turns right toward the exterior sets. The landscape shifts, distorts, the path grows muddy, stones roll beneath the soles of her shoes and puddles bring the midges of late afternoon. The light lowers, but the sky after the shower is limpid. The world is newly born.

❦

The charlatan comes to see her in the studio the next day while she's putting the finishing touches on the Sistine Chapel, using a round sable brush, hoping to see Nanni Moretti who is rumored to be in the area. The papal loggia is up, it was mounted yesterday on the *Rome* set for light tests, you should go see your cornice—they're sniffing around each other, it's tangible now, senses so sharpened they don't even need to catch a glimpse of the other to know they're within the same perimeter, sometimes vast, sometimes populated with dozens of other people, and even if they talk to others and have their backs to each other, each one knows the other is there, and it's a mystery what they're waiting for to finally slip away and touch each other—Paula stands up straighter and puts her hands on her lower back, of course, I'll check it out.

᠅

There's an archway, and then a vast esplanade slick with rain: a church, a tower, palaces, wooden houses. Everything to scale, showing a historic place, a space in time: *Firenze medievale*, say the signboards. The set, built a dozen years earlier, was meant to depict another city, Assisi, for a television series on the life of Saint Francis, *Francesco*, and the historical references had been tended to painstakingly to meet the requirements of the story—Paula makes out the rosette window of the church, the front steps in a half-moon, the horizontal bands of marble, the square shape of the belfry with its flat roof and lancet window—but it has been recycled since then, the elements reused, rerouted. It's not really Assisi here anymore, any more than Florence, Padua, or Bologna, but rather a city in northern Italy in the Middle Ages, any city, all cities, a Meccano toy that matches the actions to the moment in history, a melting pot where the fictions of cinema pile up in strata or become entwined. It's a patched-together place. Soon, during another filming, it will be Verona in summer, the peregrine falcon, the ball and the swords, a balcony at night, love and suffering, *Is the day so young*? Or maybe Ferrara, or Mantua, or Siena, for a new James Bond, and we'll see Daniel Craig running through it, climbing the tower as the bombs fall, rock climber in a smoking jacket, ziplining across the esplanade, Walther PPK between his teeth and shoes shined to a mirror.

᠅

Paula walks to the center of the square, struck by the space, the silence, the emptiness, and by the closed aspect of the set, an insularity that immediately recreates a world in itself, a stage house. There's room here, room for cranes, cameras, tracking rails, a camera crew, a multitude of extras, horses, chariots, jugglers, and fire breathers; there's room for a war, for celebrations, room to execute a traitor or dance a farandole, and you could also throw sand the way they did early on February 7, 1469, on the piazza Santa Croce in Florence, where they've gathered to wait for the appearance of the young prince on horseback, powerful and calm, gaze floating over the crowd, the long white silk cape with ermine trimming, the velvet surcoat studded with pearls, the *mazzocchio* bedecked with a pure diamond, he and the twelve young men of good birth who form his brigade, the lords of Florence, the masters, arriving in health and in number, who will soon trade in their party clothes for suits of armor and set off at a gallop, shouting, will break their lances, but who, for the moment, parade two by two, grasping the reins of their mounts with a firm hand, and it's surprising to see them sitting so tall and straight after the night of debauchery they've just had—women and men shared in drunkenness and common rooms, overturned, kneaded, pinched, stuffed, sucked, women taken standing up, skirts hiked above their waists, corset laces sliced open, the dagger blade drawn slowly up the belly between the cleavage and lifted with a snap, breasts tumbling out soft and warm, the bare shoulder gleaming in the chiaroscuro, a river pebble, and somewhere in this kaleidoscope of glints and flashes, laughs and shouts, sweat and breath, gasping of all sorts, there emerges a white throat stretched in pleasure (carotid hardened), a mouth beaded with blood, a chin streaming with alcohol, a dark and damp sex quivering like an anthill by the light of a dormer in the loft where they finally collapsed after supporting each other up each step of the ladder so as not to fall backwards, where they finally tumbled onto a bed of straw, watched over by the light of the moon, full, filled up—images that these young horsemen chase away now, sober, heads plunged in a bucket of ice water at the first crow of the cock, bodies draped in fresh linen shirts and then attired with care, these little idiots who prize costly and violent pleasures, ready to kill, ready to die, eyes empty and chins greasy, all in step behind the Magnificent where everyone can read the strange motto painted on the jousting flag, *Time Returns*; and now beautiful golden clouds have amassed in waves above the square, the light has veered to yellow, or rather chartreuse, something acidic and ferrous, and Paula heads toward the church, climbs the front steps, stops before the wooden door festooned with hammered nails; but as she gets closer the illusion of a relief disappears: the painting reasserts itself—she knocks on the door and it emits a hollow sound, the sound of a fake, and she smiles. When she reaches the tower, she examines the wall with a finger, trailing it slowly along the joints of the fiberglass blocks where, seen up close, the patina is frankly so crude the woman in the black turtleneck would never have stood for this, she thinks, feeling the lumps in the material, but a few meters on she stops short: a current of cold air hits her face. The wall tears open here, parting like the curtain on a stage, allowing a glimpse of another world, a world that suddenly appears as mysterious, as dreamlike as the set where she stands: first, the side of a vacant lot, edged with brambles and sickly grass, bits of scrap iron, and farther off, visible above the surrounding wall of Cinecittà, the nearby suburb of Rome, the sound of motors and horns in the neighboring streets, and buildings where the windows are beginning to light up, where radios are switched on, computers, the TV, where the stove is lit under a pot of water, where an alarm clock is set on a night table, where other curtains frame other gaps behind other windows, where the shutters are pulled down over a balcony with plastic tables and lawn chairs dripping, here and there a child's bicycle, a ball, and everywhere, soaked with rain and stagnating in the corners: leaves and pine needles, a cork, a pink elastic, a burnt-down match. Paula glues her brown eye to the crack, then her green eye, pupils one after the other retracted in the cold, she peers through the breach for a long time, this outside that encompasses the façades, this off-camera that incubates the set. On which side is the real world? Time returns. Paula leaves the square.

ᕷ

See the other backlots before nightfall, walk a little faster. Behind the medieval city there's a neighborhood in nineteenth-century New York, behind the palace of stone is a wooden street, one continent spills into another, eras collide, scenes compete, interlock, tear each other open, and Paula moves forward, she's the one who links these worlds, she has the eyes for it, she's the one who sees the wolfish violence of aristocratic jousts tipping over into the brutality of street gangs, velvet turning to rags, the tournament becoming a brawl, a fistfight that will end in a duel, as if only one-on-one combat settled by death could convert men into heroes and create a legend; but for Paula, violence is violence.

Far off, backlit, high wooden constructions form a wobbly wall and the wind that picks up now makes the scaffolding shake, the tarps flap, and the disjointed planks whistle, a racket something like a marina when the sea swells massive beyond the breakwater and the waves strike against the hulls, the halyards clang; makes sense, Paula thinks, this is a shore, a port, and she squints at the edge of the set of *Gangs of New York*, shot here ten years earlier, spread out over three different sets: Broadway, Five Points, and the quays of the harbor. A colossal job, which is to say, the creation of a world, months of work, the technical teams pumped, and Cinecittà which, for a time, became again what it strove to be: Hollywood on the Tiber. Those from the painting studio who had worked on it used the word *gargantuan* to describe it, they were sick of it, whacked each other on the shoulder, remember this, remember that, they imitated Scorsese, his nasal voice and machine-gun delivery, they reenacted the film, and Paula liked listening to them tell how they had recreated Five Points, the Manhattan neighborhood, with just three or four inter-sections, a few streets, and a few acres of ground; the place where they came pouring—the Irish who'd fled the famine, souls who'd fought for a place in the hull of a ship set off from Cork, who'd spit blood into ragged pelisses, discharged into the internal panic and general madness; the place where they came, free, lost, only just emerged from the nightmare of more than five centuries of slavery, the Blacks who were done with the South and headed now for the North; and also the crowd of those for whom this quagmire was a promise, for whom these tenements, suffocatingly hot in summer, frigid in winter, and gutted at the first hint of an epidemic, these teeming alleys where hunger was one's primary relationship with the world, where vice was law, this tenement from which you emerged armed and hardened for good—this was an initiation to America, an airlock where you warmed up for your life to come.

The sets weave together the images that form the weft of the world, they superimpose each other and blend together; the dried-up lake of Cinecittà—*la piscina*—allows a glimpse of the polluted swamp on which Five Points was built, a cess-pool drained in 1820 but still seeping, such that the ground of the New York neighborhood turns instantly to mud at the first spring showers, the people flounder in it, slip and skid, and Paula skids now, nearly falls forward, rights herself by windmilling her arms, looks down at her sneakers smeared with the dirt that's been leveled here, turned, rutted so the movies can be made, and everything is happening now as if she had integrated the sets: she walks on the spongy ground of Cinecittà but it's another swamp that comes back to her, a field along the Seine near Le Havre, the estuary swelled wide at this point, the Tancarville bridge high and red in the white sky, enormous, her parents small beneath it, busy; a movie set, her father had murmured as he photographed her mother in a sleeveless dress—your *cable-stayed* dress—contorting himself in all directions, playing the professional, rolling his *r*'s, darling, darling, look at me, darling you are beautiful, and she, playing the actress for the first time, swaying her hips, awkward, radiant, raising an elbow behind her head, smoking a cigarette, exaggerating the pose, and looking out toward the open, toward the port, yes, and then there's little Paula who walked toward the bank as they made their film, hypnotized by the welter of the grasses, giddy with the sharpness of the air, captivated by the purple woodlice and the pink earthworms—creatures who breathe through their skin, who descend into the thickness of the soil to aerate the earth—heading into an area of semi-aquatic thickets, feet in the water, and then, plop! a hole, she's sucked into the sludge. Her hands grab at tufts of grass without managing to use them as cordage, her arms can't lift her high enough to get her elbows and then a knee onto the edge, and she falls back in, splashing her new T-shirt, her new glasses, and then comes the flood of black and white images (a solitary hand steadily swallowed up by a misty marsh) but other images, too, in color: Pierre Richard sinking into red sand saying *if I move, I'll go even deeper, everyone knows you can't fight quicksand*—she loved that scene, she and her father knew the lines by heart—and so she stops moving, closes her mouth and her eyes, terrified at the thought of disappearing while her parents frolic in a field on the side of the road to Le Havre, at the thought of being buried without a trace, of disappearing with no witness but the gulls scattered above the river, because no driver crossing the bridge can see her, none, she is a little girl reaching a hand toward the sky, a little girl in a massive open space, completely absorbed, sucked up by the innards of the earth—until her parents turn, frisk the countryside with a glance and begin to shout her name, Paula! Paula! They catch sight of the little towhead among the underbrush and run panic-stricken to the edge of the hole, her mother lunging into the boggy crevice as her father yells stop, I'll go, the three of them soon grappling together in the mud, mashed together, rattled, her parents struggling to find the movements to free their child from the sludge, then coordinating to grab her under the arms, to hold her by the hips, there, and once they're out of the muck they collapse onto the warm grass in a heap, panting, gasping, three hearts leaping in unison inside their chests. Marie realizes the child has lost her sandal, just like in the movie! shouts Paula, widening her eyes, delighted, just like Pierre Richard in *La Chévre,* and her mother, calm, methodical, slowly lifts her mud-covered dress above her gorgeous legs to head back down into the pit, and rummages around until she extracts it—triumphant—the little sandal, also brand new.

❧

Darkness falls, the air grows laden with indigo, it's that time when nocturnal animals emerge from their burrows and brush along fences, blur the borders between worlds, and Paula slips into the set, makes out the names on the faux shopfronts, names of greasy spoons and stores that the frost has chipped off, the rain has washed away, the Roman sun has bleached, names that she hunts like treasure and prey, names that populated New York and were popping up in this very moment on computer screens in the icy rooms of Ellis Island, on databases consulted by those who wanted to know what happened, what took place, piecing together trajectories despite the gaps; and among them she automatically searches for names she might have known—Seamus O'Shaughnessy, Duane Fisher, Finbarr Peary, Svevo Krankowicz, Theodora Dawn—and just as she automatically searches for her own: Karst, the name of a landscape, a name that shows the erosion of time, the boring into the rock, the subterranean rivers, dark tunnels, and decorated rooms inside limestone ground. Paula Karst—she says her name out loud, three syllables that burst out into the atmosphere, half-opening the Cinecittà night and connecting it to the cosmos as she kicks in the debris of the slum of Five Points, avoids the broken panes of sash windows, and sticks her head through knocked-down doors just to see what's behind them, the dark cavern with a sandy floor smelling of dust, the framework of wood and metal rising thirty meters high, the narrow but curiously solid scaffolding where fragile bridges and walkways squeak, everything made of bars and perches by workers secured with carabiners, riggers who were shouted at from the ground, step lively.

⁂

Run, go back in time, back to Rome. Paula bounds across cobblestones. The last set is monumental, and juxtaposes over a space of nearly two hectares the high places of Roman history for the series *Rome*—a story gorged with sex and blood that provokes shrugs in the studio, even feigned nausea, hand clutching the belly, as if the mere name of the series made them retch. Paula makes out the platform of the Rostra, the Forum, the basilica and, further off, behind a rough wall, the loggia of *Habemus papam*, of a sculptural strangeness. Three windows, four columns, a balcony, purple curtains that fold in the evening light, a close-up angle on a dark slit. Paula moves closer, the loggia is real, decorated for the movies and technically so perfect that the smoke from her cigarette, rising in soft spirals toward the balcony, becomes a white signal, announcing the appearance of the newly appointed pope.

The work on this set was done in the great tradition of the studios, and demonstrates the skill of the crafts-people—man, it's lucky this series was shot here, the head painter had mumbled—it was his responsibility to get the set colors right, including this crimson that covers the walls, a red should not be too yellow nor too blue, but something between brick red and oxblood, *sandaloni*, that's the heart of what we do! Since then, this set had taken precedence over all the others, it had become the highlight of the tour, the final stop of a visit, the guide shouting: *back to Rome, we've come full circle!* The tourists would sometimes have visited the vestiges of the real Roman Forum that same day, walked among the ruins, and then rolled up exhausted, almost haggard, to Cinecittà, delighted to find the antique city intact (or nearly) only a few metro stops from downtown: they recognized the sites from the series and, suddenly energized, struck poses and photographed each other, like Russian dolls, in nested worlds, a *mise en abyme*.

But for Paula, who breathes on her cold fingers, the city of legislators, of conquerors and traitors is nothing but an impressive catalogue of painted perspectives, columns made of resin, statues of plaster and celluloid. Standing in the middle of the esplanade, her eyes pan the set in slow lateral scopes and each image carries the world inside it—but this world isn't Rome, it's Hollywood on the Tiber, we are here, in the dream factory, the great backstage, the tool of propaganda—*il cinema è l'arma più forte*—a landscape of cardboard calling up the parades of Il Duce and the hundreds of films shot here at the height of fascism, then rounding up the epics of the golden age of the studios, citing kitschy or legendary sequences, a mille-feuille of photograms melted down into a single image that scrolls continuously.

༕

It's the dark heart of the night. Paula takes out her phone to light the way, thinks it won't be long now before the security guards start their rounds, aiming more powerful flashlights than hers into the darkness, torches whose long-reaching beams ferret out the blind spots of the set. Now she is in the artery of a busy neighborhood in Rome, a notorious street bordered by low houses, artisanal shops, workshops. A few locked metal gates close off alleys littered with the debris of previous films, fragments of sculpted capitals, amphorae, wheels, and carts, rusting axles, a few plaster statues, and a whole jumble of planks and stones, pistons, and stakes—objects that pass from one fiction to the next, rearranged. A street that, in the night, resembles an archaeological site, or at least Paula's idea of one, and she steps off the path, gliding the light of her phone over the rubble, examining the ground as if she thought she could find some treasure there, a shard of glass, a bit of pottery, a piece of gold. These are the false ruins of real ruins, the real ruins of false ruins, and Paula goes forward as if caught in the revolving door of a palace; in this swirl, a circle of images unfurls with her as the axis, a continuous reel, mix of doors and scaffoldings, rubble of cities and shredded linens, cranes, giant chimneys, lethal cliffs, and shorelines strewn with bodies, battered countrysides, a charred, volcanic landscape where nothing can recover. Then the revolving door slows its motion, the whirlwind loosens its hold, and Paula hinges forward to catch her breath, hands on her hips—a runner spitting at the end of the cinder track. She leans against a column. This is the end, she thinks, the end of the line. The end of the fantasy, the end of great cinema. The cold of the night starts to weigh her down, and in the light of her phone, moss appears. Moss spread out in random shapes, while she thought she was walking on potholed ground, on patches of soot, moss insinuating itself between the cobblestones, sliding into the crevices of low walls, growing in the interstices of planks, a vegetal fishnet that stretches farther and farther as Paula pokes at it with her flashlight, fascinated, a thin layer spun over the ground, dense and supple as the fur of an animal, the moss that survives. Only the places remain, in the end, in the very end, this is what she thinks to herself, on the verge of tears, only the places continue, as ruins, as moss, they go on, a tarpaulin that smacks against a metal pole, empty rooms that open behind scaffolding, a slab of concrete split open by grasses. Her shoes are covered in mud and her eyes are worn out.

THE CHARLATAN'S REPUTATION ENCOUR-
ages prudence, people take it upon themselves to warn her.
He turns up everywhere, preceded by the *fama* of hedonists,
the mix of reprobation and desire we feel toward those who
are ruled by pleasure—when there's alcohol I drink, when
there's music I dance, and when there's a beautiful woman I
want to make love to her. Watch yourself, Paula, he's a bad
apple, not to be trusted—the makeup artist is leaning over
Paula's face, applying a different color of eyeshadow to each
eye, the idea being to highlight her walleyes rather than trying to mask them, the way you display a flaw to turn it into
a singularity. Paula thanks her for the advice, but all these
warnings have the opposite effect, as one might suspect, so
she goes to meet the charlatan each time he asks, and little by
little he introduces her around the studios. Son of a lighting
specialist who worked for more than thirty years on Fellini's
films, and a hairstylist who put her first rollers in Jane Fonda's
hair in *Barbarella*, he's the prince of the realm, the chron-
icler of studio drudges. Claims to be the only one to know
what the prop stockrooms contain, where objects from more
than three thousand films are heaped together, the only one
to be able to locate a Venus de Milo, a bust of Einstein, a
hoplite helmet in the De Angelis family studios—four gen-
erations of sculptors have been at Cinecittà since the Second
World War. Calls everyone by their name, compliments
the women, hugs the men. Teatro 5 is kinda my clubhouse,
he boasts to Paula who's hot on his heels as they return to the
backlots, she's put off by the sets which she finds so coarse

in broad daylight, completely fake, so far from the perfect trompe l'œil she learned in Brussels. It's totally unbelievable! she exclaims. How could you believe in it? He puts an arm around her shoulders and leads her to the Forum: at one point they sank a real ocean liner with several hundred extras to film the sinking of the *Titanic*, did you know that? They filmed ancient battle scenes by hiring thousands of extras and arming them with javelins and lances, and sometimes they actually got injured, all the better!—he shows his splendid teeth, sharp as penknives—they underestimated the movies, its resources, its own solutions, they spent the cash to make the audience believe in it: it had to *look real*. Paula listens, silent, remembers having believed, in her childhood, that the extras who died on screen were truly dying, that they turned up to play in the film precisely because they were ready to go, and being offed in a Western—falling from the roof of a saloon, downed by a Colt bullet, or having one's heart pierced by an Apache arrow—was a good way to die. It was like the movies were taking it on, somehow, to allow them to die beautifully, to bring them into being through death, and, feeling the charlatan's hand lingering on her, Paula thinks back to her father's dumbfounded expression the night she asked the question—they were leaning against each other in front of the TV, blanket over their knees, shots bursting out from all sides onscreen, probably a Spaghetti Western like the ones that were filmed in droves at Cinecittà in the sixties (nearly four hundred between 1954 and 1963, imagine! the producers taking advantage of the hard blue sky and the cheap labor, paid in lira) and Guillaume said, stunned: but Paula, it's all fake, it's a movie! And while she was remembering this decisive night, the charlatan went on, decreeing the rules of illusion learned here, unfolding one finger for each argument: a set doesn't have to be real, it has to be true—technically true, true for the movies. Or: a natural set often seems artificial onscreen, illegible, encumbered with a bunch of elements that aren't useful, that's why we create sets for each film. Or: look, you only build what the audience can see of the set, and in general you avoid the high parts, the most expensive parts, the most difficult to construct, the places where the actors never go—this is the case with the loggia of *Habemus Papam*. Later they sit down side by side on the steps of a resin temple that had survived the fall of the Roman Empire, and the charlatan removes his hand from Paula's clavicle to point out the landscape around them: you think your eye is like a camera lens, but the human eye is a tiny, ultra-mobile machine, much more complex—he points a finger at his swollen, half-open eyes, whose irises in that moment were not dark blue but a glowing brown—the eye only sees clearly for a fraction of a second but is capable of memorizing this perception, and integrating it into the next such that the brain produces a complete image, it doesn't perceive the image in a wide shot but explores it in successive touches, it selects, organizes and reconstructs that which the camera has recorded to make a whole; finally, the nature of the image, in the movies, is to permit the eye to immediately grasp the elements necessary for the understanding of the film—he leaps up, turns around: it's not coarse, *signorina*, it's actually highly technical, and adapted to your eyes.

❦

Paula is heading into the last month of her contract and she still hasn't glimpsed Nanni Moretti but suddenly things grow sharper, accelerate. She is asked to paint a marble for the interior scenes of *Habemus Papam*, shot at the Palazzo Farnese, a panel of Cipolino—significant dimensions and short deadline, figure it out sweetheart, word is you're a specialist, the set decorator pats her on the shoulder and Paula blushes violently, then steps back and closes her eyes, calling up the image of the stone and all its resonance. In the rue du Métal, she would have measured out British racing green, ultramarine blue, Van Dyke brown, yellow ocher, and black onto her palette, she would have taken pains for each step, "fleeced" her background, created the heart grain using a veinette dipped in black, yellow ocher, and green, then she would have blended the veins and softened it all with a codtail brush, added an oil glazing, but here, remembering the charlatan's lesson, she proceeds differently, preferring to attenuate the whole, giving the impression of beds of mica and the micro-folds, almond-shaped, in the rock, characteristic of this crystalline marble, light, with green sparkles—the chlorites. Do you believe in it? the charlatan asks her, appearing at her neck at the end of the day, hat in hand. I believe, she replies, and it's like throwing herself into cold water: she turns in a rush toward this face that's thirty centimeters away, toward this mouth at the height of her own, which she kisses, carried by her own momentum, a kiss that continues beyond the lips, the charlatan's mouth becoming, beneath Paula's tongue and breath, something vast and full, of such a simplicity that the moment takes on an unexpected depth, and then hands open, fingers unfold, a hat and a paintbrush fall to the ground, palms move to touch bodies, all four palms, they touch and explore, faster and faster, fingers unknotting the smock, unzipping the sweater, undoing the first buttons of the shirt, lifting the tank top, while the feet also lose patience, suddenly head out the studio door into the narrow avenue where the umbrella pines, lit from below, send up onto the walls a black netting that gathers them in tighter still; then the passage through the main gates, the descent into the metro, Paula and the charlatan moving beneath the city, mouth to mouth on the platform in the moaning tunnel, mouth to mouth against the window in the swaying train car—suspended from the horizontal bar by their arms, shameless, and—it's crazy—talking to each other, without even ungluing their lips: you okay? I'm good; my place? your place—mouth to mouth in the little elevator of the via del Bosco, then in Paula's tiny room, in the foldout bed where they're thrown against each other, mouth to mouth with the night stretched out just below the window, such that the next day their lips are edged with red, swollen; and that day, as if everything was crystallizing all at once, each person in the painters' workshop goes over to the Cipolino to see it up close, backs up and then steps forward, begins again, and the experienced painters, the show-off guys and the arrogant women, all grimace as they nod their heads, not bad, looking at Paula with new eyes, but she doesn't care, already headed to the studio next door to meet the charlatan, to get back to the Porphyry on a column that had fallen out of the trailer of a truck going much too fast on the piazza della Signoria in Florence yesterday, a set piece they're refining together, as they will refine, over the following days, their method of making love, Paula stirred by his heavy, burning body, his rough palms, the clarity of his movements, and he discovering her to be stunningly beautiful—as if, naked, she came into her full potential—and more assertive than he would have thought; he's unsettled by her divergent gaze, by her green eye that's off the rails, always elsewhere, so he never feels like he has all of her; look at me, he asks, aroused, leaning over her and placing his hands like blinders on either side of her face, look me in the eyes. And Paula, who up until then had always claimed to be disgusted by codependent relationships, professing to never mix work and emotions—as if feelings weren't everywhere, all the time, occupying the whole terrain of existence—peremptory on this point, sure of herself, probably because nothing big had happened to her yet, we must admit—she had only just begun to pierce the atmosphere of sexual license that filled the summer villa of the Paonazzo, those hands that rested on her waist, this insistence on lending her a bathing suit, for her to swim, for her to drink and let herself go, you can't work all the time, everyone needs a little pleasure the mistress of the house would say again and again, while she herself did little but clink her golden bracelets gracefully and examine Paula through half-closed lids—well, Paula's mixing everything together now.

In the evening, she goes to pick up the charlatan in the staffers' studio, watches him work as she waits for him to finish, sitting on a paint can, a hot cup of coffee in her hands, hypnotized, she wants his movements to stretch out, for them to slow time, to present one image per second, no more, so she might freeze the scene, and soon the young woman who used to split at the end of a job, close up her paint box, clack, with the solid but rather short-lived satisfaction of a job well done and properly paid, soon this young woman is nowhere to be found: even before she leaves, Paula is already looking back at Rome over her shoulder. Are you in love or something?—Kate, lids fringed with giant false lashes, a Celtic cross between her breasts—come into the light, come closer so I can see you better on the screen. Paula does, bursting into laughter, while Kate, in Glasgow, looks her over seriously, a deep crease in her forehead, then says solemnly: I've decided to move to Paris, I need to see you when you get back, this is getting ridiculous.

One day, stepping out for a smoke and discovering with surprise the winter she hadn't seen coming (enclosed as she is constantly inside the hangar), thin layer of snow over the trees, rooftops, and the hoods of cars, Paula goes right up to a group of tourists who are visiting the studios and joins them, shamelessly, hands on her hips. The guide stands in the middle of the circle, a tall, thin, slightly jaundiced-looking student with scraggly beard, wearing a short jean jacket that's far too flimsy on this freezing day; he's telling the story of the place, opening a parenthesis between the end of the Second World War and the golden age of epics, five years, a time in which Cinecittà became a refugee camp, similar to those scattered over the surface of the globe today, and probably also similar to what Five Points was to New York around 1880, in terms of acerbic promiscuity, fatigue and grime, eighteen hundred people by 1945, a crowd of Jane and John Does scattered by the war and driven here, to movie city, among them Jews who survived the camps, exiles from Dalmatia, Libyan settlers, all piled into bunkbeds in the large teatro 5, then into basic cells that were barely sectioned off from each other, the sites of cinematographic fiction recycled into sites of life, people are born, people die, people grow up inside, they drink broth, without ever finding rest—too much noise to sleep: snores and sobs, sometimes the moans of sex, other times shouts of terror that issue forth from nightmares and wake everyone—people grow bored, they stagnate. All this for five years. The name Cinecittà comes to stand for a human scrap heap.

The group of tourists walks away in silence, but Paula doesn't move. So much has happened here, hey? The charlatan's voice comes to meet her, sneakers in the snow and hands plunged into the back pockets of his jeans, shock of tousled red hair. Paula's heart contracts. Shall I pick up where he left off? I'm listening. So the charlatan concludes rapid-fire: in 1950, fiction takes hold again, the movies return to Cinecittà in the features of Deborah Kerr as a pure Roman heroine, the shooting of *Quo Vadis*, the epic that brings the studios back to life, the archetype, and some of the refugees of the war who are still eking out an existence in teatro 5, dregs of a conflict we'd like to forget that still haunts the space, some of them are hired by the production, and enter the film to become silhouettes once more, the extras of history.

WE COULD MAKE A GOOD TEAM, THE TWO
of us. It's her last night in Rome, the charlatan is naked, and
the water steams in the bathtub. From the dark of the bedroom,
Paula watches him through the half-open door, immersed
up to his neck in a surfeit of bubbles, profile filtered by the
vapor, iridescent in the lamplight, glistening, eyes closed.
At these words, she falls onto her back on the unmade bed,
fingers interlaced behind her head, elbows lifted, protruding,
two dynamic little wings, her long legs crossed at the ankle;
with her eyes on the ceiling she answers brightly: more like an
association of miscreants, no?—playful here, an actress. The
charlatan doesn't respond, but immerses himself entirely, all
at once, his butt sliding toward the front of the tub, his back
toppling backwards, head disappearing into the froth; the
foam diminishes in the splashing countercurrents, it only lasts
a few seconds and then he surfaces again, hair slicked back, as
she says, thoughtful: we could rebuild what has disappeared.
Now, he unfolds himself to vertical, solid and spumous, belly
enormous, skin glistening with fine droplets, the hair on his
chest and pubis standing up and curling again; he steps out
of the tub and comes back into the bedroom, hips encircled
by a terry cloth wrap, backlit, placid, and Paula continues:
we could bring back that which has been forgotten. The ray
of light streaming in from the bathroom, unconstrained, falls
onto the bed and divides Paula down the middle: her breasts,
belly, and sex appear in the beam—protruding spheres, convex
basin, and isosceles triangle—and she goes on speaking: we
could find what was lost. The charlatan undoes his wrap, yes,

something like that, and then starts to get dressed, holding his clothes up to the light to discern the inside from the outside, pulling on his boxers, his shirt (he hadn't unbuttoned it the night before, just pulled it over his head with the help of an already naked Paula who stood on tiptoe to hitch it up over his lifted arms, slanting her eyes to this belly revealed all at once, pale, the heavy, soft abdomen, the navel deformed into a black foliole, the sex pale, and then the fabric had slid across the room, tossed)—adds: we would be real forgers. And Paula, watching him from the bed as he gets dressed, troubled that the scene should be so real even though the room is without contours, fibrous, ghostly, concludes calmly: real painters.

IN THE END, SHE WENT HOME. SPENT TWO more years between Rome (where the charlatan, possessive and faraway, makes her work for it) and the north of Italy where she has her jobs. She gets fed up, looks for an out. The complete restoration of a *hôtel particulier* on the île Saint-Louis gives her a golden opportunity to go back to Paris. She fights for the job with surprising fervor, burns through her phone plan by calling the Russian architecture agency several times a day, and as soon as she gets the job, it takes only seconds to liquidate her Italian life—here we recognize her characteristic briskness, as though for her, decisions can only come in the form of a landslide. She will say, much later, trying to clarify the reasons for her return to France, and thinking back on the love story with the charlatan, who couldn't hold onto her in the end: I just didn't believe in it anymore.

᪣

Her parents, as you might suspect, bring out fresh sheets for her bed and open their arms. The first night they prepare a couscous royale with caramelized yellow onions, chick-peas, and Corinthian raisins, uncork a good bottle. She's the prodigal daughter, the one whose unexpected return makes her even more precious, and she reappears bilingual, colorful, cheeks bronzed by the blush of the outdoors, the one we see again like a part of ourselves—caressing the skin on her inner wrists, the timbre of her voice immediately recognizable, like the corners of her eyes, crinkled into Japanese fans—but who (we finally realize as the days go by, observing her on the slant) is in fact a stranger. Inversely, Paula is struck to see that the rue de Paradis has not changed at all, the internal clockwork of the apartment barely dampened five years later, espousing the cadence of a perpetual-motion machine. Of course, in five years, Guillaume and Marie have aged, their hair a little thinner, perhaps, their faces threaded with fine lines that are imperceptible when seen head-on but show up in relief in a sidelong light, the lenses on their glasses thicker, hips heavier, and, likely, the memory of their last sprint further in the past. But their union, perfected by time, has become as moving as a work of art: hello artists!—this is how Paula greets them in the morning, while they drink a final coffee standing in the hallway, mutually arranging their battle dress: neutral suit, dark tie, understated coat, they look deep into each other's eyes one last time before opening the apartment door and hurling themselves outside, each in the direction of their workplace, hello performers! Thirty years this has lasted, and we might consider them curious beasts, or monsters even—people ask them shamelessly what the formula is for a lasting love, all the while showing contempt for that which, in them, is simply being content with just one life even though it may be possible to lead several side by side. People compare them to a desert island, to boredom, to unbendable metal, to habit; people have their theories. But Paula approaches them like rare birds, hovers around them, stirred by this alliance that she knows to be deep and mysterious. When the initial joy of their reunion has passed, each of them settles into their habitual areas of the apartment again, Paula takes advantage of a separate entrance through the service stairs, sitting back to see what happens next.

The job on the île Saint-Louis is interrupted in the final weeks when a seventeenth-century fresco is discovered beneath layers of plaster from a previous restoration, a painting that was on the verge of disappearing even further beneath the layers of new decor, and which they are now attempting to save. It's a first for Paula, participant in the event—she puts on a mask each morning and a protective polypropylene suit, then goes to the wall, armed with a cutter, various brushes, and a "goose-wing" feather duster to scrape and reveal something that is still only a spectral presence, hidden beneath the plaster. Experts turn up to date the fresco, identify the style, draft a possible story, dramaturgy of loss and return; they use blacklights, take out magnifying glasses, sample pigments and dust, armed with equipment similar to the tools of forensics specialists at a crime site. They question Paula as well. She testifies with precision about the moment when the coating cracked, when air slipped in beneath the crust, increasing the fissures and causing a fragment of plaster no larger than an infant's fingernail to fall to the floor, a scrap of matter that no one had seen fall but which had created an access— minuscule but quite real—to the painting beneath. Then she tells them how she enlarged the hole with a scraper, the plaster crumbling in random shapes until it revealed a petal, a rose, a garden, the world progressively opening before the eyes of those who came by each day to see what was being exposed, and stood before the wall the way they would at a show, some of them making bets, hoping for a naked woman, or why not an *Odalisque* in the style of Boucher, lying on her stomach among the cushions, buttocks round and offered up, gaze provocative, a scene so scandalous they would have had to cover it in order to save a sanctimonious wife from sin, or worse, her fourteen-year-old daughter who was already quite brazen; Paula formed hypotheses as she peeled off the edges of the images little by little, uncovering pinkish whites, emerald greens, while others beside her worked now on a hunting scene in a royal forest, Fontainebleau, Compiègne, and predicted a great red deer assailed by running dogs beneath a dark oak hung with golden acorns, the neck, throat, and the antlers stretched toward the sky in a gesture both dignified and desperate while on the ground a horrible hound bit into its hooves, a scene that the person who bought the mansion around 1750 would not have liked, a scene too sentimental for his taste, fit to make children cry, to encourage the squeamishness of daughters and the lily-liveredness of sons. After two weeks of work and waiting, they uncovered a wildlife composition, stretched over a space five meters wide by three high, an idyllic landscape with a scattering of flowers, cultivated fields, lateral underbrush, rocky promontory, and background of wooded hills—but not a trace of humans anywhere. Zoological variety occupies the entire canvas, like a great catalogue in which domestic animals—horses, dogs, cows, bulls, lambs, a cat—are seen side by side with wild ones—foxes, deer, monkeys, tigers—including a few exotic celebrities such as the dodo from Mauritius, now extinct. In the middle of this animal Eden, the wind swells the manes, the curled one of a white horse with long lashes, and that of a reddish lion lifting a huge paw toward a foolish goose; in the foreground, a hawksbill sea turtle, eye turned toward the viewer, gives Paula a shiver, and she winks at it as though at a good friend. The entire workshop applauds.

❧

On the eve of her twenty-fifth birthday, Paula lifts her glass at a sawhorse table in the large salon of the *hôtel particulier*.

Projectors illuminate the ceiling where a starry vault is still drying. There's red wine, white wine, there are cherry tomatoes and parmesan shavings on paper plates, the head painter looks like Willem Dafoe—unsettling and sexy, wolf's smile—he recites a Baudelaire poem to Paula while walking on his hands, *I have more memories than if I'd lived a thousand years*, she blows out the candles stuck into a brioche, a chrome speaker emits bossa nova melodies, you can hear the Seine rolling behind the wall, lapping gently, it's June.

❧

Paula goes out onto the balcony to smoke a cigarette: in the afternoon, she had seen brush marks at the back of a cornice seven meters high, a series of little touches that were invisible from the ground, put there by those who, like her today, had climbed onto scaffolding three hundred years earlier to calibrate their painting and decorate this same cupola. The marks formed a color chart of tints, of light, of contrast, but what had unsettled her was being able to perceive the artists' research, and to follow their eye, the way in which the section had gradually turned, how this porcelain blue had gradually been loaded with black to become stormy gray—what had happened? Just then, a woman calls to her in a French with dark vowels and considerable *r*'s, shakes her hand with an exaggerated grasp while looking at her intensely—seeing the space that cleared around her as she moved toward the buffet, Paula guesses that she's the one in charge, this Russian woman everyone's been talking about, her architecture agency having just recently become a favorite of home decor magazines, and her order book, large format, including (in addition to various dachas belonging to oligarchs around Moscow)

Victoria Beckham's cottage in Lancashire, the commission for an exhibit on the Ballets Russes at the Musée d'Orsay, and, it was rumored, the orthodox church of the Sainte-Trinité on quai Branly in Paris. She asks Paula what her plans are, and for her phone number, and she probably was thinking ahead, because two years later she has someone call *that young French girl with the wandering eye* to offer her a three-month contract in Moscow, in the Mosfilm studios, where *Anna Karenina* awaits.

⁂

Paula buys the novel half-heartedly, starts to flip through it three weeks before leaving, daunted by the thickness of the volume and by the profusion of names that populate the pages—Russian names that split and overlap, multiple characters with the same first name, some English surnames—she hesitates for a few days and then dives in one morning in her room with the shades lowered, finding the ideal position from which to enter the story, curled up on a cushy couch, head vertical but legs raised, provisioned with water and cookies—Oreos that are bought expressly for her; she refines some impromptu lighting, the ray of the lamp directed onto the pages like a follow spot in the theater, lighting up a text in which she immediately grasps the palatial nature, solid exterior, immense and detailed interior, so perfectly crafted that it seems to her to have occurred in one fell swoop, to have emerged from a powerful spell; she turns the pages slowly, loses the thread at times, goes back to the top of the paragraph, countercurrent, until she reaches the spot where she had dropped it, then dives back in, astounded by the progressive crafting of love, carved out shard by shard like a hand axe from the Paleolithic era, until it becomes blade-sharp and capable of silently cleaving a heart, until it becomes a pleochroic mote of dust, a mineral fragment that changes color depending on the angle we look at it, mysterious until the end, and which will end up driving us mad.

Soon all her thinking is filtered through the novel—the book sheds light on her own life, brings back Jonas, that late afternoon in front of her building, a few months ago now, leaning against a lamppost—or, more precisely, she thinks back to the moment when she'd sensed him even before she saw him, as if something unusual, a supernumerary presence, had slid onto the set and intrinsically modified it—cigarette between his lips and hair long, brim pulled low, hands in the pockets of a sand-colored raincoat, striated in the flood of traffic, standing at the edge of the sidewalk as if he were about to cross while she, too, stood at the edge of the gutter without letting her eyes leave him for a second; and this interval it took them later to find the right size ratio, corpulence ratio, the right way to stand face to face in the middle of the sidewalk. Paula had taken Jonas's cheek in her hand, so it *is* you, and he'd smiled, shoulders hunched, how are you? I'm good, great, and they didn't say anything else, irises whirling like glass paperweights, and in Paula's room they had moved forward without colliding, as if their aptitude for living together, which they were rediscovering now, could push back the walls, widen the room; they shared a can of beer, flopped down together onto the couch, feet intermingled and eyes on the ceiling, and soon they were smoking the same cigarette, all in a momentum so free, in an exchange of words so fine—how are you, my sweeting?—that the rest of the world around them was nothing but a fabric of lies. They had left each other just yesterday in the rue de Parme, in Brussels, and last night had stretched out for five years.

And yet they've changed since the rue du Métal. Jonas is more terrestrial, even though he's still thin, his body harder, his gestures effortless as if the least movement owed its beauty to a calibrated expenditure of energy, almost animal. Something lighter in his face, cleared away, his teeth polished maybe, the whites of his eyes fresher. And Paula had grown sharpened as well, her silhouette clearer, her profile clean—rounded forehead, long aquiline nose, thin mouth, little bump of a chin. Also, she seems solid at the moment, the gold-flecked braid placed neatly over her shoulder, her voice calm, we can see that her stamina and resourcefulness have increased, that she can now take on heavy loads, climb scaffolding more quickly, paint for a long time. But the more Jonas observes her—as she moves around the bedroom, as she hangs up her coat, plugs in her phone, as she turns on the lamps, all in a fluid movement—the more she changes in his eyes, evolving in real time the way a color shifts in sunlight, and the more his face reddens, a conflagration.

What are you doing in Paris, do you have a job here? Paula asks him point-blank, and Jonas adopts the outraged demeanor of someone who's been underestimated in the strength of his feelings: I came for you! He counts on his fingers, nose in the air: how long has it been, five years? and Paula's laughter creates a clearing around them, encloses them in it together, *for me?* yes, of course, and then suddenly he says: I've stopped doing trompe l'œil, I've stopped doing sets, I'm a painter now, and all at once Paula becomes strained, not knowing how to answer, trembling, as if he had just thrown an ice-lined coat over her shoulders, as if he were officially notifying her of a separation, bodies and minds, abandoning her on the filthy shore of falsity to head off toward a truth to which she remained a stranger. She nodded her head like a mechanical doll. Then, slowing his voice down, he says, I just took a job, I need money, this will be the last one, the last ever!—and he raises a fist in the air, excited. Later, he tells Paula the story of his final year in Brussels, describes to her the free-dive into painting, each component of the world approached as a painter, without hierarchy, including the most fragmentary, the most trivial, the most evanescent or microscopic element, each one treated as a world in itself, a continuity of painting that had sent him spinning, but a year that ended in a cold, poorly lit gallery where his exhibit hadn't attracted any crowds, where even the opening was sparsely attended, a few former students from the rue du Métal who'd come in and left just as quickly, it hadn't worked out—oh, that's the least you could say, the young woman at the gallery had yipped as she poured the untouched chips and peanuts into big black garbage bags, he imitated this *petite bourgeoise* with her narrow hips and narrow mind, this trendy little creature, unmoved by his paintings, voice twitchy with bitterness. He finally flops onto the couch, lying on his back with his silt-colored skin and long fawn's lashes, and then between two puffs of a cigarette starts up again: what about you, don't you want to paint for real? Paula leaps up to open the window and bathes her face in the void, feeling her eye drifting to the side as before her the sky swarms, the diffuse rumble of the outside nearly obscuring this beloved voice that says, fervent, I want to be closer to you, I'm coming to live in Paris, and at these words she spins around—her eyes have never been so far from each other before, the left eye rolling to the edge of orbit, the right as if pricked by the head of a pin, never have they embraced so much clarity, everything is clear at the moment: to paint for real, to love for real, to really love each other, it's all the same thing. She comes back to the couch and lies down, and then they turn onto their sides, face to face, eyes open, first to blink loses the game, and she's the one who finally closes her eyes.

⅔

Anna Karenina is a good optical instrument with which to examine love, this is what Paula thinks as she closes the book, gets up, and parts two strips of the blinds to peer out at the street, the intersection, the sidewalks, the area surrounding the lamppost, looking for Jonas in the spot where he had last appeared, even though she knows he's in Dubai, flew there last spring to do the decor for a villa promised to the cousin of the emir—a thousand square meters done entirely in trompe l'œil, a hand-picked armada of international decorators and artists, and Jonas among them with his ironic smile and inimitable work ethic. Then she glances at her watch—almost time to head to the airport for her flight to Moscow.

Awake in the
Fossil Radiation

WALK WITH PAULA AS SHE LENGTHENS HER
step along a platform at the Gare d'Austerlitz. The long coat
of gray wool, the yellow scarf, the fur-lined boots, the leather
gloves, the purse, and, trailing behind her, the flame-red
wheeled suitcase she didn't even have time to put away after
her return from Moscow. It's night, still. Not many people
out, the New Year's parties are over, she gets into the first
train for Périgueux, a scant dozen people in the passenger
car, it's a bitterly cold winter. In the shuddering of the train
and the dawning day, her face lights up, and what was still
imperceptible when she first sat down, still hidden, is revealed
now as she turns her head toward the window: something
dreamy and arid, something solitary. Soon the train is cutting
through pale scrub and Paula tries to draw lines, sending
her gaze as far as possible into the depths of the landscape,
touching the vanishing point of a vale, a car that disappears
around a turn, or, as the cities draw near, someone leaning
out their window to watch the train pass. The January forest
presses in close to the window, dusted with frost. In four
hours, the Dordogne.

The ultimate replica. This is how Jonas describes the job he
had to refuse, the facsimile of the Lascaux Cave. It's after
midnight when he calls, and he's calm, pragmatic, he tells
her the salary range, says the site is in Montignac, in the
Dordogne, that she'll have to go live there, and that he needs

her answer before noon the next day. Then he whispers: this job was made for you. A furrowed cavern, red and black paintings, bulls, reindeer, the Sistine Chapel of prehistory, Paula sifts through these images as her gaze travels diagonally across the room to rest on the wheeled suitcase standing in a corner, the stickers in Cyrillic script over the zipper. She doesn't want to leave again, not yet, she just got back from Moscow barely three weeks ago. I get it, Jonas says after a silence. But to make the call last, to keep him a little longer, Paula reconsiders: what exactly is the job? Jonas, we might imagine, must have savored that moment, but doesn't let it show, as if he were trying to coax the deer on the prairie toward the palm of his hand. He takes his time. Then Paula pedals back her covers, and in one leap is at the window where the sky is dull, no stars, and she hears him strike a match: it's your chance to be prehistoric.

After they hang up, she lies back down to sleep on it, but is soon up again, crossing her legs and leaning against a pillow, reaching for the laptop to surf until dawn, skin waxy and blue, temporal veins stretched like hawsers, and somewhere in the night the name Lascaux becomes a wave, a swell whose knowing coil has scraped the bottom of time, lifted and propelled it into this subterranean world where she has never ventured before.

⁂

Her father, the following morning. Leaning against the edge of the sink, long legs crossed Gary Cooper style, a cup of coffee in hand as Paula comes and goes in the kitchen, a blur in striped pajamas—coffee maker, sugar, cupboard honey, fridge cheese, drawer knife. He guesses from her tousled hair and her chiffon eyelids that she must not have slept much. Paula sits down and summarizes Jonas's proposition while Guillaume rinses his bowl, then turns around: I saw the Lascaux Cave, the real one. Paula jumps: you saw it? When? With his eyes on the ceiling: in 1969, I was thirteen, we went in the Simca 1100, beastly heat, horrendous day. But Paula shakes her head: that's impossible, it's been closed since 1963, you couldn't have seen it. Guillaume pauses, deflated, thumb and index pressed into the corners of his eyes, then speaks again, slowly: yes, it was in 1969, I was the same age as the kids who discovered it, I loved that story, the dog who found the hole, the whole thing. But Paula frowns, no, sorry, dad, you're mistaken.

What happens next in the rue de Paradis could be compared to a little sedan (which has, up until then, been driven with respect for the rules of the road) veering into a ditch, and only the appearance of Marie in the doorframe, monolithic in a batik kimono, manages to put their home back en route, redirecting their blazing eyes to her face. Because Paula's tone—definitive, no no no, little miss know-it-all—together with the little movement of her chin, the fact that she's contesting her father's childhood memory, even denying it (because that's how it must have felt to him, the capacity for remembering something, as though suddenly he were wandering in a shapeless past and wasn't part of the same world as her), all this causes Guillaume to overheat, his glasses slide down his nose, blotches appear on his neck: I saw it, you go down some stairs and you're in the Hall of the Bulls, then there's a tunnel across from it and another on the side with a large black cow, animals everywhere, I *saw* it. He adds hand gestures to his story as though he were pointing out the way to a lost traveler, but none of his movements can divert Paula's eye, who watches the honey drip from her spoon onto her toast and repeats, categorical: you saw something else, Malraux closed that one in 1963, you can't have seen it afterwards—distant, above all not to be associated with this genitor who has a screw loose, counter his tale with something remote and upright, it's unbearable, and Guillaume's voice booms out, perforates the invisible ceiling it has not ventured past since military service and barracks role calls—he had to yell *here* when his name was called, and yell it loud—it blasts out now so loud and agitated it makes the decor tremble, and creates a few ripples in the surface of the café au lait.

Guillaume's anger dynamites whole blocks of the past, fragments with sharp angles projected before Paula, herself suddenly angular, discovering the subsoil of her father, his unstable, magmatic part. If he remembers being in Lascaux, it's because of the family incident that took place that day, his private memory recreating its own hierarchy, the shock of the encounter with rupestrian art in competition with and ultimately supplanted by an episode that was trivial, perhaps, but intense. Her father's story begins in a wonky syntax punctuated by insults aimed at her—*goddamn fool*—and then organizes itself in present tense like the Banks children's room at the snap of Mary Poppins's fingers: my mother is wearing capri pants with two slits on the calf, a white shirt with red polka dots, she looks like an *Amanita muscaria*, the blood-red interior of the car stinks of burning plastic, we're all nauseous, feel like throwing up around the bends, my father says we'll get a lemon sorbet after the caves, the five of us line up in the stairwell, then there are the bulls, the Chinese horses, the red deer, I saw all that, but my older brother gets caught just as he's about to write some graffiti on the wall with his pen knife—there were a few other things already carved there, actually, like *Marcel + Simone = ♥*, *Robert was here*, etc.—my father gives him a couple of good whacks in front of everyone, the guide hadn't seen what my brother was about to do and so my father seems crazy, volatile, I'm dying of shame, and when we get back outside my brother disappears. We think he's gone to take a piss, we hear him in the little parking lot, we're thirsty, my father opens the door for us to get in the car, I don't care, we're leaving, he'll figure out his own way back, no one disobeys me like that, he bluffs, my sister panics, says he can't possibly walk fifty kilometers, my mother stays outside, accuses my father of being a hothead, unhinged, and this goes on until finally we go looking for my brother, all four of us, my father, my mother, my sister, and me, a search party, we're like hunters, spread out a dozen meters from each other, walking forward, cupping our hands around our mouths, calling out, but there's no one; evening falls, the cave is below us, I'm scared, and when we get back to the car there he is, my brother, he's torn his pants on some barbed wire and is bleeding a little, my mother's not sure his tetanus shot is up to date and wants to go to Brive to find a pharmacy, but my father says out of the question, he's not going to cause us any more trouble and starts the car, my mother bursts into tears, I think my brother is going to die, my sister hums with her head against the window, and no one dares to mention the lemon sorbet.

With Marie having appeared at the end of the story, the sequence ends, the memory breaks up, calm returns, the bodies take up their daily gestures again, and Paula leaves the room with the feeling of having glimpsed a long black fish through a hole cut into the ice. Once she's back in her room, she calls Jonas, her voice sure: I'll take it. And then she gets ready for her journey to Lascaux.

MOVE FORWARD IN THE DIMNESS, GET YOUR bearings by sounds, by currents of air, walk along behind the metal framework, then head toward the lit-up area and come upon Paula, almost fragile, standing before the wall. A man in a fisherman's sweater and cargo pants shows her to her work station, a temporary spot, he says in a gravelly voice that reddens the vowels, each painter has to be able to work on all the panels, it could be that you start on one wall and someone else ends up taking over—this way we avoid appropriating any one piece of the replica and leaving the mark of any one particular hand in a given spot—Paula smiles faintly, she knows this speech, knows it like the back of her hand—here there's no interpretation, we are copyists, we erase ourselves before Lascaux.

※

The studios are situated in the neighborhood of the old train station in Montignac and stretch out over an immense area, large enough, in any case, to hold an out-of-the-ordinary work site: they will be painting fifty-three decorated panels, which will then be assembled in an artificial cave built at the foot of the hill, a giant puzzle that will reproduce, identically, the near-totality of the original cave.

The wall that stands before Paula is bare and uneven. Vast, seven meters long by four meters high, it imposes its stony blankness and she feels it as she approaches, scrutinizes, it's crazy! As if speaking from far away the man behind her replies loudly: the hundreds of plates that make up the relief of the cave were first made by digital milling, using data from the 3D copy made inside the cavity—a very fine, high pressure water jet sculpted the polystyrene; next, each plate was refined by hand using paper pulp to work the smallest crevice, the least bump in the relief, and then a stylus to incise the one thousand five hundred parietal engravings that exist in the cave, a massive job, precise and delicate; next, silicone elastomer was applied to take the print of the modeled relief and obtain the negative of the cave, each panel stiffened by a layer of fiberglass resin and then reinforced with a metal framework. He finally wraps up, calling her by her first name without preamble: there you have it, Paula, you should know what you'll be working on, you need to know the nature of your frame.

While he was speaking, Paula had moved even closer, brought her face right up to the panel to pore over it, touch it with a finger. That there is the stone veil—the man's voice echoes at her back and then he comes to stand beside her—they developed a special mix of white marble powder layered with acrylic resin and fiberglass in the bottom of the molds to obtain this ultrafine membrane that mimics the mineral quality of the cave, the grain and feel of it; it's also a material that should resist the climatic conditions of the replica.

The man marks out the sweep of the wall with his eyes now, hands on his hips, then declares: the time of the painters has come! Paula turns back to him: sixty, tall and stooped, little round glasses with metal frames and the voice of a country preacher as he breaks down the work she's expected to do: it's a matter of reproducing the background of the Paleolithic paintings, of creating the patina before painting the figures; it's important to move slowly, grain by grain, without resorting to pointillism, and to be exact to the quarter millimeter. Then he slows down: it's the visual ambience of the cave that's at play here, one element of its atmosphere, and the most difficult—it's important that we feel the wear and tear of time—and he rubs his thumbs against his fingers to express the inexpressible, while Paula glimpses in a flash the tremendous work of imagination that awaits her. He quickly adds: last thing, we're creating a whole, the background is as essential as the figures, I don't need to spell it out for you—no, thinks Paula, you don't.

☙

Around her, the lighting sifts down onto a familiar set: mobile scaffolding, stepladder, footboard, crates, trolleys, stool, and then books, photos, a computer on a console, a sweatshirt, a tuque with a pompom, a bottle of water, and those studio projectors that create the movie-set atmosphere she's been walking through for seven years now—you'd think you were in the rue de Parme, she muses, as the Belgian apartment comes into focus in the quicksilver of her memory, this intimate floor that moves beneath her feet wherever she goes, wherever she lives, with Jonas's shadow projected onto the walls every time. Similarly, those who enter the hangar now and let their voices and footsteps ring out inside the structure like a theater troupe, those who hold out a cool hand and are silently surprised by her dissident eye, her unbalanced beauty, are all immediately familiar to her: paint-splattered pants, dry palms, radiant eyes circumscribed by taupe circles, the importance of lunch, and the well-balanced gait of ridge walkers, those who walk the line between two worlds. It's us, the forgery people, laughs a tall woman with auburn hair who comes up to Paula and kisses her on both cheeks, holding her shoulders, before taking off her anorak: I'm a former student from the rue du Métal, we're going to be working on the same panel.

There are about twenty of them and Paula feels as though she knows them all, feels she's finding her gang again, the copyists, the bamboozlers of the real, traffickers of fiction, employed at the great replica of Lascaux because they are scenographers, stained-glass artists, costume artists, laminators, mold makers, theater makeup artists, watercolorists, movie directors, icon restorers, gilders, or mosaic artists. They spread out like performers on a stage before the curtain rises, each one takes their place in their islet of light before their wall, and soon the power of their common concentration enmeshes the entire space and Paula is caught in the web, suddenly exhilarated.

❦

Later, in a windowless room that serves as a storage space and a lab, she surveys the white plastic pails and the jars aligned on the shelves, jots down the references in her notebook, decodes: ground limestone, glass powder, clay, and calcite from the Dordogne caves, and then natural pigments similar to those in the cave, manganese oxide for the black, ochers for the browns (limonite), the reds (hematite) and the yellows (goethite). The first material, the ground, its richness. She places boxes of samples on the table taken from actual archaeological specimens from the cave, and the woman with the auburn hair works beside her, both of them preparing their powders.

The woman points to the photocopy of a watercolor color chart pinned to the wall and ponders aloud: they used fifteen different chromatic shades in Lascaux, they would have to have known where to find deposits of manganese—for the ochers all they had to do was bend down and gather some; the only unknown is that square of purple they painted on the underside of one hoof of the Great Black Cow, in the Nave, on the left wall—know what I'm talking about? She goes on without even looking up at Paula: they would have had to prepare the job, think in advance, mix up the colors; it would have taken time, likely several hours; they would either have had to add more material to thicken, or find something to liquefy with, and they may also have had to heat the pigment. They had to do exactly what we're doing. Paula stops in her tracks. All this jostles around in her brain, the information rushes in, but what unsettles her comes from elsewhere, from within language—from this *they* that keeps coming up and bouncing around between the walls of the room like a magic ball: *they* came, *they* did this, *they* did that, the direct pronoun, without reference and chock full, referring to beings that are both nearby and given over to the depths of time. *They*, as if Paula could *see* them. The woman has pulled back her hair with tortoiseshell combs, she has full lips, flat cheeks, a wide forehead with a widow's peak, a strong neck, irises like two drops of whisky—the face of a Roman goddess. She goes on: as for the paintings, before we get to style, you have to know the technical constraints *they* had to deal with, the constraints of the physical environment, of the material, and of the surface.

But have you actually seen the real cave? Paula asks her, brusque as ever with the weight of emotion, and she answers with a satisfied smile: yes, just for twenty minutes. But those twenty minutes had changed her life. She was one of the few plastic artists, a half dozen at most, who had gone down into the cave, and upon their return to the surface, nothing was the same. She had lived among the painters of prehistory, she had stood behind their eyes; a contact that had lasted twenty minutes beyond twenty thousand years. Paula listens while her hands mix the selected ochers with acrylic binders, and at the same time get mixed up in the fissures of Cerfontaine marble, the carp in the ponds at Versailles, the painted eyes of the statue of Kha behind the glass of the museum in Turin, and the ground of teatro 5 at Cinecittà: everything coexists—you have to make us feel the time, the man in the fisherman's sweater had said, and rubbed his fingers between which, indeed, time ceased to exist, became translucent, no thicker than a rolling paper.

⁊

Back at her station, Paula is warmed up, and she's used to the lighting now. The auburn woman smiles: in the studio, we are rather like they were in the cave, same temperature, roughly thirteen degrees in winter, same light—we're working under the same conditions. The next moment Paula takes out fan brushes, soft brushes and sponges, extra fine detail brushes which she's dipped into the ocher wash, she turns on the projector and goes right up to the stone veil, and now, she paints.

AS SHE LEAVES THE STUDIOS, PAULA PULLS up a map of Montignac on her phone, types in the address, and heads off on foot to the other bank of the Vézère. The wheels on her suitcase echo in the deserted streets. She rings at the door of an old house where a room came free before Christmas when the previous tenant, a young sculptor employed at Lascaux IV, had gone back to Spain. A teenager in light gray sweatpants and black sneakers opens the door and leads her upstairs, shows her the room, the closet, the light switches and the taps, round-faced and serious, pink cheeks and protruding ears, instructions delivered in the intonations of an adult. I live in the house next door, if you need anything, just come get me, my name's Valmy. Paula nods and puts her suitcase on the bed, opening it out flat, okay, if I need anything I'll ask, thanks. Then she looks out the window and the boy says: that's the hill, the colline de Lascaux, there. The cave—the real one—is inside, and Paula goes to the casement to see the dark curve rising in the distance.

※

She would have preferred a room like a box, a space in which to make a nest, one of those standard spaces quickly inhabited, but she's struck by this one: old walnut-stained wood floor, walls hung with toile de Jouy depicting hunting scenes, once again—hunters and rifles, dogs, hares, watchful deer, but also pastoral shepherds, reed pipe, swing—an old-fashioned bathroom behind a screen with a bowl-shaped sink, and this oak bed whose grain she recognizes at a glance—she takes a picture and sends it straight to Jonas—remind you of anything? A bed so massive she can't move it one centimeter but so broad that she tosses books and brochures onto it, and maps she's brought with her. She begins to pace, comes back to the window, opens it wide to the countryside—a current of cold air rushes into the room, full of the scent of the night, ferrous, but Paula stays leaning out for a while—she would have probably liked to make out the radio murmur that fills the celestial dome, the fossil radiation that bathes our existences in a very ancient light, a light of thirteen billion eight hundred million years, that light freed from matter and scattered to every corner of the cosmos in a phenomenal flash. She looks at the colline de Lascaux, then turns abruptly, closes the window, and gets into bed, still fully dressed.

WHEN SHE WAKES, THE HILL IS HIGHER AND nearer than she would have thought—she can practically touch it—and the boy's words come back to her. At that very moment—at least this is what she tells Jonas when she calls him, first thing—she begins to tap into the presence of the cave, a tangible emanation, the bulge of the hill like a lid lifted by a push from inside. That makes sense, says Jonas, the cave is there, no one can see it but everyone's thinking about it, everyone's thinking about it all the time.

～

Later, Paula rides a bicycle through the streets of Montignac, following the flow of the Vézère further and further, the air is chilly and sprinkled with miniscule frozen splinters, the ditches full of water, the countryside steams. Hardly any animals in the fields but traces here and there: grasses creased at the edges as if a fox, badger, or hare had passed through, little tufts of fur caught in the barbed wire of the fences. It's been a long time since she followed a river's course like this, integrating herself into nature, it's been a long time since she rode a bike, her thoughts leading her invariably back to Jonas, slowly at first, and quietly, the way it is when we drift, and then converging on him, faster and faster. The frequency of their calls has increased since she took this job, they are in touch several times a day, the interval between conversations diminishes, they talk about him coming to Montignac.

The path leads through a wooded area, and at the first sounds of a motor, amplified by the calm of the countryside, Paula recognizes the characteristic sound of trail bikes. Three kids zoom between the trees, skidding in the carpet of decomposing leaves. She keeps pedaling, the sound fading behind her, but just after a bend the bikes appear suddenly, thrumming, lined up like horses on the river's edge, dominating the whole path. Paula slows down: on the middle bike (a little Yamaha with Arctic blue fairing) wearing a flaming helmet, she recognizes Valmy.

Everything okay, Madame? he says, smirking. Paula puts one foot down: I'm fine, I'm going for a ride, as you can see. Then she asks: is the cave this way? Valmy looks at the other two and laughs, it's higher up, but there's nothing to see, Madame, it's closed, I already told you. They flick their wrists on the accelerators, making the bikes champ at the bit, making that noise Paula found so desirable at twelve years old, when she wanted to get as close to it as possible, and followed her cousins into the forest behind the big house, chosen and silent, while they squatted together around the customized bike they'd fixed up, feeling like men now, talking pistons and compression, cables and discs, testing the accelerator and the brakes, ignoring her presence, until the oldest said alright, I'm taking it out, put on a full-face helmet and straddled it, drove off into the forest, his yellow T-shirt like a fugitive flying banner, while the others waited for his return, worried that their elder would use his privilege to burn up all the fuel on his joyride, and Paula, ordered to get on the seat behind him, to press herself against his back and wrap her arms around his waist or she'll fall off, legs held out horizontal to avoid burning her calves on the exhaust pipe, biting her lips when the bike hits a stone and starts to shake and zigzag as if out of control, her mouth suffocated by the air the wind the dust, by the neck of this cousin she observes up close, a recent haircut revealing a clearing of white skin beneath the hairline, reduced to little cropped points that sparkle, holding back from screaming when he goes up onto the back wheel and yells *hold on*, and, finally, stopping herself from crying when the bike falls to one side. Her leg was covered with bruises for several weeks, causing her to limp, distancing her forever from these boys with their mud-spattered jeans, free as birds on their bikes in the woods.

⁂

Back in Montignac, on a roll, she takes a right turn toward the hill and soon the site of Lascaux IV appears before her. She tries to see something over the fence, but the state of progress keeps the site unreadable—piles of material and brightly colored machines, montage of cranes—and she barely manages to make out the long façade of concrete and glass designed to look like a rock shelter, numerous in the area— she had seen it from various perspectives the day before on the architectural plans hanging in the lobby of the studios. She grows cold after a moment, stopped on her bike. She should go back, but instead she continues on, carried forward by an impulse that comes from somewhere far away, and turns left after the bend to plunge into the woods.

Mist floats over the path, and the slender forest—pines, oaks, chestnut trees—becomes spectral; the air smells of moss, mushrooms, and all that proliferates beneath a layer of rotting leaves, between the roots of trees. She makes out a sealed gate flanked by a *Monument historique* sign, and a high fence, and gets off her bike to see better. The entrance to the cave must be this way, a few meters off, the silence augments the clarity, and yet Paula doesn't immediately see the stairwell that descends in a gentle slope toward the door—it's only after looking at the ground for some time that she notices the passageway, camouflaged. She looks around for a tree to climb, two meters would suffice, she wants to see the door, but all the trunks are wound with barbed wire, she has to stand on tiptoe to catch sight of the lintel, and even though it is nothing great in itself, it moves her deeply. There are shapes of absence as intense as presences, this is what she thinks to herself as she presses her forehead to the fence, leaning toward the world that opens here, concealed, no more than ten meters away, a cave where they had identified nothing less than the birthplace of art.

Paula imagines the cave underground, its withdrawn beauty, the cavalcade of animals in the Magdalenian night, and she wonders whether paintings continue to exist when there is no one left to see them.

BETWEEN JULY 14, 1948, AND APRIL 20, 1963, the Lascaux Cave, set up to receive vast numbers of tourists, was open to the public. You'd buy your ticket at the counter and head down the stairs to the bronze door guarding the cavern like the entrance to a temple. From the outset, cars could be seen bumper-to-bumper up the hill, lineups forming through the underbrush. Those who had waited so long to see it, people from the area and prehistory buffs (and sometimes these were one and the same) came first, and then it was like a kind of vast magnetization, visitors rushing in from countries farther and farther away, crossing borders, the Lascaux Cave the sole reason for the trip. A major national heritage site, a must-see, like Mont-Saint-Michel or Versailles. The number of visitors rose each year—thirty thousand in 1955, 120,000 in 1962, a daily influx of five hundred people with attendance peaking at 1,800 per day that particular summer. It's a craze. It's easy to imagine the tourists, vacationers, families from the 1950s with dads in short-sleeved shirts driving pastel-colored cars (a pale yellow Dauphine, a sky-blue Frégate, sometimes a pistachio-colored Aronde), bare-shouldered mothers in percale dresses, children in flip-flops and terry cloth shorts tripping over each other's feet, tackling each other on the sly, wild, guileful, badly behaved, eyes slipping off into the woods, sometimes a grandmother with bobbed hair or a straw boater complaining of the heat; often they were people who disliked caves, uneasy at the thought of heading into dark, dank places, into these labyrinthine galleries, and more so at the thought that the first peoples, whom they still were not keen to accept as being essentially the same as them, might have lived there—a false idea though still largely believed. Chests puffed up in the queue, complex words were uttered, words in Latin and Greek, sapiens, Paleolithic, claustrophobia, jokes cracked about homo erectus, imagining the ancestors half-naked, vigorous and bestial, nervous laughter rang out as they inched closer, likely in the next group, and they tried to ward off bad luck out loud—hope we don't get stuck in there!—the fear of a landslide that would block the exit, the ancestral fear of being buried alive surging up at the moment tickets were handed over to the guide, who, if they were lucky, was sometimes Marcel or Jacques, two of the four discoverers. Then the group entered the cave, moved forward, pressed against each other, heads nearly touching, little ones lifted up to see the paintings. All you had to do was open your eyes and you'd be captivated, overwhelmed by emotion, and you'd lower your voice just the same as in a sanctuary, overcome by the enigma, clamoring with questions, and possibly also filled with fear, caught in the circle of powerful beasts that you could feel, pulsing with life, all around. People were proud, too, proud to be there, even if they'd sometimes had to force themselves to leave the riverbanks, the city pool, the shade of the walnut tree, even if they'd had to *bust their balls*, because it was important to show this stuff to the kids, because it was culture and they wanted life to look like something.

An estimated one million people visited the Lascaux Cave in those fifteen years. A million people saw the paintings. If we apply these fifteen years of being open to the twenty thousand years of the works' existence, we get a proportional value of one minute and three seconds in twenty-four hours. One minute and three seconds is long—it's not a lightning strike, not a photographic flash, more like a long exposure, a slow infusion of light. The burning of thirteen matches in a row. A blaze that stretches out—a wonder. Indeed, they had time to make history with the cave. To connect with it, to enter into a relationship, to make of it a legend.

PAULA GRAVITATES TOWARD THE LEGEND-
ary, she goes straight for it. It excites her to read the various
versions of the discovery of Lascaux, piled up, juxtaposed, mixed
together, most of them written with a dramatic tension that
moves from darkness to light: there are the early accounts of the
discoverers themselves, those of the adults who listened to them
and recorded their testimonies, teachers or prehistorian priests,
and the accounts of scholars, of journalists who rushed to the
site early on, of poets and local town councilors, and those,
belated, of the Alsatians who went into the cave the day after
the four boys (but legend had erased them), and finally, that
of her father Guillaume, who *loved this story*. Paula takes her
place in the chain of narrators, and on the night of Epiphany,
back in her room, stuffed with frangipane, and a little tipsy
too—they had pulled the kings from the galette in the studio at
the end of the day, relaxed ambience, the work moving forward
according to the umpteenth version of the schedule; earlier
two representatives from the departmental council and one
of the directors from the tourism company Semitour Périgord
(on a visit to the site, accompanied by a reporter from the *Sud
Ouest*) had left impressed—she phones Jonas. Let me tell you
the story—and in that moment, she looks and sounds exactly
like someone speaking by the light of a fire.

⁂

She starts by synchronizing her narration with the moment
in history, stitching the hill to the world surrounding it: the

Nazi darkness striking Europe, France humiliated by defeat, the Marshal at Vichy, the French Demarcation Line that placed Montignac in the Free Zone, the refugees who came to the village—among them the Coencas, a Jewish family from Montreuil, and practically all the inhabitants of Elsenheim, in Alsace, four hundred thousand Alsatians suddenly doubling the population of the Dordogne. Then, with the phone mouthpiece right up against her lips, the sound of her voice stretching softly into the night, she begins: so it's the end of summer, and four boys are walking in the woods.

Chalky September, they climb a path on the mountainside, the ground is rough, little stones roll under their shoes, you can hear them coming from far off—the echo of their steps, the clamor of their voices. The underbrush rustles all around, ashy, the birds doze in the oaks, the snakes lie still, the ants busy themselves, everything is thirsty. It's a Thursday, September 12, 1940. The hikers are not kids anymore, but they are in search of treasure—is this how childhood perseveres? Paula pauses. She sees herself at work, tirelessly copying matter, scratching out wood, carving into marble, scraping away at the world: I, too, am looking for treasure, she thinks, this treasure that's destined for me and is just waiting to be found.

She goes on: one of them, the eldest, is the leader—it's plain to see, you can tell by his height, his broad shoulders, and by the gear he's carrying—including this lamp cobbled together with a Tecalemit grease gun, a good wick, and some petrol—also, he's the one who knows where they're going. He's a mechanic's apprentice in a garage in Montignac, eighteen years old, named Marcel, nicknamed *the convict* because he looks like Harry Baur as Jean Valjean in a version of *Les Misérables* from the thirties—the names are already swirling, those of the actors and those of the characters, those from literature poured into the movies and found again in the eyes of the inhabitants of Montignac. It's him, Marcel Ravidat, who plays the lead role, he's in command. The three others are younger: Georges Agniel is seventeen, Jacques Marsal is fourteen and Simon Coencas is thirteen—*kids*? For the three of them, this expedition is a diversion: Marcel runs into them in the streets of Montignac and recruits them, and as she tells the story Paula thinks immediately of Valmy and his friends who also like to bomb around the woods of Lascaux.

Marcel has an idea—to go back to the hole he *heard* four days before, on September 8. On that day, he had gone with a few others to the hill behind Lascaux Manor, a kilometer south of Montignac, when his dog Robot disappeared into a hollow overgrown with bushes, a cavity about a meter deep left when a large tree tore loose in a storm long before—a hole that people already knew about. Marcel goes in after his dog and discovers another hole, this one narrower. He throws in a stone, stands with an ear cocked, and estimates the depth by counting the seconds before he hears it touch bottom; and the echo of the stone that bounced and then rolled along the cone of loose scree inside probably allowed him to picture what lay beneath—it's hollow below, vast, and already there's room, something, an adventure; and maybe everything that followed, everything—this is a hypothesis that sets Paula on fire—is contained within the echoing of a stone that falls into a well and resonates ceaselessly in Marcel's ear, resonates in such an insistent and beautiful way that four days and four nights later he's on the move, geared up, with a team in tow—Paula's voice reverberates too, causes images to flow into Jonas's ear, including her face and her hands that underscore her words.

The four of them climb, heads leaning forward as if their foreheads were indicating the way, they go at a good clip but without excessive haste, have gathered sticks and whack the foliage with large loose movements, speak quietly to each other, spit, exchange thumps and blows to the balls, toss around insults, Alsatians, Lorrainians, but not a word yet about the treasure; and as she imagines them climbing the slope through the underbrush, Paula thinks of the prologue to an installment of *The Famous Five*, bold typeface and pages sewn into the hardcover binding of the Bibliothèque rose edition—do you know those books, Jonas? Paula asks suddenly: can you see Timmy the dog, yapping between the feet of the intrepid gang of kids? I see him, says Jonas, keep going.

What Marcel said to the others was that he may have found the underground passage to Lascaux Manor, and this information was enough to make them change course. The presence of a passageway between the village and the hill had been rumored for so long that each one held a clear idea of its existence, and like most of the kids in the village (and the handful of beret-wearing scholars who consult the local archives), the three kids who are listening to Marcel, impressed by Marcel—Paula knows exactly the impression a boy of eighteen can make when you're thirteen, when it's summer, the holidays, and when he puts forward a plan while you're there, wandering like a dog in a scorching yard—the three of them dream of finding it, and so they have no hesitation about entering ancient plots of land, feudal and mysterious, guarded, braving the stewards who protect them (the aristocrats, the *Parisians*—the owners—hardly ever show themselves). As is often the case, the rumor sticks to the tangled and tenacious logic of the legend: if there is a castle—and there is a castle—then there must be an underground passage. Surely they would have dug a tunnel for supplies in case a siege lasted and in case bread, water, and wax ran out, they would have thought of an emergency exit if an attack set the walls aflame and the enemy had invaded the outer walls and plunged down the spiral staircase to the dungeon, heavy in their leather but in a hurry to get it over with, they would have surely thought of what they'd need to escape with an aging father on their back, child in one hand, torch in the other to light the shaft with its ceiling so low you have to duck, pressing on in spite of seeping walls and swarms of insects, in spite of the anxiety of the labyrinth, dark dead ends and junctions that all look the same, in spite of the terror that the flame might be extinguished, that the oxygen might run out, that they might end up ensnared in a trap, buried alive; if there is a castle, they would have dug a means of escape, a corridor, at the end of which sparkles the light of the outside, the light we can make out among all others, pale sun or moonless night, breath of fresh air on the face, roots, mud, and the return to the world—images that flash in the sound of the stone that falls inside Marcel's ear.

Teenagers who climb the hill *just to see*, then, the way we raise the stakes during a round of poker just to stay in the game, to keep up with the promise of life. They reach the spot where it begins and Paula visualizes the four pairs of eyes on the ground, silently examining the chasm, too narrow to put a head through, shouting hullo, hullo, anyone there?, but large enough to let out the smell of the earth, as intimate as the smell of the folds of human skin, and then Marcel pulls out a piece of auto machinery, a leaf spring from a car's suspension, which they take turns using to enlarge the opening—this takes a good hour (the stubbornness of the eldest has infected the others and they persevere, seize the chance to display their strength). Then, once the hole is widened, they do exactly what they came here to do: they climb down—in other words, they go in to believe.

The discovery, already, is a wound—Paula pauses, she doesn't let go of the phone, but slips off her shoes, her socks, and climbs onto the bed—the outside and the inside open to each other through a hole that is scooped out—it's about twenty centimeters wide on the day of the discovery, and five by five meters only a month later—and through this contact, something is irreversibly lost. When the cone of loose scree is destroyed, the cavity loses its climatic, hydric, and thermic stopper, and the stability of the environment inside the cave is changed—the exact relation that existed between the air, water, and stone is disturbed, and a continuity of twenty thousand years collapses.

Contrary to break-ins, or speleological explorations, where the shortest and slightest usually goes first as scout for the others, Marcel is the one who enters first while the other three stay listening at the surface. His feet touch ground, he lands in the blackness, they toss down the Pigeon lamp borrowed for the occasion, and he turns it on: he's at the top of a pile of fallen rocks and is soon crawling down, pressed between the two walls, belly bruised by the stones, he inches forward—how does he hold the lamp? Jonas wonders. Then the passage widens, becomes a room, and Marcel calls out to the others who come in one by one: faint shadows on the walls of the cave, voices that lower a notch, groans, perhaps, when a stone hurts them—Jonas imagines all of it, and the hardest thing to imagine is their courage, to crawl underground into the dark. Once they're together again, they check out their surroundings, the amazing bas-relief, the flowing gours overhead, the stretches of white calcite wall: it's not the underground passageway of the castle, for the moment it's just a cave, which, in a region full of prehistoric sites, is far from unusual. They move about carefully, the walls close in around them, and now they are in a narrow gallery—at this stage of the descent, they still haven't seen anything, haven't seen the paintings, and the idea that these exist in the dark, alive, frozen, but ready to be set in motion with the least flicker of light, this idea makes Jonas shiver. At that moment, Jacques lets out a cry and points to the white vaulted ceiling: shapes so powerful they separate from the shadows and announce themselves, now stirring in the glow of the makeshift lights, these fluttering lights that heighten the impression of movement, of a procession of animals. They are not scared off—they lift their lamps high before the images: a deer, little horses, a bull. Then they follow the procession along the length of the wall until they find themselves at the end of the passage, standing before a horse lying on its back in a *U* shape, legs in the air, like the sign of the U-turn they would have to make, and soon (indeed the oil lamp begins to get hot, so hot they have to make the decision to climb back out); and Jonas imagines that the paintings themselves were what limited the time the boys could gaze upon them, one moment of amazement before the darkness closes again over a mnesic wake, a presence etched forever within each of them, and then the desire that follows, to return.

Their faces when they come out of the cave, the words they say, the sound of their sneakers on the path down the hill as night falls—Jonas can't stop thinking about it. Everything is altered, Paula tells him, the familiar landscape they know down to the last rooftop, the smallest window, the least group of trees, all of it is different from now on: unchanged on the surface, it contains a clandestine world that only they know about. She wonders if those who see them coming home can tell that something has happened to them, that everything has shifted, that their center of gravity has been reoriented to the place beneath the hill. Of course they're late for dinner, clothes dirty and bodies covered in bruises as though they've been to battle, and of course they must be tired, a little dazed, absorbed by their visions, concentrating on the promise of the next day, but nothing else marks them out from the other kids in Montignac, no transfiguration, no stutter, no fever or scar of any kind—they show no disturbance, nothing more than an unusual reserve, a silence. Do you think they had a sense from that first night of the incredible significance of their discovery? Jonas asks. Paula ignores him, she's imagining instead a collective emotion that's both powerful and vague, and the certainty of having found a treasure. The fact remains that they opted to keep the secret, saw themselves already as the protectors and guardians of the cave, and in this secret, a foursome is formed forever: Marcel, Jacques, Georges, and Simon—the young mechanic from Montignac, the son of the owner of the café-restaurant Le Bon Accueil, the boy from Nogent-sur-Marne on vacation at his grandmother's place, and the Jewish teenager taking refuge in Montignac.

The next day, though, September 13, five of them climb the hill—Simon brings his brother along, widening the circle of possessors of the secret. They've brought carbide lamps, shovels, ropes, and have decided to do a systematic exploration of the cave walls. They enter the narrow bottleneck in single file, slide down the scree, and the emotion from the day before, the vertigo of the shock, has changed: now, it's enchantment.

They're on a reconnaissance mission with wonder as their method, and Paula imagines them moving quickly, spreading out, calling to each other, caught up in a kind of exclamatory one-upmanship that must have seemed like it would go on forever. The first animal, strange, is a horse with two long thin black horns, which straightaway gives a sense of movement, indicates a direction; here the bulls, some little black horses, and four deer at a gallop, an ibex, there a black deer, then a bear at the side of a bull, heads poking up between two necks, misaligned hindquarters, manes lifting, and everything is warm, mobile, alive, sonorous, the beauty has no point, the beauty has no end, and little by little, tossed outside of themselves, they will enlarge the space of the cavern even more. Georges discovers a passage on the right side of the first chamber and calls out to the others, there's more! He heads down the tunnel that stretches for fifteen meters before opening onto another gallery, so high and steep they have to climb onto ledges to admire the paintings, more horses, a bison marked with arrows, a large cow, black and corpulent, back-to-back bison, four deer heads—or maybe it's the same one that's moving through the cave?—and the space continues on, farther and farther, another shaft appears on the right, the slanting light reveals a domed ceiling where engravings of animals intertwine, a mass of such density and agitation that it's difficult to make out individual forms. The beauty goes on. Are you there, Jonas? asks Paula.

❦

On the third day, they go back in. They still haven't told anyone. Paula imagines that the new geodesic coordinates of their existence must change their appearance now, their comportment, their sleep, their appetites—but then, it's wartime, the economic slump has delayed the school year, and they've been left to their own devices. On this day, though, they're going to take some risks. Marcel, as always, is the first to explore the hole they'd given up on the day before, beneath the dome covered in engravings: a deep hole, five meters, the rope is too short, he has to jump into the void while keeping hold of the lamp. It's crazy but he does it, he jumps, and when he stands up and turns on the light, a creature appears on the wall, a man with a bird's head, stylized in the extreme; he has four fingers, an erect penis, and is lying on his back facing a wounded bison as a rhinoceros walks away. At the bottom of this black well, the atmosphere is other, enigmatic—there's the sense that death has appeared—and Jonas, who's still listening, imagines that Marcel must have stopped and shivered, gripped by the scene, and then, quick, chased away the disquiet by climbing out of the grave, before the other three jumped down in turn. This is the final episode of the discovery—now they feel the urge to tell someone.

❧

For three days they explored the cave, three days in which they toiled at extending the known world—extending known space and time—our great work. An operation involving bags and ropes, cobbled-together lamps and torn clothes, physical risks, a descent that illuminates youth, creativity, imagination, and all that is willing to grope around in the dark.

THE DAY KATE RESURFACES, SNOW FALLS from a low sky—no reverberation, just soft flakes landing on the pavement and vanishing, their indistinct patter absorbed into the landscape. Paula feels the silent vibration of the phone just as the studios of Lascaux IV come into view. A series of emojis—sun, bikini, fish—pop up on the screen, and then a video link. She ducks under an awning to watch it, picks Kate out immediately among the people pulling on neoprene suits in the tiled changing room of a diving club, just the legs, the top falling around her waist. Then the same folks are gathered under the mast of a Boston Whaler at sea, eight or ten ruddy faces, eight or ten white bellies, and yes, Kate is wearing a triangle bikini top, and already the cetaceans inked on her arms are coming to life. She listens, concentrating, to the guy who rattles off the security measures, an instructor wearing a pair of black lace-up trunks and an old white T-shirt, speaking in a Marseillais accent, Ray-Ban aviators reflecting an expectant sky. The image dips and rises with the waves, and Paula, who's starting to feel seasick, lifts her eyes to the colline de Lascaux long enough to steady herself: Kate had gone to swim with the whales off La Réunion. She gives the thumbs-up sign to the camera, saying *let's go to the real world!* and takes an exaggerated inhale, puffing up her chest and shoulders, perched on the edge of the boat, then falls backwards into the water, holding her diving mask against her face with both hands. The other passengers follow, each leap creating points of perforation between sky and sea, craters of spray. The next shot in the film is underwater, abyssal, mythological: Kate floats ten meters above a humpback whale who weaves slowly through a cathedral's volume, disappearing into blue thickness, then re-emerging later from another direction, shadowy and immense. So colossal—twenty-five tons and fifteen meters long, a four-story building—that it reconfigures the scale of the world. Kate is suddenly minute, a tiny backlit shadow against the translucent ceiling, barely a piece of seaweed. The animal inhabits the ocean in all its dimensions, comes and goes in a state of great calm, its presence revealing a world without interruption, a fluid continuity where everything coexists—the realm of time. Now and then the whale rises to the surface and its back suddenly occupies her entire field of vision, but Kate doesn't panic, she observes the safety instructions, moves her flippers as one in a becoming-mermaid stroke. The creature rinses its skin in the sun, sucks up the tubers that have grown on its jaws, breathes, and in this movement shows its pale belly before sinking again below the sea, that overwhelming belly. Paula, gripped by the video, swallows in terror when the whale turns to face her—from a spectral shadow it becomes clear in a nanosecond, mortal—but on the screen, carried in the pelagic, Kate continues to shed her human appearance, continues to cease being Kate in order to approach this huge fish that fascinates her. And when the whale finally begins to sing, when it lets this sound be heard, bass frequency capable of crossing insane distances (it has even been rumored that the sound could cross the ocean from shore to shore), capable of identifying prey or obstacles a thousand leagues away through echolocation, a fog engulfs the mask, and Paula thinks to herself that Kate must be crying.

They grow impatient at the surface, the other divers have reboarded the boat and are already comparing videos and photos, showing each other the technical possibilities of their devices, listing the storage capacity and number of pixels in a clamor of enthusiasm, while below, immersed, Kate awaits the creature's return—it had just disappeared into the blue where the ocean remains turned in on itself, wildly dark. Next we see her taking off her mask on the bridge of the Boston, spitting out her snorkel and kissing a guy full on the mouth, someone Paula identifies as the property manager from avenue Foch—bald spots pinking through, signet ring on his middle finger, meticulous movements as he unzips Kate's suit at the back. At the end of the video, she's sitting on a bench in the prow, hands on her hips, thighs marbled, and she speaks into the camera in English, voice halting, Paula doesn't understand the details but gets the gist: the world has been re-dimensioned, the large, the small, the sense of proportion, everything is altered; the eye of the whale had swiveled toward her beneath the fold of its eyelid, had shifted in its socket when Kate swam five or six meters below, a moment of contact that changed everything. Kate's pupils are dilated and her black suit lies at her feet, empty and disarticulated, like the shed skin of a snake.

THE COMPLETE FACSIMILE, THE PERFECT copy. People even speak of a cloning of the cave and Paula often thinks back to Jonas's words the night he called to tell her about the job on Lascaux IV: the ultimate replica—the job of a lifetime, he had added. But Paula had never copied without having contact with the original, had never reproduced a subject that she couldn't position herself, never painted the portrait of something she had never seen—and that you have no chance of seeing, I should tell you, says the auburn woman, who she's working with—the privilege of having seen the cave swells her like a balloon. Paula shrugs, she intends to have her turn in that cave, she can wait, she has all the time in the world. One minute and three seconds on the inside, that's all she asks.

⁂

The clone, in this case, is first digital—this is what the man in the fisherman's sweater explains to Paula, taking the time to break down the graphic software designed from the 3D model used to cast the panels, and which she would have access to for painting. People had descended into the cavity equipped with high-performance scanners and had recorded the position of three or four billion points in order to reproduce the very tissue of the epidermis, the skin of the cave. Next came the complete photographic documenting, including the cramped Chamber of the Felines, which would not be copied—twenty thousand high-res shots. Then the man in the fisherman's sweater places one on top of the other to show Paula how they had put together the volumetric data from the scans and the photographic images to obtain the 3D model of Lascaux. His voice suddenly speeds up and he lands a hand on his sternum: in a certain way, the facsimile will be more real than the original, it will be more accurate, will recreate, for example, the initial hole and the cone of loose scree at the entrance to the cave, the slope down which the discoverers climbed, which, although impossible to scan and copy, had been drawn up by an archaeologist, then built by the plastic artists. He concludes: in fact, the entrance is the only part of the replica that came from the imagination. Paula lowers her eyes to the plans, silent, while he adds, stroking his beard: so in some ways, the artisans who've come to work on the plastic arts of Lascaux IV have to create the archaeology of the replica, they have to go back in time, climb back up the path of the images.

&

The first image, Paula imagines, is drawn on a piece of paper folded in four and stuffed into the hip pocket of a boy who heads back down the hill in September 1940 and goes straight to Léon Laval, retired teacher, renowned figure in Montignac and archaeology enthusiast. Jacques had confided the cave's discovery to him, but in order to believe it, Laval had asked Georges Estréguil, a friend of the group and a good artist, to go in and bring back a sketch; the image hits its mark, and the very next day Laval goes into the cave and emerges, overcome. The second image, lurching along in a bike basket, heads toward Brive on September 20. The person pedaling, Maurice Thaon, is a young guy, thirty years old, who has also gone into the cave to draw, and is now rushing to bring his work to Abbé Breuil, an eminent historian of the period and international specialist in wall paintings, who was also a distant cousin. Once again, the image sets off a chain of events, and on September 21, Breuil is in Lascaux, where he authenticates the cave. The third image is a nearly transparent piece of paper—florist's paper—on which Breuil, using a method he refined in the caves of the Southwest and in Altamira in northern Spain, traced a large cat from the Chamber of Felines and a horse from the Axial Gallery. But his sight is declining: he had injured his right eye in July on a hazelnut branch as he was walking through the forest, and his left eye was already weak, so what could he see? (Paula places a hand over her right eye, she knows something about this.) The time has come to authenticate Lascaux, and this tracing may be the crowning touch on the report that Breuil sends the Académie des inscriptions et belles lettres a month later, in which he baptizes the cave *the Sistine Chapel of the Périgord.*

🦌

The images precede the cave, they prance around, and Paula goes along with them. News of the discovery spreads at breakneck speed, transmitted by voices on the radio (nasal, a little stiff), and soon visitors flock to the town. The entire population of Montignac and its surroundings climb the hill, where, on certain October days in 1940, a thousand people can be seen, people who are curious, or friends, or people who once lived in the village, the elite among prehistorians, canons and priests, local notables, a procession escorted by a few animals, insects, pollens, microorganisms, and other minute presences invisible to the naked eye. The discoverers set up camp on location in order to protect the cave—they are guides, for two francs a visit. The press comes, the first articles speak of a "Versailles of prehistory," and the black and white photos already illustrate the legend: the forest of Lascaux is the bivouac of young adventurers who live free, sleep in tents, speak one on one with scholars and poets, a lock of hair over their eyes, pipes in their mouths. Soon the four discoverers dwindle to two: Georges goes back to the capital in early October for the school year, and Simon has already left Montignac to return to Montreuil—he and his sister will be the sole survivors of their family, who are detained in Drancy, deported, and then sent to Auschwitz.

※

The cave is there, stunning, intact. Its miraculous coolness abolishes time, and the humans of prehistory are there, so near—and yet unknown. Nothing could be more thrilling. For the artists, photographers, reporters, documentarists, and filmmakers, the period that precedes the public opening is a honeymoon. Starting in October 1940, all these characters make themselves at home in Lascaux, settle in with their equipment, contort themselves to photograph the frescoes, lit up again by carbide lamps. There are the ones who produce surveys, often at the request of Breuil—Maurice Thaon is hired by the École des Beaux-Arts to take the first scientific records; Fernand Windels, editor and photographer living as a refugee in Montignac, goes into the cave with his large expanding camera; there are the ones who film the legend—in 1942, a movie, *La Nuit des temps*, features Laval and the discoverers as themselves; and there are the ones who work for the press—in January 1941, a first photographic essay by Pierre Ichac, published in *L'Illustration*, shows Abbé Breuil standing in front of the walls, very pope of prehistory, beret on his head and staff in hand; in 1947, photographer Ralph Morse and his wife Ruth set up an electric generator imported from England inside the cave to light the paintings with powerful projectors—for the first time the radiance of the colors in the Paleolithic paintings will be seen, and the report published in *LIFE* magazine extends Lascaux's fame overseas, making it world-renowned. In 1948, a report by Norbert Casteret and photographed by Maynard Owen Williams, published in *National Geographic*, consecrates the site. In the general euphoria, it's still hardly noticeable that all the work undertaken by the cave's owner (a curious thing, but Lascaux *belongs* to someone, to the de la Rochefoucauld family) with the aim of making it a tourist attraction is altering the place in irreversible ways. A bronze door, an entryway, and a stairway are built, the ground is lowered to cement a pathway for visitors, lighting is installed, and ten years later a ventilation system as well. In the last account from the period of initial revelation, Georges Bataille sets himself up in the cave in 1954 to write his great book *Lascaux ou la naissance de l'art*: the photos of underground sessions depict him in a princely light, seated in the Hall of Bulls with publisher Albert Skira and both of their wives, Diane and Rosabianca, or posing alone facing the walls, or standing with Jacques and Marcel as they point out the spot where they first saw the paintings, trying to identify the exact place where the art first appeared to the teens, the precise spot of its birthplace; and while Bataille is in residence, all these things happen here: creation, writing, lighting, photographing of the chambers, smoking too, the cave inhabited by the poet suddenly becoming again what it was twenty thousand years before—a studio.

※

From the moment of its discovery, the cave has produced images. Paula sees it as a magical factory: its doors open and images emerge; they close and still the images slip out through the cracks. Image-vehicles designed to carry its presence to the outside world. Paula downloads digital folders of the tracings, begun in 1952 and continued for more than ten years by Abbé Glory (another priest!). Although she imagines him as irritable, monomaniacal, and difficult, Paula thinks to herself that she would have liked to watch him at his nocturnal work—because he had to wait for all the visitors to leave before he could light the walls, place his tracing paper, and copy each stroke, each mark, in the silence of the cave; he would emerge at three in the morning and head through the woods to a neighboring house, exhausted—one hip aches. By night, he climbs in and traces, by day, always on all fours, in socks, he traces onto a film of cellophane, assembles his tracings like a puzzle, stretches them onto a drawing board, has another look, verifies the precision on site before correcting again with pencil, and then reduces the scale of his tracings with a camera lucida. All of it obsessive, fastidious, fervent. Thousands of hours of work. The tracing of the parietal engraving, less spectacular than the painting itself but still remarkable, will thus be the work of this underground man, who looks on, powerless, as the site is degraded through tourism—in a photo from 1957, taken in the Hall of Bulls, four workers are assembled around a jackhammer, the ground is full of holes, channels for electrical cables, and on the left stands Abbé Glory, stricken.

❧

By 1963, the party is over. Cave overheating, humidity becoming acidic, walls oxidizing, algae proliferating, and a *green sickness* followed quickly by a *white sickness*—formation of calcite crystals that threaten to render the paintings opaque. The thousands of visitors had infected, polluted, and damaged the cave. André Malraux, Minister of Cultural Affairs, orders the owner to close the cave—and those who had planned to visit in summer '63 write letters of protest: what about us, how are we going to see it? To satisfy these rejected visitors and keep the tourist flow coming to the village, the town hall sets up the first virtual visit of the cave: a slide show with commentary by two of the discoverers, Ravidat and Marsal. As for the owner, the closing meant the loss of a financial godsend—a solution had to be found for them too. An initial project is launched in 1971, a strange presentation mixing the real and the false, using natural caves to showcase copies, a project that was abandoned when, after the caves were sold to the state in 1972 (the owner retaining the sole right to sell access to photographs, tracings, and copies of the works), the facsimiles entered the picture. Lascaux II, created a few dozen meters from the original site, restores to the cave its original character: neither scientific tracing nor photography, it is a work of art. A work by sculptors and painters, and among them Monique Peytral who, rather than *erasing* herself before these painters from prehistory—Paula frowns—tried to put herself in their shoes, to incorporate their art, and is soon painting using their techniques, learning from them, in their presence, using pigments analogous to theirs, spending long stretches of time immersed in the cave, until she herself becomes prehistoric.

The financing gives out, the site is shut down, starts up again, the facsimile is only partial—only one side of the cave, the Hall of Bulls and the Axial Gallery are copied—and yet, the work is so mind-blowing that the discoverers themselves express their admiration on opening day, in July 1983, and then visitors turn up in droves, the parking lots fill, the queues lengthen, the hill is flooded with people once again. From the start, people are prepared to make the trip to admire a forgery, and in fact, they don't really care, they barely think about it, they come to Lascaux because this name has been synonymous with wonder for decades now, and at the end of the first season, the number of tickets sold surpasses the annual number of visitors to the real cave.

⁂

Until this point, people had kept up their hopes of seeing the real one: in 1967, it was opened each day to five visitors from a waiting list maintained at the ministry, people of patience and endurance, who trusted the state and projected themselves into the future; even small groups of tourists were still permitted access in the summers of '69 and '70—and Paula thinks back to her father, who could have seen it after all, who *did* see it, then, and promises herself she'll call him to tell him. Though poised at the brink of loss, Lascaux hadn't disappeared completely—this wasn't yet the absolute void of destruction. But in 2001, it was over, finished: Lascaux shall be protected. The cave had produced its own fungus (*Ochroconis lascauxensis*), the walls were covered in white patches, the ceilings in black splotches, total panic. The procession of animals was cordoned off underground, and aside from the rare scholar, a few artists working on the facsimiles, engineers in charge of the 3D copies and, according to established ritual, the President of the Republic (he disappears inside to the clicking of cameras, becoming for a moment the national witness, the one whose face we scrutinize when he re-emerges, the light in his eyes proving that the paintings really are there, that the engravings still exist), no one else goes in.

It was likely believed to be eternal, indestructible, indifferent to time, as if the walls were not, like every other rock surface, subject to atmospheric pressures and organisms present in any biotope, and likely people didn't realize to what extent the walls were alive. In other words: mortal, vulnerable. From then on, the history of the cave became mixed up with that of preservation in subterranean environments, punctuated by crises, then stabilized, the cave convalescing after the final scare of 2007, when it brushed up against catastrophe in the form of a fungus. Its only occupants now are the teams of scientists and officials tackling the issues of safeguarding, observation, measuring, surveying, each incursion strictly limited and carried out according to a drastic protocol—suits are required, and overshoes, masks, and hygiene caps.

But the cave is all the more desirable for being invisible, and copies follow copies: Lascaux III explants the cave from the hill to reveal it to the whole world, where it travels in the form of mobile walls, and Lascaux IV, aiming for a complete copy, wall art and mineral decor included, will be the last. Little by little, the cave is no longer the object of copying, but has become the laboratory of the art of replicas, generating more and more precise technologies, a world of points to measure, data to collect, paintings to duplicate, odors to reproduce, lights to simulate, a world in the form of a puzzle, whether the assembled panels are made of paper or resin. Prehistorians become artists, artists become scholars, archaeologists imagine scenographies, each one shifts their axis, each one travels into the landscape of the other. *To replicate* the cave is to render it visible in order to create its portrait. It is to bring it back into being. It is also to experience it, the way we experience an aftershock a little while after a seismic shift.

 ❧

Submerged in the images, Paula doesn't hear her phone, though it's been vibrating constantly since lunch. When she lifts her head, the blue hour has spread through the room, she's dizzy, eyes heavy, can barely make out the drawings, photos, all these documents gathered left right and center and heaped up on her bed forming a single continuum now, at once irradiant and obscure. Her phone lights up silently, a single pulsation, and she finds the dozen messages that accumulate on the screen—one from Kate, most from Jonas, all stamped with exclamation marks of urgency. Paula calls back without turning on the light, Jonas picks up but she can't quite make out his voice, there's a hubbub of noise around him as if he were standing in the middle of a dense crowd. What's happening? Jonas understands, at the sound of her voice, that she doesn't know anything yet, that she's still in another world, and he steels himself to tell her what happened that very morning, in rue Nicolas-Appert: the attack on *Charlie Hebdo*, the two terrorists armed with machine guns who burst into the newsroom, the twelve people dead. The assassination of the illustrators.

JONAS ARRIVES THE NEXT MORNING, AT THE
hour when the night grows slack, releasing the birdsong.
Signaled by a text, Paula goes down to wait for him in the
square below the house, she hurtles down the sloping street
wrapped in a white shawl with sequins, feet bare inside her
boots, the skin of her face hardened by the icy air, hair electric.
The lights of the car find her immediately in the half-light,
leaning against a wall, and when the motor is turned off in
the parking lot, she hears the door click, the trunk slam,
and then Jonas appears. He walks toward her, same swaying
gait, same fur-lined army jacket he wore in Senzeilles on the
day of the Beauchâteau quarry, and as he gets nearer, she
feels that the space is re-forming around them, that they are
progressively becoming the center, like the rotation axis of a
record on a turntable. They kiss each other's faces, temples,
corners of the eyes, anywhere, and then Paula takes his hand
to lead him to her place, guiding him by his waist toward
the house, come, it's this way.

In the bedroom, Jonas puts down his bag and glances
out the window at the hill that you can just begin to make out,
splashes his face and neck with cold water and then lies down
on his back and closes his eyes. He's been driving all night.
He'd sent a message, I'm coming, and he'd come. Paula looks
at him: his presence, as before in the rue de Parme, completes
the room, crowns it, even though only a moment ago he had
not been missing from this place. She lies down beside him
but has barely placed her head on the pillow when Jonas
opens his eyes and turns toward her. They look at each other,

speechless, breathless, take in each micro-movement of their bodies, everything that recedes, rises, dips, accelerates. Time flies and there's nothing left but to master it, to catch up to it. And so they blink in the same moment and everything that has been held back is suddenly unleashed.

They undress in a hurry, barely lifting themselves from the bed, drop their clothes on the floor, and even though it's collected, concentrated, this moment also splits in two, two speeds are flush: the earthly embrace, linked to yesterday's shock and the desire to become one (like the hunger for sex after a funeral), and then the cosmic embrace, that of resonance, born of the orbits that whirl in a sky as ordered as music paper. Shock produces a kind of clarity: they are clear, of a violent clarity, one and the other, new and sharpened, exploring pleasure like the sensitive wall of a cave, using their whole bodies, their skin, their palms, their tongues, their lashes, as if they are painting each other, as if they have become brushes and are shading each other, polishing, rubbing, tracing, embellishing blue veins and beauty marks, folds of the groin and backs of the knees; they take shape and come closer, their skin soon haloed by the same light, shining with the same soft illumination, and they are the ones who make an impression on the little pink-nosed hunters on the wallpaper, the far-off deer, the dogs who pick up the scent of hawthorn—they make love as if they were straying through a side passage from the underground gallery in which they find themselves, and uncovering a whole other gallery that is even more vast, as if this could only occur once, as if they are discoverers.

❧

When they come out of the bedroom in the early afternoon the weather has mellowed, the air is moist, the sky a pearly gray. Paula looks at Jonas over the car hood, I'm not working today, I want to take you to see something. They head in the direction of Les Eyzies, drive without turning on the radio, without looking at their phones where messages continue to pour in—Kate sending broken-heart emojis, tearful faces, angry faces, she wants to know if they'll be in Paris on Sunday—while they silently join the landscape of the people of prehistory, the land of caves and rock shelters formed in limestone deposits, the place of hollowed cliffs, of karst. A country whose marvelous names Paula had only recently learned: Bernifal, Font-de-Gaume, Combarelles. You'd think the names were dressed up, says Jonas, driving fast, names of heroes from novels. And Paula replies: you say them out loud and you feel like you're dancing with someone. Later, they stop in front of a restaurant in a town called Laugerie-Basse. Paula asks Jonas to wait for her, goes inside and, seeing her come back out, vibrant, her white shawl around her shoulders, a set of keys in hand, he wants to pull her toward him right then and there. We're going to the valley of the Gorge d'Enfer! she says, getting back into the car.

※

The world seems to cleave open before them—there's no one else on the road, they are alone in the landscape. Soon they park at the roadside and the instant they get out it starts to pour, a ringing and icy rain whose sound swells in space. Paula opens the gate and they enter the valley as you'd enter a noble, abandoned palace, push their way inside, the grass comes up to their knees; they walk along a narrow path between wild bushes, thorns, Paula walking ahead, following instructions she memorized when she picked up the keys. A door appears on their right in a wall that sections off the path to a rock shelter, and Paula says: we're here. When she opens it, daylight enters in a single ray—an eyelid opening a crack—and the secrecy of the place, hidden away beneath the cliff, nestled in the dark, tucked away, multiplies their surprise when, in the very same instant, they lift their heads toward the vaulted ceiling and discover the fish.

⁊

Jonas strikes a match and holds it up toward the ceiling like a torch, and the fish stirs. Paula, here is your treasure, is what he says to her, while the rain pours into the subterranean room. The golden fish caught in the fisherman's net.

A twenty-five-thousand-year-old fish, from the Upper Paleolithic Period, an era when the first people had come to populate Europe, those people who were ancestors to Paula and Jonas. Over a meter long, it was a catch so magnificent and rare that they had wanted to make an image of it—Paula thinks of fishers who pose proudly before the camera, brandishing their fish high—an image that was itself so marvelous, sculpted and engraved in bas-relief, enhanced with red, that attempts had been made to detach it from the ceiling, to carry it off, to sell it, the looters' perforations forming now a kind of frame for a tableau that presaged naturalist engravings in which a fish was, just like here, usually represented in profile, detailed, eye open. This one, a salmon with a kype (a male, then, vigorous), was a reminder that the Vézère had flowed here in Paleolithic times too, that this shelter had been the riverbank, and the salmon spawn had fed the camp.

Paula and Jonas are standing before time itself. The fish above their heads reveals the memory accumulated at the bottom of the oceans, the erosion of limestone, the movement of rivers, the migration of humans, these lengths of time that coexist with the state of shock their country is in now, the anger, sorrow, the twenty-four-hour news channels that bail out time all day long while the two terrorists continue on their deadly run; it connects the history of the world to their fragile human life.

After one minute and three seconds, Paula breaks the silence and murmurs that they should go, they have to take the keys back now, and they step out again hand in hand into the pounding rain. As they close the doorway to the valley, Jonas takes Paula's face in his hands and asks her to imagine a time when humans would be nothing but a distant memory, a time when they would be no more than myths, legends, specters in the stories of creatures that now walked the earth—who can believe in humans anymore, Paula?

IN THE SILENCE OF THE STUDIOS AT NOON,
Paula looks at the images of the black deer she's preparing to
paint, and then ties on her apron. Before her stands the panel,
the wall she goes up to until she's close enough to hear her
own breath. The more she looks at it, the more the complex
profusion of shapes reveals itself, the infinitesimal texture
echoing a limitless space. She turns on the projector and uses
reference marks on the surface of the coated resin rock to adjust
with exactitude a first image from the 3D digital copy, and
projects the animal—the black deer suddenly stands before her
eyes, so real she jumps: it's here, elegant and graphic, seeming
to lean on one of its front hooves to tilt back its head, black
antlers angled, their edges starred like whirling helixes, like
parabolic reflectors, the diffuse red shroud around its nostrils
suggesting the warmth of its breath, but also sound, a bellow
of presence, short and coarse, or maybe a bellow of triumph,
of challenge. Paula stares at its eye: the black mark of the
iris is deftly circled with white, as white as the snowy valley
she walked through that very morning, leaving the camp at
dawn with others like her, admitted to their ranks for the
first time, a day she'd long been waiting for; she rolls up her
tools in a leather case, the blizzard picks up a powdery layer
of recent snow, visibility is low, she walks quickly even though
her furs weigh her down, doesn't want to be left behind, she's
afraid of the woolly rhinoceros and its hunger in winter;
the others move silently, armed, they know where they're
going, scale the scree of rocks at the foot of the hill, climb its
craggy slope and reach an opening where the strongest and

most agile go in first and inspect the room; then the others follow, and they set up the studio. First a fire—and maybe then older paintings appear, scaffolding for what's to come. A few unwrap hollow stones and braided plants—juniper, lichen—brought as burners and wicks; others collect them, make them on the spot, and then the stones are spread with grease, flames are lit, the room brightens and they spread out. Paula is impressed, and warm. She's led to a white wall covered in limestone—here's where you'll be painting—and she nods in assent, kneels and unrolls her case, taking out her materials: leather stencils, swabs, brushes, and a perforated stick to be used for mixing and blowing the colors in this part of the cave; she sets out the ochers she spent a long time preparing the day before, and little pebbles of manganese she gathered along the river last summer, looks for a stone to use as a mortar and begins to grind her materials, to grate them with the flint blade and gather up the powder, and then, for a palette, she unwraps a tortoise shell from a piece of leather. She steps outside to add a little snow, which melts immediately, then pours in her color and mixes. A young man appears at her side then, silent love has been running between them for a long time now—he's going to paint a horse with a black mane, and its gallop will follow the movement of the wall, will ride along the relief of the stone—they look at each other. And then, caught in the ray of the projector, filtered through the luminous reproduction of photography, spun with furrows and lighter veins, integrated into the flat surfaces of the painting, herself furrowed with underground rivers, with dark galleries and ornamented rooms, Paula melts into the image, prehistoric and parietal.

NOTE ON SOURCES

Page 50: This quote is fictionalized from *Decorative Painting the Van Der Kelen Way*, by Denise Van Der Kelen (Paris: Éditions Vial, 2010), page 242.

A NOTE ABOUT THE AUTHOR

Maylis de Kerangal is the author of several novels, including
Naissance d'un pont (published in English as *Birth of a Bridge*),
which won the Prix Médicis in 2010; *Réparer les vivants*,
whose U.S. English translation, *The Heart*, was one of *The
Wall Street Journal*'s Top Ten Novels of 2016; and *Un chemin
de tables*, whose English translation, *The Cook*, was a *New
York Times Book Review* Editors' Choice. She lives in Paris.

A NOTE ABOUT THE TRANSLATOR

Jessica Moore is the author of the books *Everything, Now* and
The Whole Singing Ocean. Her translation of *Turkana Boy*, by
Jean-François Beauchemin, received a PEN/Heim Translation Fund Grant, and her translation of Maylis de Kerangal's
Réparer les vivants, published as *Mend the Living*, was long-
listed for the 2016 Man Booker International Prize and won
the U.K.'s Wellcome Prize in 2017.